A.D. 2076

Fact: President Hugo Allen Winkler and his robot look-alike are both present at the July 4th tercentennial celebration.

Fact: An assassin's disintegrator fires.

Unknown: Which one of the "Presidents" has survived?

THE TERCENTENARY INCIDENT

"Totally top-flight Asimov."
                                    —*South Bend Tribune*

"Clearly number among the best things he's written."   —*S. F. Booklog*

THE BICENTENNIAL MAN
and Other Stories

Isaac Asimov

A FAWCETT CREST BOOK ● NEW YORK

Acknowledgments:

"The Prime of Life" © 1966 by Mercury Press, Inc.
"Feminine Intuition" © 1969 by Mercury Press, Inc.
"Waterclap" Copyright © 1970 by Universal Publishing and Distributing Corporation
"That Thou Art Mindful of Him" Copyright © 1974 by Mercury Press, Inc.
"Stranger in Paradise" Copyright © 1974 by UPD Publishing Corporation
"The Life and Times of Multivac" © 1975 The New York Times Company
"The Winnowing" Copyright © 1976 by The Condé Nast Publications, Inc.
"The Bicentennial Man" Copyright © 1976 by Random House, Inc.
"Marching In" Copyright © 1976 by ABC Leisure Magazines, Inc.
"The Tercentenary Incident" © 1976 by Isaac Asimov
"Birth of a Notion" Copyright © 1976 by Ultimate Publishing Co., Inc.

THE BICENTENNIAL MAN AND OTHER STORIES

THIS BOOK CONTAINS THE COMPLETE TEXT OF THE ORIGINAL HARDCOVER EDITION.

Published by Fawcett Crest Books, a unit of CBS Publications, the Consumer Publishing Division of CBS Inc., by arrangement with Doubleday and Company, Inc.

ISBN: 0-449-23573-4

Selection of the Science Fiction Book Club

Printed in the United States of America

10 9 8 7 6 5 4 3 2 1

Contents

Dedicated to:
Judy-Lynn del Rey,
and the swath she is cutting in our field

Here I am with another collection of science fiction stories, and I sit here and think, with more than a little astonishment, that I have been writing and publishing science fiction now for just three-eighths of a century. This isn't bad for someone who only admits to being in his late youth—or a little over thirty, if pinned down.

It seems longer than that, I imagine, to most people who have tried to follow me from book to book and from field to field. As the flood of words continues year after year with no visible signs of letting up, the most peculiar misapprehensions naturally arise.

Just a few weeks ago, for instance, I was at a librarian's convention signing books, and some of the kindly remarks I received were:

"I can't believe you're still alive!"

"But how can you possibly look so young?"

"Are you really only one person?"

It goes even beyond that. In a review of one of my books* in the December 1975 *Scientific American*, I was described as: "Once a Boston biochemist, now label and linchpin of a New York corporate authorship—"

Dear me! *Corporate* authorship? Merely the linchpin and label?

It's not so. I'm sorry, if my copious output makes it seem impossible, but I'm alive, I'm young, and I'm only one person.

In fact, I'm an absolutely one-man operation. I have no assistants of any kind. I have no agent, no business manager, no research aides, no secretary, no stenographer. I do all my own typing, all my own proofreading, all my own indexing, all my own research, all my own letter writing, all my own telephone answering.

I like it that way. Since I don't have to deal with other people, I can concentrate more properly on my work, and get more done.

*ASIMOV ON CHEMISTRY (Doubleday, 1974), and it was a very favorable review.

I was already worrying about this misapprehension concerning myself ten years ago. At that time, *The Magazine of Fantasy and Science Fiction* (commonly known as *F & SF*) was planning a special Isaac Asimov issue for October 1966. I was asked for a new story to be included and I obliged,† but I also wrote a short poem on my own initiative.

That poem appeared in the special issue and it has never appeared anywhere else—until now. I'm going to include it here because it's appropriate to my thesis. Then, too, seven years after the poem appeared, I recited it to a charming maiden, who, without any sign of mental effort, immediately suggested a change that was so inevitable, and so great an improvement, that I have to get the poem into print again in order to make that change.

I originally called the poem I'M IN THE PRIME OF LIFE, YOU ROTTEN KID! Edward L. Ferman, editor of *F & SF*, shortened that to THE PRIME OF LIFE. I like the longer version much better, but I decided it would look odd on the contents page, so I'm keeping the shorter version. (Heck!)

†That story was THE KEY, and it appears in my collection ASIMOV'S MYSTERIES (Doubleday, 1968).

1

The Prime of Life

It was, in truth, an eager youth
    Who halted me one day.
He gazed in bliss at me, and this
    Is what he had to say:

"Why, mazel tov, it's Asimov,
    A blessing on your head!
For many a year, I've lived in fear
    That you were long since dead.

Or if alive, one fifty-five
    Cold years had passed you by,
And left you weak, with poor physique,
    Thin hair and rheumy eye.

For sure enough, I've read your stuff
    Since I was but a lad
And couldn't spell or hardly tell
    The good yarns from the bad.

My father, too, was reading you
    Before he met my Ma.
For you he yearned, once he had learned
    About you from *his* Pa.

Since time began, you wondrous man,
    My ancestors did love
That s.f. dean and writing machine
    The aged Asimov."

I'd had my fill. I said, "Be still!
    I've kept my old-time spark.
My step is light, my eye is bright,
    My hair is thick and dark."

His smile, in brief, spelled disbelief,
    So this is what I did;
I scowled, you know, and with one blow,
    I killed that rotten kid.

The change I mentioned occurs in the first line of the second stanza. I had it read, originally, "Why, stars above, it's Asimov," but the aforementioned maiden saw at once it ought to be "mazel tov." This is a Hebrew phrase meaning "good fortune" and it is used by Jews as a joyful greeting on jubilant occasions—as a meeting with me should surely be.

Ten years have passed since I wrote the poem and, of course, the impression of incredible age which I leave among those who know me only from my writings is now even stronger. When this poem was written, I had published a mere 66 books, and now, ten years later, the score stands at 175, so that it's been a decade of constant mental conflagration.

Just the same, I've kept my old-time spark even yet. My step is still light and my eye is still bright. What's more, I'm as suave in my conversations with young women as I have ever been (which is very suave indeed). That bit about my hair being "thick and dark" must be modified, however. There is no danger of baldness but, oh me, I am turning gray. In recent years, I have grown a generous pair of fluffy sideburns, and they are almost white.

And how that you know the worst about me, let's go on to the stories themselves or, rather (for you are not quite through with me), to my introductory comments to the first story.

The beginning of FEMININE INTUITION is tied up with Judy-Lynn Benjamin, whom I met at the World Science Fiction Convention in New York City in 1967. Judy-Lynn has to be seen to be believed—an incredibly intelligent, quick-witted, hard-driving woman who seems to be burning constantly with a bright radioactive glow.

She was managing editor of *Galaxy* in those days.

On March 21, 1971, she married that lovable old curmudgeon Lester del Rey, and knocked off all his rough edges in two seconds flat. At present, as Judy-Lynn del Rey, she is a senior editor at Ballantine Books and is generally recognized (especially by me) as one of the top editors in the business.*

Back in 1968, when Judy-Lynn was still at *Galaxy*, we were sitting in a bar in a New York hotel and she introduced me, I remember, to something called a "grasshopper." I told her I didn't drink because I had no capacity for alcohol, but she said I would like this one, and the trouble is I did.

It's a green cocktail with crème de menthe, and cream, and who knows what else in it, and it is delicious. I only had one on this occasion, so I merely graduated to a slightly higher than normal level of the loud bonhomie that usually characterizes me and was still sober enough to talk business.†

Judy-Lynn suggested I write a story about a *female* robot. Well, of course, my robots are sexually neutral, but they all have masculine names and I treat them all as males. The turn-about suggestion was good.

I said, "Gee, that's an interesting idea," and was awfully pleased, because Ed Ferman had asked me for a story with which to celebrate the twentieth anniversary of *Fantasy and Science Fiction* and I had agreed, but, at the moment, did not have an idea in my head.

On February 8, 1969, in line with the suggestion, I began FEMININE INTUITION. When it was done, Ed took it and the

---

*You may have noticed that this book is dedicated to her.
†A year or so later during the course of a science fiction convention, Judy-Lynn persuaded me to have *two* grasshoppers and I was instantly reduced to a kind of wild drunken merriment, and since then no one lets me have grasshoppers any more. Just as well!

story was indeed included in the October 1969 *Fantasy and Science Fiction*, the twentieth-anniversary issue. It appeared as the lead novelette, too.

Between the time I sold it, however, and the time it appeared, Judy-Lynn said casually to me one day, "Did you ever do anything about my idea that you write a story about a female robot?"

I said enthusiastically, "Yes, I did, Judy-Lynn, and Ed Ferman is going to publish it. Thanks for the suggestion."

Judy-Lynn's eyes opened wide and she said in a very dangerous voice, "Stories based on my ideas go to *me*, you dummy. You don't sell them to the competition."

She went on to expound on that theme for about half an hour and my attempts to explain that Ed had asked me for a story *before* the time of the suggestion and that she had never quite made it clear that she wanted the story for herself were brushed aside with scorn.

Anyway, Judy-Lynn, here's the story again, and I'm freely admitting that the suggestion of a female robot was yours. Does that make everything all right? (No, I didn't think so.)

2

Feminine Intuition

The Three Laws of Robotics:

1. *A robot may not injure a human being or, through inaction, allow a human being to come to harm.*
2. *A robot must obey the orders given it by human beings except where such orders would conflict with the First Law.*
3. *A robot must protect its own existence as long as*

> *such protection does not conflict with the First or*
> *Second Law.*

For the first time in the history of United States Robots and Mechanical Men, Inc., a robot had been destroyed through accident on Earth itself.

No one was to blame. The air vehicle had been demolished in mid-air and an unbelieving investigating committee was wondering whether they really dared announce the evidence that it had been hit by a meteorite. Nothing else could have been fast enough to prevent automatic avoidance; nothing else could have done the damage short of a nuclear blast and that was out of the question.

Tie that in with a report of a flash in the night sky just before the vehicle had exploded—and from Flagstaff Observatory, not from an amateur—and the location of a sizable and distinctly meteoric bit of iron freshly gouged into the ground a mile from the site and what other conclusion could be arrived at?

Still, nothing like that had ever happened before and calculations of the odds against it yielded monstrous figures. Yet even colossal improbabilities can happen sometimes.

At the offices of United States Robots, the hows and whys of it were secondary. The real point was that a robot had been destroyed.

That, in itself, was distressing.

The fact that JN-5 had been a prototype, the first, after four earlier attempts, to have been placed in the field, was even more distressing.

The fact that JN-5 was a radically new type of robot, quite different from anything ever built before, was abysmally distressing.

The fact that JN-5 had apparently accomplished something before its destruction that was incalculably important and that that accomplishment might now be forever gone, placed the distress utterly beyond words.

It seemed scarcely worth mentioning that, along with the robot, the Chief Robopsychologist of United States Robots had also died.

Clinton Madarian had joined the firm ten years before. For five of those years, he had worked uncomplainingly under the grumpy supervision of Susan Calvin.

Madarian's brilliance was quite obvious and Susan Calvin

had quietly promoted him over the heads of older men. She wouldn't, in any case, have deigned to give her reasons for this to Research Director Peter Bogert, but as it happened, no reasons were needed. Or, rather, they were obvoius.

Madarian was utterly the reverse of the renowned Dr. Calvin in several very noticeable ways. He was not quite as overweight as his distinct double chin made him appear to be, but even so he was overpowering in his presence, where Susan had gone nearly unnoticed. Madarian's massive face, his shock of glistening red-brown hair, his ruddy complexion and booming voice, his loud laugh, and most of all, his irrepressible self-confidence and his eager way of announcing his successes, made everyone else in the room feel there was a shortage of space.

When Susan Calvin finally retired (refusing, in advance, any cooperation with respect to any testimonial dinner that might be planned in her honor with so firm a manner that no announcement of the retirément was even made to the news services) Madarian took her place.

He had been in his new post exactly one day when he initiated the JN project.

It had meant the largest commitment of funds to one project that United States Robots had ever had to weigh, but that was something which Madarian dismissed with a genial wave of the hand.

"Worth every penny of it, Peter," he said. "And I expect you to convince the Board of Directors of that."

"Give me reasons," said Bogert, wondering if Madarian would. Susan Calvin had never given reasons.

But Madarian said, "Sure," and settled himself easily into the large armchair in the Director's office.

Bogert watched the other with something that was almost awe. His own once-black hair was almost white now and within the decade he would follow Susan into retirement. That would mean the end of the original team that had built United States Robots into a globe-girdling firm that was a rival of the national governments in complexity and importance. Somehow neither he nor those who had gone before him ever quite grasped the enormous expansion of the firm.

But this was a new generation. The new men were at ease with the Colossus. They lacked the touch of wonder that would have them tiptoeing in disbelief. So they moved ahead, and that was good.

Madarian said, "I propose to begin the construction of robots without constraint."

"Without the Three Laws? Surely—"

"No, Peter. Are those the only constraints you can think of? Hell, you contributed to the design of the early positronic brains. Do I have to tell you that, quite aside from the Three Laws, there isn't a pathway in those brains that isn't carefully designed and fixed? We have robots planned for specific tasks, implanted with specific abilities."

"And you propose—"

"That at every level below the Three Laws, the paths be made open-ended. It's not difficult."

Bogert said dryly, "It's not difficult, indeed. Useless things are never difficult. The difficult thing is fixing the paths and making the robot useful."

"But why is that difficult? Fixing the paths requires a great deal of effort because the Principle of Uncertainty is important in particles the mass of positrons and the uncertainty effect must be minimized. Yet why must it? If we arrange to have the Principle just sufficiently prominent to allow the crossing of paths unpredictably—"

"We have an unpredictable robot."

"We have a *creative* robot," said Madarian, with a trace of impatience. "Peter, if there's anything a human brain has that a robotic brain has never had, it's the trace of unpredictability that comes from the effects of uncertainty at the subatomic level. I admit that this effect has never been demonstrated experimentally within the nervous system, but without that the human brain is not superior to the robotic brain in principle."

"And you think that if you introduce the effect into the robotic brain, the human brain will become not superior to the robotic brain in principle."

"That," said Madarian, "is exactly what I believe."

They went on for a long time after that.

The Board of Directors clearly had no intention of being easily convinced.

Scott Robertson, the largest shareholder in the firm, said, "It's hard enough to manage the robot industry as it is, with public hostility to robots forever on the verge of breaking out into the open. If the public gets the idea that robots will be uncontrolled . . . Oh, don't tell me about the Three Laws. The average man won't believe the Three Laws will protect him if he as much as hears the word 'uncontrolled.'"

"Then don't use it," said Madarian. "Call the robot—call it 'intuitive."

"An intuitive robot," someone muttered. "A girl robot?"

A smile made its way about the conference table.

Madarian seized on that. "All right. A girl robot. Our robots are sexless, of course, and so will this one be, but we always act as though they're males. We give them male pet names and call them he and him. Now this one, if we consider the nature of the mathematical structuring of the brain which I have proposed, would fall into the JN-coordinate system. The first robot would be JN-1, and I've assumed that it would be called John-1. . . . I'm afraid that is the level of originality of the average roboticist. But why not call it Jane-1, damn it? If the public has to be let in on what we're doing, we've constructing a feminine robot with intuition."

Robertson shook his head, "What difference would that make? What you're saying is that you plan to remove the last barrier which, in principle, keeps the robotic brain inferior to the human brain. What do you suppose the public reaction will be to that?"

"Do you plan to make that public?" said Madarian. He thought a bit and then said, "Look. One thing the general public believes is that women are not as intelligent as men."

There was an instant apprehensive look on the face of more than one man at the table and a quick look up and down as though Susan Calvin were still in her accustomed seat.

Madarian said, "If we announce a female robot, it doesn't matter what she is. The public will automatically assume she is mentally backward. We just publicize the robot as Jane-1 and we don't have to say another word. We're safe."

"Actually," said Peter Bogert quietly, "there's more to it than that. Madarian and I have gone over the mathematics carefully and the JN series, whether John or Jane, would be quite safe. They would be less complex and intellectually capable, in an orthodox sense, than many another series we have designed and constructed. There would only be the one added factor of, well, let's get into the habit of calling it 'intuition.'"

"Who knows what it would do?" muttered Robertson.

"Madarian has suggested one thing it can do. As you all know, the Space Jump has been developed in principle. It is possible for men to attain what is, in effect, hyper-speeds beyond that of light and to visit other stellar systems and return in negligible time—weeks at the most."

Robertson said, "That's not new to us. It couldn't have been done without robots."

"Exactly, and it's not doing us any good because we can't use the hyper-speed drive except once as a demonstration, so that U. S. Robots gets little credit. The Space Jump is risky, it's fearfully prodigal of energy and therefore it's enormously expensive. If we were going to use it anyway, it would be nice if we could report the existence of a habitable planet. Call it a psychological need. Spend about twenty billion dollars on a single Space Jump and report nothing but scientific data and the public wants to know why their money was wasted. Report the existence of a habitable planet, and you're an interstellar Columbus and no one will worry about the money."

"So?"

"So where are we going to find a habitable planet? Or put it this way—which star within reach of the Space Jump as presently developed, which of the three hundred thousand stars and star systems within three hundred light-years has the best chance of having a habitable planet? We've got an enormous quantity of details on every star in our three-hundred-light-year neighborhood and a notion that almost every one has a planetary system. But which has a *habitable* planet? Which do we visit? . . . We don't know."

One of the directors said, "How would this Jane robot help us?"

Madarian was about to answer that, but he gestured slightly to Bogert and Bogert understood. The Director would carry more weight. Bogert didn't particularly like the idea; if the JN series proved a fiasco, he was making himself prominent enough in connection with it to insure that the sticky fingers of blame would cling to him. On the other hand, retirement was not all that far off, and if it worked, he would go out in a blaze of glory. Maybe it was only Madarian's aura of confidence, but Bogert had honestly come to believe it would work.

He said, "It may well be that somewhere in the libraries of data we have on those stars, there are methods for estimating the probabilities of the presence of Earth-type habitable planets. All we need to do is understand the data properly, look at them in the appropriate creative manner, make the correct correlations. We haven't done it yet. Or if some astronomer has, he hasn't been smart enough to realize what he has.

"A JN-type robot could make correlations far more rapidly and far more precisely than a man could. In a day, it would make and discard as many correlations as a man could in ten years. Furthermore, it would work in truly random fashion, whereas a man would have a strong bias based on preconception and on what is already believed."

There was a considerable silence after that. Finally Robertson said, "But it's only a matter of probability, isn't it? Suppose this robot said, 'The highest-probability habitable-planet star within so-and-so light-years is Squidgee-17,' or whatever, and we go there and find that a probability is only a probability and that there are no habitable planets after all. Where does that leave us?"

Madarian struck in this time. "We still win. We know how the robot came to the conclusion because it—she—will tell us. It might well help gain enormous insight into astronomical detail and make the whole thing worthwhile even if we don't make the Space Jump at all. Besides, we can then work out the five most probable sites of planets and the probability that one of the five has a habitable planet may then be better than 0.95. It would be almost sure—"

They went on for a long time after that.

The funds granted were quite insufficient, but Madarian counted on the habit of throwing good money after bad. With two hundred million about to be lost irrevocably when another hundred million could save everything, the other hundred million would surely be voted.

Jane-1 was finally built and put on display. Peter Bogert studied it—her—gravely. He said, "Why the narrow waist? Surely that introduces a mechanical weakness?"

Madarian chuckled. "Listen, if we're going to call her Jane, there's no point in making her look like Tarzan."

Bogert shook his head. "Don't like it. You'll be bulging her higher up to give the appearance of breasts next, and that's a rotten idea. If women start getting the notion that robots may look like women, I can tell you exactly the kind of perverse notions they'll get, and you'll *really* have hostility on their part."

Madarian said, "Maybe you're right at that. No woman wants to feel replaceable by something with none of her faults. Okay."

Jane-2 did not have the pinched waist. She was a somber robot which rarely moved and even more rarely spoke.

Madarian had only occasionally come rushing to Bogert with items of news during her construction and that had been a sure sign that things were going poorly. Madarian's ebullience under success was overpowering. He would not hesitate to invade Bogert's bedroom at 3 A.M. with a hot-flash item rather than wait for the morning. Bogert was sure of that.

Now Madarian seemed subdued, his usually florid expression nearly pale, his round cheeks somehow pinched. Bogert said, with a feeling of certainty, "She won't talk."

"Oh, she talks." Madarian sat down heavily and chewed at his lower lip. "Sometimes, anyway," he said.

Bogert rose and circled the robot. "And when she talks, she makes no sense, I suppose. Well, if she doesn't talk, she's no female, is she?"

Madarian tried a weak smile for size and abandoned it. He said, "The brain, in isolation, checked out."

"I know," said Bogert.

"But once that brain was put in charge of the physical apparatus of the robot, it was necessarily modified, of course."

"Of course," agreed Bogert unhelpfully.

"But unpredictably and frustratingly. The trouble is that when you're dealing with n-dimensional calculus of uncertainty, things are—"

"Uncertain?" said Bogert. His own reaction was surprising him. The company investment was already most sizable and almost two years had elapsed, yet the results were, to put it politely, disappointing. Still, he found himself jabbing at Madarian and finding himself amused in the process.

Almost furtively, Bogert wondered if it weren't the absent Susan Calvin he was jabbing at. Madarian was so much more ebullient and effusive than Susan could ever possibly be—when things were going well. He was also far more vulnerably in the dumps when things weren't going well, and it was precisely under pressure that Susan never cracked. The target that Madarian made could be a neatly punctured bull's-eye as recompense for the target Susan had never allowed herself to be.

Madarian did not react to Bogert's last remark any more than Susan Calvin would have done; not out of contempt, which would have been Susan's reaction, but because he did not hear it.

He said argumentatively, "The trouble is the matter of recognition. We have Jane-2 correlating magnificently. She can correlate on any subject, but once she's done so, she can't recognize a valuable result from a valueless one. It's not an easy problem, judging how to program a robot to tell a significant correlation when you don't know what correlations she will be making."

"I presume you've thought of lowering the potential at the W-21 diode junction and sparking across the—"

"No, no, no, no—" Madarian faded off in to a whispering diminuendo. "You can't just have it spew out everything. We can do that for ourselves. The point is to have it recognize the crucial correlation and draw the conclusion. Once that is done, you see, a Jane robot would snap out an answer by intuition. It would be something we couldn't get ourselves except by the oddest kind of luck."

"It seems to me," said Bogert dryly, "that if you had a robot like that, you would have her do routinely what, among human beings, only the occasional genius is capable of doing."

Madarian nodded vigorously. "Exactly, Peter. I'd have said so myself if I weren't afraid of frightening off the execs. Please don't repeat that in their hearing."

"Do you really want a robot genius?"

"What are words? I'm trying to get a robot with the capacity to make random correlations at enormous speeds, together with a key-significance high-recognition quotient. And I'm trying to put *those* words into positronic field equations. I thought I had it, too, but I don't. Not yet."

He looked at Jane-2 discontentedly and said, "What's the best significance you have, Jane?"

Jane-2's head turned to look at Madarian but she made no sound, and Madarian whispered with resignation, "She's running that into the correlation banks."

Jane-2 spoke tonelessly at last. "I'm not sure." It was the first sound she had made.

Madarian's eyes rolled upward. "She's doing the equivalent of setting up equations with indeterminate solutions."

"I gathered that," said Bogert. "Listen, Madarian, can you go anywhere at this point, or do we pull out now and cut our losses at half a billion?"

"Oh, I'll get it," muttered Madarian.

Jane-3 wasn't it. She was never as much as activated and Madarian was in a rage.

It was human error. His own fault, if one wanted to be entirely accurate. Yet though Madarian was utterly humiliated, others remained quiet. Let he who has never made an error in the fearsomely intricate mathematics of the positronic brain fill out the first memo of correction.

Nearly a year passed before Jane-4 was ready. Madarian was ebullient again. "She does it," he said. "She's got a good high-recognition quotient."

He was confident enough to place her on display before the Board and have her solve problems. Not mathematical problems; any robot could do that; but problems where the terms were deliberately misleading without being actually inaccurate.

Bogert said afterward, "That doesn't take much, really."

"Of course not. It's elementary for Jane-4, but I had to show them something, didn't I?"

"Do you know how much we've spent so far?"

"Come on, Peter, don't give me that. Do you know how much we've got back? These things don't go on in a vacuum, you know. I've had over three years of hell over this, if you want to know, but I've worked out new techniques of calculation that will save us a minimum of fifty thousand dollars on every type of positronic brain we design, from now on in forever. Right?"

"Well—"

"Well me no wells. It's so. And it's my personal feeling that n-dimensional calculus of uncertainty can have any number of other applications if we have the ingenuity to find them, and my Jane robots *will* find them. Once I've got exactly what I want, the new JN series will pay for itself inside of five years, even if we triple what we've invested so far."

"What do you mean by 'exactly what you want'? What's wrong with Jane-4?"

"Nothing. Or nothing much. She's on the track, but she can be improved and I intend to do so. I thought I knew where I was going when I designed her. Now I've tested her and I *know* where I'm going. I intend to get there."

Jane-5 was it. It took Madarian well over a year to produce her and there he had no reservations; he was utterly confident.

Jane-5 was shorter than the average robot, slimmer. Without being a female caricature as Jane-1 had been, she managed to possess an air of femininity about herself despite the absence of a single clearly feminine feature.

"It's the way she's standing," said Bogert. Her arms were

held gracefully and somehow the torso managed to give the impression of curving slightly when she turned.

Madarian said, "Listen to her. . . . How do you feel, Jane?"

"In excellent health, thank you," said Jane-5, and the voice was precisely that of a woman; it was a sweet and almost disturbing contralto.

"Why did you do that, Clinton?" said Peter, startled and beginning to frown.

"Psychologically important," said Madarian. "I want people to think of her as a woman; to treat her as a woman; to *explain*."

"What people?"

Madarian put his hands in his pockets and stared thoughtfully at Bogert. "I would like to have arrangements made for Jane and myself to go to Flagstaff."

Bogert couldn't help but note that Madarian didn't say Jane-5. He made use of no number this time. She was *the* Jane. He said doubtfully, "To Flagstaff? Why?"

"Because that's the world center for general planetology, isn't it? It's where they're studying the stars and trying to calculate the probability of habitable planets, isn't it?"

"I know that, but it's on Earth."

"Well, and I surely know that."

"Robotic movements on Earth are strictly controlled. And there's no need for it. Bring a library of books on general planetology here and let Jane absorb them."

"*No!* Peter, will you get it through your head that Jane isn't the ordinary logical robot; she's intuitive."

"So?"

"So how can we tell what she needs, what she can use, what will set her off? We can use any metal model in the factory to read books; that's frozen data and out of date besides. Jane must have living information; she must have tones of voice, she must have side issues; she must have total irrelevancies even. How the devil do we know what or when something will go click-click inside her and fall into a pattern? If we knew, we wouldn't need her at all, would we?"

Bogert began to feel harassed. He said, "Then bring the men here, the general planetologists."

"Here won't do any good. They'll be out of their element. They won't react naturally. I want Jane to watch them at work; I want her to see their instruments, their offices, their desks, everything about them that she can. I want you to arrange to have her transported to Flagstaff. And I'd really like not to discuss it any further."

For a moment he almost sounded like Susan. Bogert winced, and said, "It's complicated making such an arrangement. Transporting an experimental robot—"

"Jane isn't experimental. She's the fifth of the series."

"The other four weren't really working models."

Madarian lifted his hands in helpless frustration. "Who's forcing you to tell the government that?"

"I'm not worried about the government. It can be made to understand special cases. It's public opinion. We've come a long way in fifty years and I don't propose to be set back twenty-five of them by having you lose control of a—"

"I won't lose control. You're making foolish remarks. Look! U. S. Robots can afford a private plane. We can land quietly at the nearest commercial airport and be lost in hundreds of similar landings. We can arrange to have a large ground car with an enclosed body meet us and take us to Flagstaff. Jane will be crated and it will be obvious that some piece of thoroughly non-robotic equipment is being transported to the labs. We won't get a second look from anyone. The men at Flagstaff will be alerted and will be told the exact purpose of the visit. They will have every motive to cooperate and to prevent a leak."

Bogert pondered. "The risky part will be the plane and the ground car. If anything happens to the crate—"

"Nothing will."

"We might get away with it if Jane is deactivated during transport. Then even if someone finds out she's inside—"

"No, Peter. That can't be done. Uh-uh. Not Jane-5. Look, she's been free-associating since she was activated. The information she possesses can be put in freeze during deactivation but the free associations never. No, sir, she can't ever be deactivated."

"But, then, if somehow it is discovered that we are transporting an activated robot—"

"It won't be found out."

Madarian remained firm and the plane eventually took off. It was a late-model automatic Computo-jet, but it carried a human pilot—one of U. S. Robots' own employees—as back-up. The crate containing Jane arrived at the airport safely, was transferred to the ground car, and reached the Research Laboratories at Flagstaff without incident.

Peter Bogert received his free call from Madarian not more than an hour after the latter's arrival at Flagstaff. Madarian was ecstatic and, characteristically, could not wait to report.

The message arrived by tubed laser beam, shielded, scrambled, and ordinarily impenetrable, but Bogert felt exasperated. He knew it could be penetrated if someone with enough technological ability—the government, for example—was determined to do so. The only real safety lay in the fact that the government had no reason to try. At least Bogert hoped so.

He said, "For God's sake, do you have to call?"

Madarian ignored him entirely. He burbled, "It was an inspiration. Sheer genius, I tell you."

For a while, Bogert stared at the receiver. Then he shouted incredulously, "You mean you've got the answer? Already?"

"No, no! Give us time, damn it. I mean the matter of her voice was an inspiration. Listen, after we were chauffeured from the airport to the main administration building at Flagstaff, we uncrated Jane and she stepped out of the box. When that happened, every man in the place stepped back. Scared! Nitwits! If even scientists can't understand the significance of the Laws of Robotics, what can we expect of the average untrained individual? For a minute there I thought: This will all be useless. They won't talk. They'll be keying themselves for a quick break in case she goes berserk and they'll be able to think of nothing else."

"Well, then, what are you getting at?"

"So then she greeted them routinely. She said, 'Good afternoon, gentlemen. I am so glad to meet you.' And it came out in this beautiful contralto. . . . That was it. One man straightened his tie, and another ran his fingers through his hair. What really got me was that the oldest guy in the place actually checked his fly to make sure it was zipped. They're all crazy about her now. All they needed was the voice. She isn't a robot any more; she's a girl."

"You mean they're talking to her?"

"*Are* they talking to her! I should say so. I should have programmed her for sexy intonations. They'd be asking her for dates right now if I had. Talk about conditioned reflex. Listen, men respond to voices. At the most intimate moments, are they looking? It's the voice in your ear—"

"Yes, Clinton, I seem to remember. Where's Jane now?"

"With them. They won't let go of her."

"Damn! Get in there with her. Don't let her out of your sight, man."

Madarian's calls thereafter, during his ten-day stay at Flagstaff, were not very frequent and became progressively less exalted.

Jane was listening carefully, he reported, and occasionally she responded. She remained popular. She was given entry everywhere. But there were no results.

Bogert said, "Nothing at all?"

Madarian was at once defensive. "You can't say nothing at all. It's impossible to say nothing at all with an intuitive robot. You don't know what might not be going on inside her. This morning she asked Jensen what he had for breakfast."

"Rossiter Jensen the astrophysicist?"

"Yes, of course. As it turned out, he didn't have breakfast that morning. Well, a cup of coffee."

"So Jane's learning to make small talk. That scarcely makes up for the expense—"

"Oh, don't be a jackass. It wasn't small talk. Nothing is small talk for Jane. She asked because it had something to do with some sort of cross-correlation she was building in her mind."

"What can it possibly—"

"How do I know? If I knew, I'd be a Jane myself and you wouldn't need her. But it has to mean something. She's programmed for high motivation to obtain an answer to the question of a planet with optimum habitability/distance and—"

"Then let me know when she's done that and not before. It's not really necessary for me to get a blow-by-blow description of possible correlations."

He didn't really expect to get notification of success. With each day, Bogert grew less sanguine, so that when the notification finally came, he wasn't ready. And it came at the very end.

That last time, when Madarian's climactic message came, it came in what was almost a whisper. Exaltation had come complete circle and Madarian was awed into quiet.

"She did it," he said. "She did it. After I all but gave up, too. After she had received everything in the place and most of it twice and three times over and never said a word that sounded like anything. . . . I'm on the plane now, returning. We've just taken off."

Bogert managed to get his breath. "Don't play games, man. You have the *answer?* Say so, if you have. Say it plainly."

"She has the answer. She's given me the answer. She's given

me the names of three stars within eighty light-years which, she says, have a sixty to ninety per cent chance of possessing one habitable planet each. The probability that at least one has is 0.972. It's almost certain. And that's just the least of it. Once we get back, she can give us the exact line of reasoning that led her to the conclusion and I predict that the whole science of astrophysics and cosmology will—"

"Are you sure—"

"You think I'm having hallucinations? I even have a witness. Poor guy jumped two feet when Jane suddenly began to reel out the answer in her gorgeous voice—"

And that was when the meteorite struck and in the thorough destruction of the plane that followed. Madarian and the pilot were reduced to gobbets of bloody flesh and no usable remnant of Jane was recovered.

The gloom at U. S. Robots had never been deeper. Robertson attempted to find consolation in the fact that the very completeness of the destruction had utterly hidden the illegalities of which the firm had been guilty.

Peter shook his head and mourned. "We've lost the best chance U. S. Robots ever had of gaining an unbeatable public image; of overcoming the damned Frankenstein complex. What it would have meant for robots to have one of them work out the solution to the habitable-planet problem, after other robots had helped work out the Space Jump. Robots would have opened the galaxy to us. And if at the same time we could have driven scientific knowledge forward in a dozen different directions as we surely would have . . . Oh, God, there's no way of calculating the benefits to the human race, and to us of course."

Robertson said, "We could build other Janes, couldn't we? Even without Madarian?"

"Sure we could. But can we depend on the proper correlation again? Who knows how low-probability that final result was? What if Madarian had had a fantastic piece of beginner's luck? And then to have an even more fantastic piece of bad luck? A meteorite zeroing in . . . It's simply unbelievable—"

Robertson said in a hesitating whisper, "It couldn't have been—meant. I mean, if we weren't meant to know and if the meteorite was a judgment—from—"

He faded off under Bogert's withering glare.

Bogert said, "It's not a dead loss, I suppose. Other Janes are bound to help us in some ways. And we can give other robots feminine voices, if that will help encourage public acceptance—though I wonder what the women would say. If we only knew what Jane-5 had said!"

"In that last call, Madarian said there was a witness."

Bogert said, "I know; I've been thinking about that. Don't you suppose I've been in touch with Flagstaff? Nobody in the entire place heard Jane say anything out of the ordinary, anything that sounded like an answer to the habitable-planet problem, and certainly anyone there should have recognized the answer if it came—or at least recognized it as a possible answer."

"Could Madarian have been lying? Or crazy? Could he have been trying to protect himself—"

"You mean he may have been trying to save his reputation by pretending he had the answer and then gimmick Jane so she couldn't talk and say, 'Oh, sorry, something happened accidentally. Oh, darn!' I won't accept that for a minute. You might as well suppose he had arranged the meteorite."

"Then what do we do?"

Bogert said heavily, "Turn back to Flagstaff. The answer *must* be there. I've got to dig deeper, that's all. I'm going there and I'm taking a couple of the men in Madarian's department. We've got to go through that place top to bottom and end to end."

"But, you know, even if there were a witness and he had heard, what good would it do, now that we don't have Jane to explain the process?"

"Every little something is useful. Jane gave the names of the stars; the catalogue numbers probably—none of the named stars has a chance. If someone can remember her saying that and actually remember the catalogue number, or have heard it clearly enough to allow it to be recovered by Psycho-probe if he lacked the conscious memory—then we'll have something. Given the results at the end, and the data fed Jane at the beginning, we might be able to reconstruct the line of reasoning; we might recover the intuition. If that is done, we've saved the game—"

Bogert was back after three days, silent and thoroughly depressed. When Robertson inquired anxiously as to results, he shook his head. "Nothing!"

"Nothing?"

"Absolutely nothing. I spoke with every man in Flagstaff—

every scientist, every technician, every student—that had had anything to do with Jane; everyone that had as much as seen her. The number wasn't great; I'll give Madarian credit for that much discretion. He only allowed those to see her who might conceivably have had planetological knowledge to feed her. There were twenty-three men altogether who had seen Jane and of those only twelve had spoken to her more than casually.

"I went over and over all that Jane had said. They remembered everything quite well. They're keen men engaged in a crucial experiment involving their specialty, so they had every motivation to remember. And they were dealing with a talking robot, something that was startling enough, and one that talked like a TV actress. They couldn't forget."

Robertson said, "Maybe a Psycho-probe—"

"If one of them had the vaguest thought that something had happened, I would screw out his consent to Probing. But there's nothing to leave room for an excuse, and to Probe two dozen men who make their living from their brains can't be done. Honestly, it wouldn't help. If Jane had mentioned three stars and said they had habitable planets, it would have been like setting up sky rockets in their brains. How could any one of them forget?"

"Then maybe one of them is lying," said Robertson grimly. "He wants the information for his own use; to get the credit himself later."

"What good would that do him?" said Bogert. "The whole establishment knows exactly why Madarian and Jane were there in the first place. They know why I came there in the second. If at any time in the future any man now at Flagstaff suddenly comes up with a habitable-planet theory that is startlingly new and different, yet valid, every other man at Flagstaff and every man at U. S. Robots will know at once that he had stolen it. He'd never get away with it."

"Then Madarian himself was somehow mistaken."

"I don't see how I can believe that either. Madarian had an irritating personality—all robopsychologists have irritating personalities, I think, which must be why they work with robots rather than with men—but he was no dummy. He *couldn't* be wrong in something like this."

"Then—" But Robertson had run out of possibilities. They had reached a blank wall and for some minutes stared at it disconsolately.

Finally Robertson stirred. "Peter—"

"Well?"

"Let's ask Susan."

Bogert stiffened. "What!"

"Let's ask Susan. Let's call her and ask her to come in."

"Why? What can she possibly do?"

"I don't know. But she's a robopsychologist, too, and she might understand Madarian better than we do. Besides, she— Oh, hell, she always had more brains than any of us."

"She's nearly eighty."

"And you're seventy. What about it?"

Bogert sighed. Had her abrasive tongue lost any of its rasp in the years of her retirement? He said, "Well, I'll ask her."

Susan Calvin entered Bogert's office with a slow look around before her eyes fixed themselves on the Research Director. She had aged a great deal since her retirement. Her hair was a fine white and her face seemed to have crumpled. She had grown so frail as to be almost transparent and only her eyes, piercing and uncompromising, seemed to remain of all that had been.

Bogert strode forward heartily, holding out his hand. "Susan!"

Susan Calvin took it, and said, "You're looking reasonably well, Peter, for an old man. If I were you, I wouldn't wait till next year. Retire now and let the young men get to it. . . . And Madarian is dead. Are you calling me in to take over my old job? Are you determined to keep the ancients till a year past actual physical death?"

"No, no, Susan. I've called you in—" He stopped. He did not, after all, have the faintest idea of how to start.

But Susan read his mind now as easily as she always had. She seated herself with the caution born of stiffened joints and said, "Peter, you've called me in because you're in bad trouble. Otherwise you'd sooner see me dead than within a mile of you."

"Come, Susan—"

"Don't waste time on pretty talk. I never had time to waste when I was forty and certainly not now. Madarian's death and your call to me are both unusual, so there must be a connection. Two unusual events without a connection is too low-probability to worry about. Begin at the beginning and don't worry about revealing yourself to be a fool. That was revealed to me long ago."

Bogert cleared his throat miserably and began. She listened

carefully, her withered hand lifting once in a while to stop him so that she might ask a question.

She snorted at one point. "Feminine intuition? Is that what you wanted the robot for? You men. Faced with a woman reaching a correct conclusion and unable to accept the fact that she is your equal or superior in intelligence, you invent something called feminine intuition."

"Uh, yes, Susan, but let me continue—"

He did. When she was told of Jane's contralto voice, she said, "It is a difficult choice sometimes whether to feel revolted at the male sex or merely to dismiss them as contemptible."

Bogert said, "Well, let me go on—"

When he was quite done, Susan said, "May I have the private use of this office for an hour or two?"

"Yes, but—"

She said, "I want to go over the various records—Jane's programming, Madarian's calls, your interviews at Flagstaff. I presume I can use that beautiful new shielded laser-phone and your computer outlet if I wish."

"Yes, of course."

"Well, then, get out of here, Peter."

It was not quite forty-five minutes when she hobbled to the door, opened it, and called for Bogert.

When Bogert came, Robertson was with him. Both entered and Susan greeted the latter with an unenthusiastic "Hello, Scott."

Bogert tried desperately to gauge the results from Susan's face, but it was only the face of a grim old lady who had no intention of making anything easy for him.

He said cautiously, "Do you think there's anything you can do, Susan?"

"Beyond what I have already done? No! There's nothing more."

Bogert's lips set in chagrin, but Robertson said, "What have you already done, Susan?"

Susan said, "I've thought a little; something I can't seem to persuade anyone else to do. For one thing, I've thought about Madarian. I knew him, you know. He had brains but he was a very irritating extrovert. I thought you would like him after me, Peter."

"It was a change," Bogert couldn't resist saying.

"And he was always running to you with results the very

minute he had them, wasn't he?"

"Yes, he was."

"And yet," said Susan, "his last message, the one in which he said Jane had given him the answer, was sent from the plane. Why did he wait so long? Why didn't he call you while he was still at Flagstaff, immediately after Jane had said whatever it was she said?"

"I suppose," said Peter, "that for once he wanted to check it thoroughly and—well, I don't know. It was the most important thing that had ever happened to him; he might for once have wanted to wait and be sure of himself."

"On the contrary; the more important it was, the less he would wait, surely. And if he could manage to wait, why not do it properly and wait till he was back at U. S. Robots so that he could check the results with all the computing equipment this firm could make available to him? In short, he waited too long from one point of view and not long enough from another."

Robertson interrupted. "Then you think he was up to some trickery—"

Susan looked revolted. "Scott, don't try to compete with Peter in making inane remarks. Let me continue. . . . A second point concerns the witness. According to the records of that last call, Madarian said, 'Poor guy jumped two feet when Jane suddenly began to reel out the answer in her gorgeous voice.' In fact, it was the last thing he said. And the question is, then, why should the witness have jumped? Madarian had explained that all the men were crazy about that voice, and they had had ten days with the robot—with Jane. Why should the mere act of her speaking have startled them?"

Bogert said, "I assumed it was astonishment at hearing Jane give an answer to a problem that has occupied the minds of planetologists for nearly a century."

"But they were *waiting* for her to give that answer. That was why she was there. Besides, consider the way the sentence is worded. Madarian's statement makes it seem the witness was startled, not astonished, if you see the difference. What's more, that reaction came 'when Jane suddenly began' —in other words, at the very start of the statement. To be astonished at the content of what Jane said would have required the witness to have listened awhile so that he might absorb it. Madarian would have said he had jumped two feet *after* he had heard Jane say thus-and-so. It would be 'after' not 'when' and the word 'suddenly' would not be included."

Bogert said uneasily, "I don't think you can refine matters down to the use or non-use of a word."

"I can," said Susan frostily, "because I am a robopsychologist. And I can expect Madarian to do so, too, because *he* was a robopsychologist. We have to explain those two anomalies, then. The queer delay before Madarian's call and the queer reaction of the witness."

"Can *you* explain them?" asked Robertson.

"Of course," said Susan, "since I use a little simple logic. Madarian called with the news without delay, as he always did, or with as little delay as he could manage. If Jane had solved the problem at Flagstaff, he would certainly have called from Flagstaff. Since he called from the plane, she must clearly have solved the problem after he had left Flagstaff."

"But then—"

"Let me finish. Let me finish. Was Madarian not taken from the airport to Flagstaff in a heavy, enclosed ground car? And Jane, in her crate, with him?"

"Yes."

"And presumably, Madarian and the crated Jane returned from Flagstaff to the airport in the same heavy, enclosed ground car. Am I right?"

"Yes, of course!"

"And they were not alone in the ground car, either. In one of his calls, Madarian said, 'We were chauffeured from the airport to the main administration building,' and I suppose I am right in concluding that if he was chauffeured, then that was because there was a chauffeur, a human driver, in the car."

"Good God!"

"The trouble with you, Peter, is that when you think of a witness to a planetological statement, you think of planetologists. You divide up human beings into categories, and despise and dismiss most. A robot cannot do that. The First Law says, 'A robot may not injure a *human being* or, through inaction, allow a *human being* to come to harm.' *Any* human being. That is the essence of the robotic view of life. A robot makes no distinction. To a robot, all men are truly equal, and to a robopsychologist who must perforce deal with men at the robotic level, all men are truly equal, too.

"It would not occur to Madarian to say a truck driver had heard the statement. To you a truck driver is not a scientist but is a mere animate adjunct of a truck, but to Madarian he was a man and a witness. Nothing more. Nothing less."

Bogert shook his head in disbelief. "But you are *sure?*"

"Of course I'm sure. How else can you explain the other point; Madarian's remark about the startling of the witness? Jane was crated, wasn't she? But she was *not* deactivated. According to the records, Madarian was always adamant against ever deactivating an intuitive robot. Moreover, Jane-5, like any of the Janes, was extremely non-talkative. Probably it never occurred to Madarian to order her to remain quiet within the crate; and it was within the crate that the pattern finally fell into place. Naturally she began to talk. A beautiful contralto voice suddenly sounded from inside the crate. If you were the truck driver, what would you do at that point? Surely you'd be startled. It's a wonder he didn't crash."

"But if the truck driver was the witness, why didn't he come forward—"

"Why? Can he possibly know that anything crucial had happened, that what he heard was important? Besides, don't you suppose Madarian tipped him well and asked him not to say anything? Would you *want* the news to spread that an activated robot was being transported illegally over the Earth's surface?"

"Well, will he remember what was said?"

"Why not? It might seem to you, Peter, that a truck driver, one step above an ape in your view, can't remember. But truck drivers can have brains, too. The statements were most remarkable and the driver may well have remembered some. Even if he gets some of the letters and numbers wrong, we're dealing with a finite set, you know, the fifty-five hundred stars or star systems within eighty light-years or so—I haven't looked up the exact number. You can make the correct choices. And if needed, you will have every excuse to use the Psychoprobe—"

The two men stared at her. Finally Bogert, afraid to believe, whispered, "But how can you be *sure?*"

For a moment, Susan was on the point of saying: Because I've called Flagstaff, you fool, and because I spoke to the truck driver, and because he told me what he had heard, and because I've checked with the computer at Flagstaff and got the only three stars that fit the information, and because I have those names in my pocket.

But she didn't. Let him go through it all himself. Carefully, she rose to her feet, and said sardonically, "How can I be sure? . . . Call it feminine intuition."

Do not fear, Gentle Readers, that my misunderstanding of Judy-Lynn's intentions destroyed a friendship. The Asimovs and the del Reys live less than a mile apart, and frequent each other often. Although Judy-Lynn never hesitates to bounce me off the nearest wall, we all are, have been, and will remain, the very best of friends.

Sometime in mid-1969, Doubleday called me up to ask if I would write a science fiction story that could serve as the basis of a movie. I didn't want to, because I don't like to get tangled up with the visual media directly. They've got money, but that's all they've got. But Doubleday pressed me and I don't like to refuse Doubleday. I agreed.

Then eventually I had dinner with a very pleasant gentleman who was involved with the motion picture company and who wanted to discuss the story with me.

He told me he wanted an undersea setting and that suited me. He then went on to describe with considerable enthusiasm the nature of the characters he wanted in the story, and the events he thought would be necessary. As he spoke, my spirits sank. The fact was that I didn't want the hero he described; I didn't want, with even greater intensity, the heroine he described; and most of all, I didn't want the events he described.

I have always found myself unable, however, to express a negative reaction to people, especially face to face. I did my best to smile and act interested.

The next day I called up Doubleday. It might not be too late. I asked if the contract had been signed. Yes, indeed, it had, and a large advance had been paid over, of which most was to be turned over to me.

I didn't think there was room for my spirits to sink lower, but they did. I *had* to write the story.

"Well, then," I said, "if what I write is unacceptable, would you return the advance?"

"We don't have to," I was told. "The advance is unconditional. If they don't like your story, we still keep the advance."

"No," I said. "I don't want it that way. If what I do is unacceptable, I want the entire advance returned. Take your share of it out of my royalties."

Doubleday doesn't like to refuse me anything either, so they agreed, although they made it plain they would return their share and not take anything out of my royalties.

That meant I was under no obligation to do anything but my best, as I conceived that best to be. On September 1, 1969, I began to write WATERCLAP and I did it my way. I

knew exactly what the movie people wanted and I didn't give
it to them. Naturally, they rejected it when it was done and
every cent they had advanced was returned to them.

This was a huge relief to me, you can well imagine.

And there is a world outside Hollywood, too. Ejler Jakobs-
son of *Galaxy* liked the story as I had written it, so it appeared
in the May 1970 issue of that magazine. He paid me far less
than the movie people would have, but then, all he bought
was the story.

3

Waterclap

Stephen Demerest looked at the textured sky. He kept looking at it and found the blue opaque and revolting.

Unwarily, he had looked at the Sun, for there was nothing
to blank it out automatically, and then he had snatched his
eyes away in panic. He wasn't blinded; just a few afterimages.
Even the Sun was washed out.

Involuntarily, he thought of Ajax's prayer in Homer's
Iliad. They were fighting over the body of Patroclus in the
mist and Ajax said, "O Father Zeus, save the Achaeans out of
this mist! Make the sky clean, grant us to see with our eyes!
Kill us in the light, since it is thy pleasure to kill us!"

Demerest thought: Kill us in the light—

Kill us in the clear light on the Moon, where the sky is
black and soft, where the stars shine brightly, where the
cleanliness and purity of vacuum make all things sharp.

—Not in this low-clinging, fuzzy blue.

He shuddered. It was an actual physical shudder that
shook his lanky body, and he was annoyed. He was going to

die. He was sure of it. And it wouldn't be under the blue, either, come to think of it, but under the black—but a different black.

It was as though in answer to that thought that the ferry pilot, short, swarthy, crisp-haired, came up to him and said, "Ready for the black, Mr. Demerest?"

Demerest nodded. He towered over the other as he did over most of the men of Earth. They were thick, all of them, and took their short, low steps with ease. He himself had to feel his footsteps, guide them through the air; even the impalpable bond that held him to the ground was textured.

"I'm ready," he said. He took a deep breath and deliberately repeated his earlier glance at the Sun. It was low in the morning sky, washed out by dusty air, and he knew it wouldn't blind him. He didn't think he would ever see it again.

He had never seen a bathyscaphe before. Despite everything, he tended to think of it in terms of prototypes, an oblong balloon with a spherical gondola beneath. It was as though he persisted in thinking of space flight in terms of tons of fuel spewed backward in fire, and an irregular module feeling its way, spiderlike, toward the Lunar surface.

The bathyscaphe was not like the image in his thoughts at all. Under its skin, it might still be buoyant bag and gondola, but it was all engineered sleekness now.

"My name is Javan," said the ferry pilot. "Omar Javan."

"Javan?"

"Queer name to you? I'm Iranian by descent; Earthman by persuasion. Once you get down there, there are no nationalities." He grinned and his complexion grew darker against the even whiteness of his teeth. "If you don't mind, we'll be starting in a minute. You'll be my only passenger, so I guess you carry weight."

"Yes," said Demerest dryly. "At least a hundred pounds more than I'm used to."

"You're from the Moon? I thought you had a queer walk on you. I hope it's not uncomfortable."

"It's not exactly comfortable, but I manage. We exercise for this."

"Well, come on board." He stood aside and let Demerest walk down the gangplank. "I wouldn't go to the Moon myself."

"You go to Ocean-Deep."

"About fifty times so far. That's different."

Demerest got on board. It was cramped, but he didn't mind

that. It might be a space module except that it was more—well, textured. There was that word again. There was the clear feeling everywhere that mass didn't matter. Mass was held up; it didn't have to be hurled up.

They were still on the surface. The blue sky could be seen greenishly through the clear thick glass. Javan said, "You don't have to be strapped in. There's no acceleration. Smooth as oil, the whole thing. It won't take long; just about an hour. You can't smoke."

"I don't smoke," said Demerest.

"I hope you don't have claustrophobia."

"Moon-men don't have claustrophobia."

"All that open—"

"Not in our cavern. We live in a"—he groped for the phrase —"a Lunar-Deep, a hundred feet deep."

"A hundred feet!" The pilot seemed amused, but he didn't smile. "We're slipping down now."

The interior of the gondola was fitted into angles but here and there a section of wall beyond the instruments showed its basic sphericity. To Javan, the instruments seemed to be an extension of his arms; his eyes and hands moved over them lightly, almost lovingly.

"We're all checked out," he said, "but I like a last-minute look-over; we'll be facing a thousand atmospheres down there." His finger touched a contact, and the round door closed massively inward and pressed against the beveled rim it met.

"The higher the pressure, the tighter that will hold," said Javan. "Take your last look at sunlight, Mr. Demerest."

The light still shone through the thick glass of the window. It was wavering now; there was water between the Sun and them now.

"The last look?" said Demerest.

Javan snickered. "Not the *last* look. I mean for the trip. . . . I suppose you've never been on a bathyscape before."

"No, I haven't. Have many?"

"Very few," admitted Javan. "But don't worry. It's just an underwater balloon. We've introduced a million improvements since the first bathyscaphe. It's nuclear-powered now and we can move freely by water jet up to certain limits, but cut it down to basics and it's still a spherical gondola under buoyancy tanks. And it's still towed out to sea by a mother ship because it needs what power it carries too badly to waste it on surface travel. Ready?"

"Ready."

The supporting cable of the mother ship flicked away and the bathyscaphe settled lower; then lower still, as sea water fed into the buoyancy tanks. For a few moments, caught in surface currents, it swayed, and then there was nothing. The bathyscaphe sank slowly through a deepening green.

Javan relaxed. He said, "John Bergen is head of Ocean-Deep. You're going to see him?"

"That's right."

"He's a nice guy. His wife's with him."

"She is?"

"Oh, sure. They have women down there. There's a bunch down there, fifty people. Some stay for months."

Demerest put his finger on the narrow, nearly invisible seam where door met wall. He took it away and looked at it. He said, "It's oily."

"Silicone, really. The pressure squeezes some out. It's supposed to. . . . Don't worry. Everything's automatic. Everything's fail-safe. The first sign of malfunction, any malfunction at all, our ballast is released and up we go."

"You mean nothing's ever happened to these bathyscaphes?"

"What can happen?" The pilot looked sideways at his passenger. "Once you get too deep for sperm whales, nothing can go wrong."

"Sperm whales?" Demerest's thin face creased in a frown.

"Sure, they dive as deep as half a mile. If they hit a bathyscaphe—well, the walls of the buoyancy chambers aren't particularly strong. They don't have to be, you know. They're open to the sea and when the gasoline, which supplies the buoyancy, compresses, sea water enters."

It was dark now. Demerest found his gaze fastened to the viewport. It was light inside the gondola, but it was dark in that window. And it was not the darkness of space; it was a thick darkness.

Demerest said sharply, "Let's get this straight, Mr. Javan. You are not equipped to withstand the attack of a sperm whale. Presumably you are not equipped to withstand the attack of a giant squid. Have there been any actual incidents of that sort?"

"Well, it's like this—"

"No games, please, and don't try ragging the greenhorn. I am asking out of professional curiosity. I am head safety engineer at Luna City and I am asking what precautions this bathyscaphe can take against possible collision with large creatures."

Javan looked embarrassed. He muttered, "Actually, there have been no incidents."

"Are any expected? Even as a remote possibility?"

"Anything is remotely possible. But actually sperm whales are too intelligent to monkey with us and giant squid are too shy."

"Can they see us?"

"Yes, of course. We're lit up."

"Do you have floodlights?"

"We're already past the large-animal range, but we have them, and I'll turn them on for you."

Through the black of the window there suddenly appeared a snow-storm, an inverted upward-falling snowstorm. The blackness had come alive with stars in three-dimensional array and all moving upward.

Demerest said, "What's that?"

"Just crud. Organic matter. Small creatures. They float, don't move much, and they catch the light. We're going down past them. They seem to be going up in consequence."

Demerest's sense of perspective adjusted itself and he said, "Aren't we dropping too quickly?"

"No, we're not. If we were, I could use the nuclear engines, if I wanted to waste power; or I could drop some ballast. I'll be doing that later, but for now everything is fine. Relax, Mr. Demerest. The snow thins as we dive and we're not likely to see much in the way of spectacular life forms. There are small angler fish and such but they avoid us."

Demerest said, "How many do you take down at a time?"

"I've had as many as four passengers in this gondola, but that's crowded. We can put two bathyscaphes in tandem and carry ten, but that's clumsy. What we really need are trains of gondolas, heavier on the nukes—the nuclear engines—and lighter on the buoyancy. Stuff like that is on the drawing board, they tell me. Of course, they've been telling me that for years."

"There are plans for large-scale expansion of Ocean-Deep, then?"

"Sure, why not? We've got cities on the continental shelves, why not on the deep-sea bottom? The way I look at it, Mr. Demerest, where man can go, he will go and he should go. The Earth is ours to populate and we will populate it. All we need to make the deep sea habitable are completely maneuverable 'scaphes. The buoyancy chambers slow us, weaken us, and complicate the engineering."

"But they also save you, don't they? If everything goes wrong at once, the gasoline you carry will still float you to the surface. What would do that for you if your nuclear engines go wrong and you had no buoyancy?"

"If it comes to that, you can't expect to eliminate the chances of accident altogether, not even fatal ones."

"I know that very well," said Demerest feelingly.

Javan stiffened. The tone of his voice changed. "Sorry. Didn't mean anything by that. Tough about that accident."

"Yes," said Demerest. Fifteen men and five women had died. One of the individuals listed among the "men" had been fourteen years old. It had been pinned down to human failure. What could a head safety engineer say after that?

"Yes," he said.

A pall dropped between the two men, a pall as thick and as turgid as the pressurized sea water outside. How could one allow for panic and for distraction and for depression all at once? There were the Moon-Blues—stupid name—but they struck men at inconvenient times. It wasn't always noticeable when the Moon-Blues came but it made men torpid and slow to react.

How many times had a meteorite come along and been averted or smothered or successfully absorbed? How many times had a Moonquake done damage and been held in check? How many times had human failure been backed up and compensated for? How many times had accidents *not* happened?

But you don't pay off on accidents not happening. There were twenty dead—

Javan said (how many long minutes later?), "There are the lights of Ocean-Deep!"

Demerest could not make them out at first. He didn't know where to look. Twice before, luminescent creatures had flicked past the windows at a distance and with the floodlights off again, Demerest had thought them the first sign of Ocean-Deep. Now he saw nothing.

"Down there," said Javan, without pointing. He was busy now, slowing the drop and edging the 'scaphe sideways.

Demerest could hear the distant sighing of the water jets, steam-driven, with the steam formed by the heat of momentary bursts of fusion power.

Demerest thought dimly: Deuterium is their fuel and it's

all around them. Water is their exhaust and it's all around them.

Javan was dropping some of his ballast, too, and began a kind of distant chatter. "The ballast used to be steel pellets and they were dropped by electromagnetic controls. Anywhere up to fifty tons of it were used in each trip. Conservationists worried about spreading rusting steel over the ocean floor, so we switched to metal nodules that are dredged up from the continental shelf. We put a thin layer of iron over them so they can still be electromagnetically handled and the ocean bottom gets nothing that wasn't sub-ocean to begin with. Cheaper, too. . . . But when we get out real nuclear 'scaphes, we won't need ballast at all."

Demerest scarcely heard him. Ocean-Deep could be seen now. Javan had turned on the floodlights and far below was the muddy floor of the Puerto Rican Trench. Resting on that floor like a cluster of equally muddy pearls was the spherical conglomerate of Ocean-Deep.

Each unit was a sphere such as the one in which Demerest was now sinking toward contact, but much larger, and as Ocean-Deep expanded—expanded—expanded, new spheres were added.

Demerest thought: They're only five and a half miles from home, not a quarter of a million.

"How are we going to get through?" asked Demerest.

The 'scaphe had made contact. Demerest heard the dull sound of metal against metal but then for minutes there had been nothing more than a kind of occasional scrape as Javan bent over his instruments in rapt concentration.

"Don't worry about that," Javan said at last, in belated answer. "There's no problem. The delay now is only because I have to make sure we fit tightly. There's an electromagnet joint that holds at every point of a perfect circle. When the instruments read correctly, that means we fit over the entrance door."

"Which then opens?"

"It would if there were air on the other side, but there isn't. There's sea water, and that has to be driven out. *Then* we enter."

Demerest did not miss this point. He had come here on this, the last day of his life, to give that same life meaning and he intended to miss nothing.

He said, "Why the added step? Why not keep the air lock,

if that's what it is, a real air lock, and have air in it at all times?"

"They tell me it's a matter of safety," said Javan. "*Your* specialty. The interface has equal pressure on both sides at all times, *except* when men are moving across. This door is the weakest point of the whole system, because it opens and closes; it has joints; it has seams. You know what I mean?"

"I do," murmured Demerest. There was a logical flaw here and that meant there was a possible chink through which— but later.

He said, "Why are we waiting now?"

"The lock is being emptied. The water is being forced out."

"By air."

"Hell, no. They can't afford to waste air like that. It would take a thousand atmospheres to empty the chamber of its water, and filling the chamber with air at that density, even temporarily, is more air than they can afford to expend. Steam is what does it."

"Of course. Yes."

Javan said cheerfully, "You heat the water. No pressure in the world can stop water from turning to steam at a temperature of more than 374° C. And the steam forces the sea water out through a one-way valve."

"Another weak point," said Demerest.

"I suppose so. It's never failed yet. The water in the lock is being pushed out now. When hot steam starts bubbling out the valve, the process automatically stops and the lock is full of overheated steam."

"And then?"

"And then we have a whole ocean to cool it with. The temperature drops and the steam condenses. Once that happens, ordinary air can be let in at a pressure of one atmosphere and *then* the door opens."

"How long must we wait?"

"Not long. If there were anything wrong, there'd be sirens sounding. At least, so they say. I never heard one in action."

There was silence for a few minutes, and then there was a sudden sharp clap and a simultaneous jerk.

Javan said, "Sorry, I should have warned you. I'm so used to it I forgot. When the door opens, a thousand atmospheres of pressure on the other side forces us hard against the metal of Ocean-Deep. No electromagnetic force can hold us hard enough to prevent that last hundredth-of-an-inch slam."

Demerest unclenched his fist and released his breath. He said, "Is everything all right?"

"The walls didn't crack, if that's what you mean. It sounds like doom, though, doesn't it? It sounds even worse when I've got to leave and the air lock fills up again. Be prepared for that."

But Demerest was suddenly weary. Let's get on with it, he thought. I don't want to drag it out. He said, "Do we go through now?"

"We go through."

The opening in the 'scaphe wall was round and small; even smaller than the one through which they had originally entered. Javan went through it sinuously, muttering that it always made him feel like a cork in a bottle.

Demerest had not smiled since he entered the 'scaphe. Nor did he really smile now, but a corner of his mouth quirked as he thought that a skinny Moon-man would have no trouble.

He went through also, feeling Javan's hands firmly at his waist, helping him through.

Javan said, "It's dark in here. No point in introducing an additional weakness by wiring for lighting. But that's why flashlights were invented."

Demerest found himself on a perforated walk, its stainless metallic surface gleaming dully. And through the perforations he could make out the wavering surface of water.

He said, "The chamber hasn't been emptied."

"You can't do any better, Mr. Demerest. If you're going to use steam to empty it, you're left with that steam, and to get the pressures necessary to do the emptying that steam must be compressed to about one-third the density of liquid water. When it condenses, the chamber remains one-third full of water—but it's water at just one-atmosphere pressure. . . . Come on, Mr. Demerest."

John Bergen's face wasn't entirely unknown to Demerest. Recognition was immediate. Bergen, as head of Ocean-Deep for nearly a decade now, was a familiar face on the TV screens of Earth—just as the leaders of Luna City had become familiar.

Demerest had seen the head of Ocean-Deep both flat and in three dimensions, in black-and-white and in color. Seeing him in life added little.

Like Javan, Bergen was short and thickset; opposite in

structure to the traditional (already traditional?) Lunar pattern of physiology. He was fairer than Javan by a good deal and his face was noticeably asymmetrical, with his somewhat thick nose leaning just a little to the right.

He was not handsome. No Moon-man would think he was, but then Bergen smiled and there was a sunniness about it as he held out his large hand.

Demerest placed his own thin one within, steeling himself for a hard grip, but it did not come. Bergen took the hand and let it go, then said, "I'm glad you're here. We don't have much in the way of luxury, nothing that will make our hospitality stand out, we can't even declare a holiday in your honor— but the spirit is there. Welcome!"

"Thank you," said Demerest softly. He remained unsmiling now, too. He was facing the enemy and he knew it. Surely Bergen must know it also and, since he did, that smile of his was hypocrisy.

And at that moment a clang like metal against metal sounded deafeningly and the chamber shuddered. Demerest leaped back and staggered against the wall.

Bergen did not budge. He said quietly, "That was the bathyscaphe unhitching and the waterclap of the air lock filling. Javan ought to have warned you."

Demerest panted and tried to make his racing heart slow. He said, "Javan did warn me. I was caught by surprise anyway."

Bergen said, "Well, it won't happen again for a while. We don't often have visitors, you know. We're not equipped for it and so we fight off all kinds of big wheels who think a trip down here would be good for their careers. Politicians of all kinds, chiefly. Your own case is different of course."

Is it? thought Demerest. It had been hard enough to get permission to make the trip down. His superiors back at Luna City had not approved in the first place and had scouted the idea that a diplomatic interchange would be of any use. ("Diplomatic interchange" was what they had called it.) And when he had overborne them, there had been Ocean-Deep's own reluctance to receive him.

It had been sheer persistence alone that had made his present visit possible. In what way then was Demerest's case different?

Bergen said, "I suppose you have your junketing problems on Luna City, too?"

"Very little," said Demerest. "Your average politician isn't as anxious to travel a half-million-mile round trip as he is to travel a ten-mile one."

"I can see that," agreed Bergen, "and it's more expensive out to the Moon, of course. . . . In a way, this is the first meeting of inner and outer space. No Ocean-man has ever gone to the Moon as far as I know and you're the first Moon-man to visit a sub-sea station of any kind. No Moon-man has ever been to one of the settlements on the continental shelf."

"It's a historic meeting, then," said Demerest, and tried to keep the sarcasm out of his voice.

If any leaked through, Bergen showed no sign. He rolled up his sleeves as though to emphasize his attitude of informality (or the fact that they were very busy, so that there would be little time for visitors?) and said, "Do you want coffee? I assume you've eaten. Would you like to rest before I show you around? Do you want to wash up, for that matter, as they say euphemistically?"

For a moment, curiosity stirred in Demerest; yet not entirely aimless curiosity. Everything involving the interface of Ocean-Deep with the outside world could be of importance. He said, "How are sanitary facilities handled here?"

"It's cycled mostly; as it is on the Moon, I imagine. We can eject if we want to or have to. Man has a bad record of fouling the environment, but as the only deep-sea station, what we eject does no perceptible damage. Adds organic matter." He laughed.

Demerest filed that away, too. Matter was ejected; there was therefore ejection tubes. Their workings might be of interest and he, as a safety engineer, had a right to be interested.

"No, he said, "I don't need anything at the moment. If you're busy—"

"That's all right. We're always busy, but I'm the least busy, if you see what I mean. Suppose I show you around. We've got over fifty units here, each as big as this one, some bigger—"

Demerest looked about. Again, as in the 'scaphe, there were angles everywhere, but beyond the furnishings and equipment there were signs of the inevitable spherical outer wall. Fifty of them!

"Built up," went on Bergen, "over a generation of effort. The unit we're standing in is actually the oldest and there's been some talk of demolishing and replacing it. Some of the men say we're ready for second-generation units, but I'm not sure.

It would be expensive—everything's expensive down here—and getting money out of the Planetary Project Council is always a depressing experience."

Demerest felt his nostrils flare involuntarily and a spasm of anger shot through him. It was a thrust, surely. Luna City's miserable record with the PPC must be well known to Bergen.

But Bergen went on, unnoticing. "I'm a traditionalist, too—just a little bit. This is the first deep-sea unit ever constructed. The first two people to remain overnight on the floor of an ocean trench slept here with nothing else beyond this bare sphere except for a miserable portable fusion unit to work the escape hatch. I mean the air lock, but we called it the escape hatch to begin with—and just enough controls for the purpose. Reguera and Tremont, those were the men. They never made a second trip to the bottom, either; stayed Topside forever after. Well, well, they served their purpose and both are dead now. And here we are with fifty people and with six months as the usual tour of duty. I've spent only two weeks Topside in the last year and a half."

He motioned vigorously to Demerest to follow him, slid open a door which moved evenly into a recess, and took him into the next unit. Demerest paused to examine the opening. There were no seams that he could notice between the adjacent units.

Bergen noted the other's pause and said, "When we add on our units, they're welded under pressure into the equivalent of a single piece of metal and then reinforced. We can't take chances, as I'm sure you understand, since I have been given to understand that you're the head safe—"

Demerest cut him off. "Yes," he said. "We on the Moon admire your safety record."

Bergen shrugged. "We've been lucky. Our sympathy, by the way, on the rotten break you fellows had. I mean that fatal—"

Demerest cut him off again. "Yes."

Bergen, the Moon-man decided, was either a naturally voluble man or else was eager to drown him in words and get rid of him.

"The units," said Bergen, "are arranged in a highly branched chain—three-dimensional actually. We have a map we can show you, if you're interested. Most of the end units represent living-sleeping quarters. For privacy, you know. The working units tend to be corridors as well, which is one of the embarrassments of having to live down here.

"This is our library; part of it, anyway. Not big, but it's got our records, too, on carefully indexed and computed microfilm, so that for its kind it's not only the biggest in the world, but the best and the only. And we have a special computer to handle the references to meet our needs exactly. It collects, selects, coordinates, weighs, then gives us the gist.

"We have another library, too, book films and even some printed volumes. But that's for amusement."

A voice broke in on Bergen's cheerful flow. "John? May I interrupt?"

Demerest started; the voice had come from behind him. Bergen said, "Annette! I was going to get you. This is Stephen Demerest of Luna City. Mr. Demerest, may I introduce my wife, Annette?"

Demerest had turned. He said stiffly, a little mechanically, "I'm pleased to meet you, Mrs. Bergen." But he was staring at her waistline.

Annette Bergen seemed in her early thirties. Her brown hair was combed simply and she wore no makeup. Attractive, not beautiful, Demerest noted vaguely. But his eyes kept returning to that waistline.

She shrugged a little. "Yes, I'm pregnant, Mr. Demerest. I'm due in about two months."

"Pardon me," Demerest muttered. "So rude of me. . . . I didn't—" He faded off and felt as though the blow had been a physical one. He hadn't expected women, though he didn't know why. He *knew* there would have to be women in Ocean-Deep. And the ferry pilot had said Bergen's wife was with him.

He stammered as he spoke. "How many women are there in Ocean-Deep, Mr. Bergen?"

"Nine at the moment," said Bergen. "All wives. We look forward to a time when we can have the normal ratio of one to one, but we still need workers and researchers primarily, and unless women have important qualifications of *some* sort—"

"They all have important qualifications of *some* sort, dear," said Mrs. Bergen. "You could keep the men for longer duty if—"

"My wife," said Bergen, laughing, "is a convinced feminist but is not above using sex as an excuse to enforce equality. I keep telling her that that is the feminine way of doing it and not the feminist way, and she keeps saying—Well, that's why she's pregnant. You think it's love, sex mania, yearning for motherhood? Nothing of the sort. She's going to have a baby down here to make a philosophical point."

Annette said coolly, "Why not? Either this is going to be home for humanity or it isn't going to be. If it *is*, then we're going to have babies here, that's all. I want a baby born in Ocean-Deep. There are babies born in Luna City, aren't there, Mr. Demerest?"

Demerest took a deep breath. "*I* was born in Luna City, Mrs. Bergen."

"And well she knew it," muttered Bergen.

"And you are in your late twenties, I think?" she said.

"I am twenty-nine," said Demerest.

"And well she knew that, too," said Bergen with a short laugh. "You can bet she looked up all possible data on you when she heard you were coming."

"That is quite beside the point," said Annette. "The point is that for twenty-nine years at least children have been born in Luna City and no children have been born in Ocean-Deep."

"Luna City, my dear," said Bergen, "is longer-established. It is over half a century old; we are not yet twenty."

"Twenty years is quite enough. It takes a baby nine months."

Demerest interposed, "Are there any children in Ocean-Deep?"

"No," said Bergen. "No. Someday, though."

"In two months, anyway," said Annette Bergen positively.

The tension grew inside Demerest and when they returned to the unit in which he had first met Bergen, he was glad to sit down and accept a cup of coffee.

"We'll eat soon," said Bergen matter-of-factly. "I hope you don't mind sitting here meanwhile. As the prime unit, it isn't used for much except, of course, for the reception of vessels, an item I don't expect will interrupt us for a while. We can talk, if you wish."

"I *do* wish," said Demerest.

"I hope I'm welcome to join in," said Annette.

Demerest looked at her doubtfully, but Bergen said to him, "You'll have to agree. She's fascinated by you and by Moon-men generally. She thinks they're—uh—*you're* a new breed, and I think that when she's quite through being a Deep-woman she wants to be a Moon-woman."

"I just want to get a word in edgewise, John, and when I get that in, I'd like to hear what Mr. Demerest has to say. What do you think of us, Mr. Demerest?"

Demerest said cautiously, "I've asked to come here, Mrs. Bergen, because I'm a safety engineer. Ocean-Deep has an enviable safety record—"

"Not one fatality in almost twenty years," said Bergen cheerfully. "Only one death by accident in the C-shelf settlements and none in transit by either sub or 'scaphe. I wish I could say, though, that this was the result of wisdom and care on our part. We do our best, of course, but the breaks have been with us—"

"John," said Annette, "I really wish you'd let Mr. Demerest speak."

"As a safety engineer," said Demerest, "I can't afford to believe in luck and breaks. We cannot stop Moon-quakes or large meteorites out at Luna City, but we are designed to minimize the effects even of those. There are no excuses or there should be none for human failure. We have not avoided that on Luna City; our record recently has been"—his voice dropped—"bad. While humans are imperfect, as we all know, machinery should be designed to take that imperfection into account. We lost twenty men and women—"

"I know. Still, Luna City has a population of nearly one thousand, doesn't it? Your survival isn't in danger."

"The people on Luna City number nine hundred and seventy-two, including myself, but our survival is in danger. We depend on Earth for essentials. That need not always be so; it wouldn't be so right now if the Planetary Project Council could resist the temptation toward pygmy economies—"

"There, at least, Mr. Demerest," said Bergen, "we see eye to eye. We are not self-supporting either, and we could be. What's more, we can't grow much beyond our present level unless nuclear 'scaphes are built. As long as we keep that buoyancy principle, we are limited. Transportation between Deep and Top is slow; slow for men; slower still for matériel and supplies. I've been pushing, Mr. Demerest, for—"

"Yes, and you'll be getting it now, Mr. Bergen, won't you?"

"I hope so, but what makes you so sure?"

"Mr. Bergen, let's not play around. You know very well that Earth is committed to spending a fixed amount of money on expansion projects—on programs designed to expand the human habitat—and that it is not a terribly large amount. Earth's population is not going to lavish resources in an effort to expand either outer space or inner space if it thinks this will cut into the comfort and convenience of Earth's prime habitat, the land surface of the planet."

Annette broke in. "You make it sound callous of Earthmen, Mr. Demerest, and that's unfair. It's only human, isn't it, to want to be secure? Earth is overpopulated and it is only slowly reversing the havoc inflicted on the planet by the Mad Twentieth. Surely man's original home must come first, ahead of either Luna City or Ocean-Deep. Heavens, Ocean-Deep is almost *home* to me, but I can't want to see it flourish at the expense of Earth's land."

"It's not an either-or, Mrs. Bergen," said Demerest earnestly. "If the ocean and outer space are firmly, honestly, and intelligently exploited, it can only redound to Earth's benefit. A small investment will be lost but a large one will redeem itself with profit."

Bergen held up his hand. "Yes, I know. You don't have to argue with me on that point. You'd be trying to convert the converted. Come, let's eat. I tell you what. We'll eat here. If you'll stay with us overnight, or several days for that matter—you're quite welcome—there will be ample time to meet everybody. Perhaps you'd rather take it easy for a while, though."

"Much rather," said Demerest. "Actually, I want to stay here. . . . I would like to ask, by the way, why I met so few people when we went through the units."

"No mystery," said Bergen genially. "At any given time, some fifteen of our men are asleep and perhaps fifteen more are watching films or playing chess or, if their wives are with them—"

"Yes, John," said Annette.

"—And it's customary not to disturb them. The quarters are constricted and what privacy a man can have is cherished. A few are out at sea; three right now, I think. That leaves a dozen or so at work in here and you met them."

"I'll get lunch," said Annette, rising.

She smiled and stepped through the door, which closed automatically behind her.

Bergen looked after her. "That's a concession. She's playing woman for your sake. Ordinarily, it would be just as likely for me to get the lunch. The choice is not defined by sex but by the striking of random lightning."

Demerest said, "The doors between units, it seems to me, are of dangerously limited strength."

"Are they?"

"If an accident happened, and one unit was punctured—"

"No meteorites down here," said Bergen, smiling.

"Oh yes, wrong word. If there were a leak of any sort, for any reason, then could a unit or a group of units be sealed off against the full pressure of the ocean?"

"You mean, in the way that Luna City can have its component units automatically sealed off in case of meteorite puncture in order to limit damage to a single unit."

"Yes," said Demerest with a faint bitterness. "As did *not* happen recently."

"In theory, we could do that, but the chances of accident are much less down here. As I said, there are no meteorites and, what's more, there are no currents to speak of. Even an earthquake centered immediately below us would not be damaging since we make no fixed or solid contact with the ground beneath us and are cushioned by the ocean itself against the shocks. So we can afford to gamble on no massive influx."

"Yet if one happened?"

"Then we could be helpless. You see, it is not so easy to seal off component units here. On the Moon, there is a pressure differential of just one atmosphere; one atmosphere inside and the zero atmosphere of vacuum outside. A thin seal is enough. Here at Ocean-Deep the pressure differential is roughly a thousand atmospheres. To secure absolute safety against that differential would take a great deal of money and you know what you said about getting money out of PPC. So we gamble and so far we've been lucky."

"And we haven't," said Demerest.

Bergen looked uncomfortable, but Annette distracted both by coming in with lunch at this moment.

She said, "I hope, Mr. Demerest, that you're prepared for Spartan fare. All our food in Ocean-Deep is prepackaged and requires only heating. We specialize in blandness and nonsurprise here, and the non-surprise of the day is a bland chicken à la king, with carrots, boiled potatoes, a piece of something that looks like a brownie for dessert, and, of course, all the coffee you can drink."

Demerest rose to take his tray and tried to smile. "It sounds very like Moon fare, Mrs. Bergen, and I was brought up on that. We grow our own micro-organismic food. It is patriotic to eat that but not particularly enjoyable. We hope to keep improving it, though."

"I'm sure you *will* improve it."

Demerest said, as he ate with a slow and methodical chewing, "I hate to ride my specialty, but how secure are you against mishaps in your air-lock entry?"

"It *is* the weakest point of Ocean-Deep," said Bergen. He had finished eating, well ahead of the other two, and was half through with his first cup of coffee. "But there's got to be an interface, right? The entry is as automatic as we can make it and as fail-safe. Number one: there has to be contact at every point about the outer lock before the fusion generator begins to heat the water within the lock. What's more, the contact has to be metallic and of a metal with just the magnetic permeability we use on our 'scaphes. Presumably a rock or some mythical deep-sea monster might drop down and make contact at just the right places; but if so, nothing happens.

"Then, too, the outer door doesn't open until the steam has pushed the water out and then condensed; in other words, not till both pressure and temperature have dropped below a certain point. At the moment the outer door begins to open, a relatively slight increase in internal pressure, as by water entry, will close it again."

Demerest said, "But then, once men have passed through the lock, the inner door closes behind them and sea water must be allowed into the lock again. Can you do that gradually against the full pressure of the ocean outside?"

"Not very." Bergen smiled. "It doesn't pay to fight the ocean too hard. You have to roll with the punch. We slow it down to about one-tenth free entry but even so it comes in like a rifle shot—louder, a thunderclap, or waterclap, if you prefer. The inner door can hold it, though, and it is not subjected to the strain very often. Well, wait, you heard the waterclap when we first met, when Javan's 'scaphe took off again. Remember?"

"I remember," said Demerest. "But here is something I don't understand. You keep the lock filled with ocean at high pressure at all times to keep the outer door without strain. But that keeps the inner door at full strain. Somewhere there has to be strain."

"Yes, indeed. But if the outer door, with a thousand-atmosphere differential on its two sides, breaks down, the full ocean in all its millions of cubic miles tries to enter and that would be the end of all. If the inner door is the one under strain and it gives, then it will be messy indeed, but the only water that enters Ocean-Deep will be the very limited quantity in the lock and its pressure will drop at once. We will have plenty of time for repair, for the outer door will certainly hold a long time."

"But if both go simultaneously—"

"Then we are through." Bergen shrugged. "I need not tell you that neither absolute certainty nor absolute safety exists. You have to live with some risk and the chance of double and simultaneous failure is so microscopically small that it can be lived with easily."

"If all your mechanical contrivances fail—"

"They fail safe," said Bergen stubbornly.

Demerest nodded. He finished the last of his chicken. Mrs. Bergen was already beginning to clean up. "You'll pardon my questions, Mr. Bergen, I hope."

"You're welcome to ask. I wasn't informed, actually, as to the precise nature of your mission here. 'Fact finding' is a weasel phrase. However, I assume there is keen distress on the Moon over the recent disaster and as safety engineer you rightly feel the responsibility of correcting whatever short-comings exist and would be interested in learning, if possible, from the system used in Ocean-Deep."

"Exactly. But, see here, if all your automatic contrivances fail safe for some reason, for any reason, you would be alive, but all your escape-hatch mechanisms would be sealed permanently shut. You would be trapped inside Ocean-Deep and would exchange a slow death for a fast one."

"It's not likely to happen but we'd *hope* we could make repairs before our air supply gave out. Besides we *do* have a manual backup system."

"Oh?"

"Certainly. When Ocean-Deep was first established and this was the only unit—the one we're sitting in now—manual controls were all we had. *That* was unsafe, if you like. There they are, right behind you—covered with friable plastic."

"In emergency, break glass," muttered Demerest, inspecting the covered setup.

"Pardon me?"

"Just a phrase commonly used in ancient fire-fighting systems . . . Well, do the manuals still work, or has the system been covered with your friable plastic for twenty years to the point where it has all decayed into uselessness with no one noticing?"

"Not at all. It's periodically checked, as all our equipment is. That's not my job personally, but I know it is done. If any electrical or electronic circuit is out of its normal working condition, lights flash, signals sound, everything happens but a nuclear blast. . . . You know, Mr. Demerest, we are as curious about Luna City as you are about Ocean-Deep. I presume you would be willing to invite one of our young men—"

"How about a young woman?" interposed Annette at once.

"I am sure you mean yourself, dear," said Bergen, "to which I can only answer that you are determined to have a baby here and to keep it here for a period of time after birth, and that effectively eliminates you from consideration."

Demerest said stiffly, "We hope you will send men to Luna City. We are anxious to have you understand our problems."

"Yes, a mutual exchange of problems and of weeping on each other's shoulders might be of great comfort to all. For instance, you have one advantage on Luna City that I wish we could have. With low gravity and a low pressure differential, you can make your caverns take on any irregular and angular fashion that appeals to your aesthetic sense or is required for convenience. Down here we're restricted to the sphere, at least for the foreseeable future, and our designers develop a hatred for the spherical that surpasses belief. Actually it isn't funny. It breaks them down. They eventually resign rather than continue to work spherically."

Bergen shook his head and leaned his chair back against a microfilm cabinet. "You know," he continued, "when William Beebe built the first deep-set chamber in history in the 1930s—it was just a gondola suspended from a mother ship by a half-mile cable, with no buoyancy chambers and no engines, and if the cable broke, good night, only it never did. . . . Anyway, what was I saying? Oh, when Beebe built his first deep-sea chamber, he was going to make it cylindrical; you know, so a man would fit in it comfortably. After all, a man is essentially a tall, skinny cylinder. However, a friend of his argued him out of that and into a sphere on the very sensible grounds that a sphere would resist pressure more efficiently than any other possible shape. You know who that friend was?"

"No, I'm afraid I don't."

"The man who was President of the United States at the time of Beebe's descents—Franklin D. Roosevelt. All these spheres you see down here are the great-grandchildren of Roosevelt's suggestion."

Demerest considered that briefly but made no comment. He returned to the earlier topic. "We would particularly like someone from Ocean-Deep," he said, "to visit Luna City because it might lead to a great enough understanding of the need, on Ocean-Deep's part, for a course of action that might involve considerable self-sacrifice."

"Oh?" Bergen's chair came down flat-leggedly on all fours. "How's that?"

"Ocean-Deep is a marvelous achievement; I wish to detract nothing from that. I can see where it will become greater still, a wonder of the world. *Still*—"

"Still?"

"Still, the oceans are only a part of the Earth; a major part, but only a part. The deep sea is only part of the ocean. It is inner space indeed; it works inward, narrowing constantly to a point."

"I think," broke in Annette, looking rather grim, "that you're about to make a comparison with Luna City."

"Indeed I am," said Demerest. "Luna City represents outer space, widening to infinity. There is nowhere to go down here in the long run; everywhere to go out there."

"We don't judge by size and volume alone, Mr. Demerest," said Bergen. "The ocean is only a small part of Earth, true, but for that very reason it is intimately connected with over five billion human beings. Ocean-Deep is experimental but the settlements on the continental shelf already deserve the name of cities. Ocean-Deep offers mankind the chance of exploiting the whole planet—"

"Of polluting the whole planet," broke in Demerest excitedly. "Of raping it, of ending it. The concentration of human effort to Earth itself is unhealthy and even fatal if it isn't balanced by a turning outward to the frontier."

"There is nothing at the frontier," said Annette, snapping out the words. "The Moon is dead, all the other worlds out there are dead. If there are live worlds among the stars, light-years away, they can't be reached. This ocean is *living*."

"The Moon is living, too, Mrs. Bergen, and if Ocean-Deep allows it, the Moon will become an independent world. We Moon-men will then see to it that other worlds are reached and made alive and, if mankind but has patience, we will reach the stars. We! We! It is only we Moon-men, used to space, used to a world in a cavern, used to an engineered environment, who could endure life in a spaceship that may have to travel centuries to reach the stars."

"Wait, wait, Demerest," said Bergen, holding up his hand.

"Back up! What do you mean, if Ocean-Deep allows it? What have we to do with it?"

"You're competing with us, Mr. Bergen. The Planetary Project Commission will swing your way, give you more, give us less, because in the short term, as your wife says, the ocean is alive and the Moon, except for a thousand men, is not; because you are a half-dozen miles away and we a quarter of a million; because you can be reached in an hour and we only in three days. And because you have an ideal safety record and we have had—misfortunes."

"The last, surely, is trivial. Accidents can happen any time, anywhere."

"But the trivial can be used," said Demerest angrily. "It can be made to manipulate emotions. To people who don't see the purpose and the importance of space exploration, the death of Moon-men in accidents is proof enough that the Moon is dangerous, that its colonization is a useless fantasy. Why not? It's their excuse for saving money and they can then salve their consciences by investing part of it in Ocean-Deep instead. That's why I said the accident on the Moon had threatened the survival of Luna City even though it killed only twenty people out of nearly a thousand."

"I don't accept your argument. There has been enough money for both for a score of years."

"Not enough money. That's exactly it. Not enough investment to make the Moon self-supporting in all these years, and then they use that lack of self-support against us. Not enough investment to make Ocean-Deep self-supporting either. . . . But now they can give you enough if they cut us out altogether."

"Do you think that will happen?"

"I'm almost sure it will, unless Ocean-Deep shows a statesmanlike concern for man's future."

"How?"

"By refusing to accept additional funds. By not competing with Luna City. By putting the good of the whole race ahead of self-interest."

"Surely you don't expect us to dismantle—"

"You won't have to. Don't you see? Join us in explaining that Luna Ctiy is essential, that space exploration is the hope of mankind; that you will wait, retrench, if necessary."

Bergen looked at his wife and raised his eyebrows. She shook her head angrily. Bergen said, "You have a rather romantic view of the PPC, I think. Even if I made noble, self-sacrificing speeches, who's to say they would listen? There's a great deal more involved in the matter of Ocean-Deep than my opinion and my statements. There are economic considerations and public feeling. Why don't you relax, Mr. Demerest? Luna City won't come to an end. You'll receive funds, I'm sure of it. I tell you, I'm sure of it. Now let's break this up—"

"No, I've got to convince you one way or another that I'm serious. If necessary, Ocean-Deep must come to a halt unless the PPC can supply ample funds for both."

Bergen said, "Is this some sort of official mission, Mr. Demerest? Are you speaking for Luna City officially, or just for yourself?"

"Just for myself, but maybe that's enough, Mr. Bergen."

"I don't think it is. I'm sorry, but this is turning out to be unpleasant. I suggest that, after all, you had better return Topside on the first available 'scaphe."

"Not yet! Not yet!" Demerest looked about wildly, then rose unsteadily and put his back against the wall. He was a little too tall for the room and he became conscious of life receding. One more step and he would have gone too far to back out.

He had told them back on the Moon that there would be no use talking, no use negotiating. It was dog-eat-dog for the available funds and Luna City's destiny must not be aborted; not for Ocean-Deep; not for Earth; no, not for all of Earth, since mankind and the Universe came even before the Earth. Man must outgrow his womb and—

Demerest could hear his own ragged breathing and the inner turmoil of his whirling thoughts. The other two were looking at him with what seemed concern. Annette rose and said, "Are you ill, Mr. Demerest?"

"I am *not* ill. Sit down. I'm a safety engineer and I want to teach you about safety. Sit *down*, Mrs. Bergen."

"Sit down, Annette," said Bergen. "I'll take care of him." He rose and took a step forward.

But Demerest said, "No. Don't you move either. I have something right here. You're too naïve concerning human dangers, Mr. Bergen. You guard against the sea and against mechanical failure and you don't search your human visitors, do you? I have a weapon, Bergen."

Now that it was out and he had taken the final step, from which there was no returning, for he was now dead whatever he did, he was quite calm.

Annette said, "Oh, John," and grasped her husband's arm. "He's—"

Bergen stepped in front of her. "A weapon? Is that what that thing is? Now slowly, Demerest, slowly. There's nothing to get hot over. If you want to talk, we will talk. What is that?"

"Nothing dramatic. A portable laser beam."

"But what do you want to do with it?"

"Destroy Ocean-Deep."

"But you can't, Demerest. You know you can't. There's only so much energy you can pack into your fist and any laser you can hold can't pump enough heat to penetrate the walls."

"I know that. This packs more energy than you think. It's Moon-made and there are some advantages to manufacturing the energy unit in a vacuum. But you're right. Even so, it's designed only for small jobs and requires frequent recharging. So I don't intend to try to cut through a foot-plus of alloy steel. . . . But it will do the job indirectly. For one thing, it will keep you two quiet. There's enough energy in my fist to kill two people."

"You wouldn't kill us," said Bergen evenly. "You have no reason."

"If by that," said Demerest, "you imply that I am an un-reasoning being to be somehow made to understand my madness, forget it. I have every reason to kill you and I *will* kill you. By laser beam if I have to, though I would rather not."

"What good will killing us do you? Make me understand. Is it that I have refused to sacrifice Ocean-Deep funds? I couldn't do anything else. I'm not really the one to make the decision. And if you kill me, that won't help you force the decision in your direction, will it? In fact, quite the contrary. If a Moon-man is a murderer, how will that reflect on Luna City? Consider human emotions on Earth."

There was just an edge of shrillness in Annette's voice as she joined in. "Don't you see there will be people who will say that Solar radiation on the Moon has dangerous effects? That the genetic engineering which has reorganized your bones and muscles has affected mental stability? Consider the word 'lunatic,' Mr. Demerest. Men once believed the Moon brought madness."

"I am not mad, Mrs. Bergen."

"It doesn't matter," said Bergen, following his wife's lead smoothly. "Men will say that you were; that all Moon-men are; and Luna City will be closed down and the Moon itself closed to all further exploration, perhaps forever. Is that what you want?"

"That might happen if they thought I killed you, but they won't. It will be an accident." With his left elbow, Demerest broke the plastic that covered the manual controls.

"I know units of this sort," he said. "I know exactly how it works. Logically, breaking that plastic should set up a warning flash—after all, it might be broken by accident—and then someone would be here to investigate, or, better yet, the controls should lock until deliberately released to make sure the break was not merely accidental."

He paused, then said, "But I'm sure no one will come; that no warning has taken place. Your manual system is not failsafe because in your heart you were sure it would never be used."

"What do you plan to do?" said Bergen.

He was tense and Demerest watched his knees carefully, and said, "If you try to jump toward me, I'll shoot at once, and then keep right on with what I'm doing."

"I think maybe you're giving me nothing to lose."

"You'll lose time. Let me go right on without interference and you'll have some minutes to keep on talking. You may even be able to talk me out of it. There's my proposal. Don't interfere with me and I will give you your chance to argue."

"But what do you plan to do?"

"This," said Demerest. He did not have to look. His left hand snaked out and closed a contact. "The fusion unit will now pump heat into the air lock and the steam will empty it. It will take a few minutes. When it's done, I'm sure one of those little red-glass buttons will light."

"Are you going to—"

Demerest said, "Why do you ask? You know that I must be intending, having gone this far, to flood Ocean-Deep?"

"But why? Damn it, why?"

"Because it will be marked down as an accident. Because your safety record will be spoiled. Because it will be a complete catastrophe and will wipe you out. And PPC will then turn from you, and the glamor of Ocean-Deep will be gone. We will get the funds; we will continue. If I could bring that to pass in some other way, I would, but the needs of Luna City are the needs of mankind and those are paramount."

"You will die, too," Annette managed to say.

"Of course. Once I am forced to do something like this,

would I *want* to live? I'm not a murderer."

"But you will be. If you flood this unit, you will flood all of Ocean-Deep and kill everyone in it—and doom those who are out in their subs to slower death. Fifty men and women —an unborn child—"

"That is not my fault," said Demerest, in clear pain. "I did not expect to find a pregnant woman here, but now that I have, I can't stop because of that."

"But you must stop," said Bergen. "Your plan won't work unless what happens can be shown to be an accident. They'll find you with a beam emitter in your hand and with the manual controls clearly tampered with. Do you think they won't deduce the truth from that?"

Demerest was feeling very tired. "Mr. Bergen, you sound desperate. Listen—When the outer door opens, water under a thousand atmospheres of pressure will enter. It will be a massive battering ram that will destroy and mangle everything in its path. The walls of the Ocean-Deep units will remain but everything inside will be twisted beyond recognition. Human beings will be mangled into shredded tissue and splintered bone and death will be instantaneous and unfelt. Even if I were to burn you to death with the laser there would be nothing left to show it had been done, so I won't hesitate, you see. This manual unit will be smashed anyway; anything I can do will be erased by the water."

"But the beam emitter, the laser gun. Even damaged, it will be recognizable," said Annette.

"We use such things on the Moon, Mrs. Bergen. It is a common tool; it is the optical analogue of a jackknife. I could kill you with a jackknife, you know, but one would not deduce that a man carrying a jackknife, or even holding one with the blade open, was necessarily planning murder. He might be whittling. Besides, a Moon-made laser is not a projectile gun. It doesn't have to withstand an internal explosion. It is made of thin metal, mechanically weak. After it is smashed by the waterclap I doubt that it will make much sense as an object."

Demerest did not have to think to make these statements. He had worked them out within himself through months of self-debate back on the Moon.

"In fact," he went on, "how will the investigators ever know what happened in here? They will send 'scaphes down to inspect what is left of Ocean-Deep, but how can they get inside without first pumping the water out? They will, in effect, have to build a new Ocean-Deep and that would take

—how long? Perhaps, given public reluctance to waste money, they might never do it at all and content themselves with dropping a laurel wreath on the dead walls of the dead Ocean-Deep."

Bergen said, "The men on Luna City will know what you have done. Surely one of them will have a conscience. The truth will be known."

"One truth," said Demerest, "is that I am not a fool. No one on Luna City knows what I planned to do or will suspect what I have done. They sent me down here to negotiate cooperation on the matter of financial grants. I was to argue and nothing more. There's not even a laser-beam emitter missing up there. I put this one together myself out of scrapped parts. . . . And it works. I've tested it."

Annette said slowly, "You haven't thought it through. Do you know what you're doing?"

"I've thought it through. I know what I'm doing. . . . And I know also that you are both conscious of the lit signal. I'm aware of it. The air lock is empty and time's up, I'm afraid."

Rapidly, holding his beam emitter tensely high, he closed another contact. A circular part of the unit wall cracked into a thin crescent and rolled smoothly away.

Out of the corner of his eye, Demerest saw the gaping darkness, but he did not look. A dankly salt vapor issued from it; a queer odor of dead steam. He even imagined he could hear the flopping sound of the gathered water at the bottom of the lock.

Demerest said, "In a rational manual unit, the outer door ought to be frozen shut now. With the inner door open, nothing ought to make the outer door open. I suspect, though, that the manuals were put together too quickly at first for that precaution to have been taken, and it was replaced too quickly for that precaution to have been added. And if I need further evidence of that, you wouldn't be sitting there so tensely if you knew the outer door wouldn't open. I need touch one more contact and the waterclap will come. We will feel nothing."

Annette said, "Don't push it just yet. I have one more thing to say. You said we would have time to persuade you."

"While the water was being pushed out."

"Just let me say this. A minute. A *minute*. I said you didn't know what you were doing. You don't. You're destroying the space program, the *space* program. There's more to space than *space.*" Her voice had grown shrill.

Demerest frowned. "What are you talking about? Make sense, or I'll end it all. I'm tired. I'm frightened. I want it over."

Annette said, "You're not in the inner councils of the PPC. Neither is my husband. But I am. Do you think because I am a woman that I'm secondary here? I'm not. You, Mr. Demerest, have your eyes fixed on Luna City only. My husband has his fixed on Ocean-Deep. Neither of you know *anything.*

"Where do you expect to go, Mr. Demerest, if you had all the money you wanted? Mars? The asteroids? The satellites of the gas giants? These are all small worlds; all dry surfaces under a blank sky. It may be generations before we are ready to try for the stars and till then we'd have only pygmy real estate. Is that your ambition?

"My husband's ambition is no better. He dreams of pushing man's habitat over the ocean floor, a surface not much larger in the last analysis than the surface of the Moon and the other pygmy worlds. We of the PPC, on the other hand, want more than either of you, and if you push that button, Mr. Demerest, the greatest dream mankind has ever had will come to nothing."

Demerest found himself interested despite himself, but he said, "You're just babbling." It was possible, he knew, that somehow they had warned others in Ocean-Deep, that any moment someone would come to interrupt, someone would try to shoot him down. He was, however, staring at the only opening, and he had only to close one contact, without even looking, in a second's movement.

Annette said, "I'm not babbling. You know it took more than rocket ships to colonize the Moon. To make a successful colony possible, men had to be altered genetically and adjusted to low gravity. You are a product of such genetic engineering."

"Well?"

"And might not genetic engineering also help men to greater gravitational pull? What is the largest planet of the Solar System, Mr. Demerest?"

"Jupi—"

"Yes, Jupiter. Eleven times the diameter of the Earth; forty times the diameter of the Moon. A surface a hundred and twenty times that of the Earth in area; sixteen hundred times that of the Moon. Conditions so different from anything we can encounter anywhere on the worlds the size of Earth or less that any scientist of any persuasion would give half his life for a chance to observe at close range."

"But Jupiter is an impossible target."

"Indeed?" said Annette, and even managed a faint smile. "As impossible as flying? Why is it impossible? Genetic engineering could design men with stronger and denser bones, stronger and more compact muscles. The same principles that enclose Luna City against the vacuum and Ocean-Deep against the sea can also enclose the future Jupiter-Deep against its ammoniated surroundings."

"The gravitational field—"

"Can be negotiated by nuclear-powered ships that are now on the drawing board. You don't know that but I do."

"We're not even sure about the depth of the atmosphere. The pressures—"

"The pressures! The *pressures!* Mr. Demerest, look about you. Why do you suppose Ocean-Deep was *really* built? To exploit the ocean? The settlements on the continental shelf are doing that quite adequately. To gain knowledge of the deep-sea bottom? We could do that by 'scaphe easily and we could then have spared the hundred billion dollars invested in Ocean-Deep so far.

"Don't you see, Mr. Demerest, that Ocean-Deep must mean something more than that? The purpose of Ocean-Deep is to devise the ultimate vessels and mechanisms that will suffice to explore and colonize *Jupiter.* Look about you and see the beginnings of a Jovian environment; the closest approach we can come to it on Earth. It is only a faint image of mighty Jupiter, but it's a beginning.

"Destroy this, Mr. Demerest, and you destroy any hope for Jupiter. On the other hand, let us live and we will, together, penetrate and settle the brightest jewel of the Solar System. And long before we can reach the limits of Jupiter, we will be ready for the stars, for the Earth-type planets circling them, *and* the Jupiter-type planets, too. Luna City won't be abandoned because *both* are necessary for this ultimate aim."

For the moment, Demerest had altogether forgotten about that last button. He said, "Nobody on Luna City has heard of this."

"*You* haven't. There are those on Luna City who know. If you had told them of your plan of destruction, they would have stopped you. Naturally, we can't make this common knowledge and only a few people anywhere can know. The public supports only with difficulty the planetary projects now in progress. If the PPC is parsimonious it is because public opinion limits its generosity. What do you suppose public opinion would say if they thought we were aiming toward Jupiter? What a super-boondoggle that would be in their eyes. But we continue and what money we can save and make use of we place in the various facets of Project Big World."

"Project Big World?"

"Yes," said Annette. "You know now and I have committed a serious security breach. But it doesn't matter, does it? Since we're all dead and since the project is, too."

"Wait now, Mrs. Bergen."

"If you change your mind now, don't think you can ever talk about Project Big World. That would end the project just as effectively as destruction here would. And it would end both your career and mine. It might end Luna City and Ocean-Deep, too—so now that you know, maybe it makes no difference anyway. You might just as well push that button."

"I said wait—" Demerest's brow was furrowed and his eyes burned with anguish. "I don't know—"

Bergen gathered for the sudden jump as Demerest's tense alertness wavered into uncertain introspection, but Annette grasped her husband's sleeve.

A timeless interval that might have been ten seconds long followed and then Demerest held out his laser. "Take it," he said. "I'll consider myself under arrest."

"You can't be arrested," said Annette, "without the whole story coming out." She took the laser and gave it to Bergen. "It will be enough that you return to Luna City and keep silent. Till then we will keep you under guard."

Bergen was at the manual controls. The inner door slid shut and after that there was the thunderous waterclap of the water returning into the lock.

Husband and wife were alone again. They had not dared say a word until Demerest was safely put to sleep under the watchful eyes of two men detailed for the purpose. The unexpected waterclap had roused everybody and a sharply bowdlerized account of the incident had been given out.

The manual controls were now locked off and Bergen said, "From this point on, the manuals will have to be adjusted to fail-safe. And visitors will have to be searched."

"Oh, John," said Annette. "I think people are insane. There we were, facing death for us and for Ocean-Deep; just the end of everything. And I kept thinking—I must keep calm; I mustn't have a miscarriage."

"You kept calm all right. You were magnificent. I mean, Project Big World! I never conceived of such a thing, but by —by—*Jove*, it's an attractive thought. It's wonderful."

"I'm sorry I had to say all that, John. It was all a fake, of course. I made it up. Demerest wanted me to make something up really. He wasn't a killer or destroyer; he was, according to his own overheated lights, a patriot, and I suppose he was telling himself he must destroy in order to save —a common enough view among the small-minded. But he *said* he would give us time to talk him out of it and I think he was praying we would manage to do so. He wanted us to think of something that would give him the excuse to save in order to save, and I gave it to him. . . . I'm sorry I had to fool you, John."

"You didn't fool me."

"I didn't?"

"How could you? I knew you weren't a member of PPC."

"What made you so sure of that? Because I'm a woman?"

"Not at all. Because *I'm* a member, Annette, and *that's* confidential. And, if you don't mind, I will begin a move to initiate exactly what you suggested—Project Big World."

"Well!" Annette considered that and, slowly, smiled. "Well! That's not bad. Women do have their uses."

"Something," said Bergen, smiling also, "I have never denied."

Ed Ferman of *F & SF* and Barry Malzberg, one of the brightest of the new generation of science fiction writers, had it in mind in early 1973 to prepare an anthology in which a number of different science fiction themes were carried to their ultimate conclusion. For each story they tapped some writer who was associated with a particular theme, and for a story on the subject of robotics, they wanted me, naturally.

I tried to beg off with my usual excuses concerning the state of my schedule, but they said if I didn't do it there would be no story on robotics at all, because they wouldn't ask anyone else. That shamed me into agreeing to do it.

I then had to think up a way of reaching an ultimate conclusion. There had always been one aspect of the robot theme I had never had the courage to write, although the late John Campbell and I had sometimes discussed it.

In the first two Laws of Robotics, you see, the expression "human being" is used, and the assumption is that a robot can recognize a human being when he sees one. But what is a human being? Or, as the Psalmist asks of God, "What is man that thou art mindful of him?"

Surely, if there's any doubt as to the definition of man, the Laws of Robotics don't necessarily hold. So I wrote THAT THOU ART MINDFUL OF HIM, and Ed and Barry were very happy with it—and so was I. It not only appeared in the anthology, which was entitled *Final Stage*, but was also published in the May 1974 issue of *F & SF*.

4

That Thou Art Mindful of Him

The Three Laws of Robotics:

   1. A robot may not injure a human being or, through inaction, allow a human being to come to harm.
   2. A robot must obey the orders given it by human beings except where such orders would conflict with the First Law.
   3. A robot must protect its own existence, as long as such protection does not conflict with the First or Second Law.

Keith Harriman, who had for twelve years now been Director of Research at United States Robot and Mechanical Men, Inc., found that he was not at all certain whether he was doing right. The tip of his tongue passed over his plump but rather pale lips and it seemed to him that the holographic image of the great Susan Calvin, which stared unsmilingly down upon him, had never looked so grim before.

Usually he blanked out that image of the greatest roboticist in history because she unnerved him. (He tried thinking of the image as "it" but never quite succeeded.) This time he didn't quite dare to and her long-dead gaze bored into the side of his face.

It was a dreadful and demeaning step he would have to take.

Opposite him was George Ten, calm and unaffected either by Harriman's patent uneasiness or by the image of the patron saint of robotics glowing in its niche above.

Harriman said, "We haven't had a chance to talk this out, really, George. You haven't been with us that long and I haven't had a good chance to be alone with you. But now I would like to discuss the matter in some detail."

"I am perfectly willing to do that," said George. "In my stay at U. S. Robots, I have gathered the crisis has something to do with the Three Laws."

"Yes. You know the Three Laws, of course."

"I do."

"Yes, I'm sure you do. But let us dig even deeper and consider the truly basic problem. In two centuries of, if I may say so, considerable success, U. S. Robots has never managed to persuade human beings to accept robots. We have placed robots only where work is required that human beings cannot do, or in environments that human beings find unacceptably dangerous. Robots have worked mainly in space and that has limited what we have been able to do."

"Surely," said George Ten, "this represents a broad limit, and one within which U. S. Robots can prosper."

"No, for two reasons. In the first place, the boundaries set for us inevitably contract. As the Moon colony, for instance, grows more sophisticated, its demand for robots decreases and we expect that, within the next few years, robots will be banned on the Moon. This will be repeated on every world colonized by mankind. Secondly, true prosperity is impossible without robots on Earth. We at U. S. Robots firmly believe that human beings need robots and must learn to live with their mechanical analogues if progress is to be maintained."

"Do they not? Mr. Harriman, you have on your desk a computer input which, I understand, is connected with the organization's Multivac. A computer is a kind of sessile robot; a robot brain not attached to a body—"

"True, but that also is limited. The computers used by mankind have been steadily specialized in order to avoid too humanlike an intelligence. A century ago we were well on the way to artificial intelligence of the most unlimited type through the use of great computers we called Machines. Those Machines limited their action of their own accord. Once they had solved the ecological problems that had threatened human society, they phased themselves out. Their own continued existence would, they reasoned, have placed them in the role of a crutch to mankind and, since they felt this would harm human beings, they condemned themselves by the First Law."

"And were they not correct to do so?"

"In my opinion, no. By their action, they reinforced mankind's Frankenstein complex; its gut fears that any artificial man they created would turn upon its creator. Men fear that robots may replace human beings."

"Do you not fear that yourself?"

"I know better. As long as the Three Laws of Robotics exist, they cannot. They can serve as *partners* of mankind; they can share in the great struggle to understand and wisely direct the laws of nature so that together they can do more than mankind can possibly do alone; but always in such a way that robots serve human beings."

"But if the Three Laws have shown themselves, over the course of two centuries, to keep robots within bounds, what is the source of the distrust of human beings for robots?"

"Well"—and Harriman's graying hair tufted as he scratched his head vigorously—"mostly superstition, of course. Unfortunately, there are also some complexities involved that antirobot agitators seize upon."

"Involving the Three Laws?"

"Yes. The Second Law in particular. There's no problem in the Third Law, you see. It is universal. Robots must always sacrifice themselves for human beings, any human beings."

"Of couse," said George Ten.

"The First Law is perhaps less satisfactory, since it is always possible to imagine a condition in which a robot must perform either Action A or Action B, the two being mutually exclusive, and where either action results in harm to human beings. The robot must therefore quickly select which action results in the least harm. To work out the positronic paths of the robot brain in such a way as to make that selection possible is not easy. If Action A results in harm to a talented young artist and B results in equivalent harm to five elderly people of no paticular worth, which action should be chosen."

"Action A," said George Ten. "Harm to one is less than harm to five."

"Yes, so robots have always been designed to decide. To expect robots to make judgments of fine points such as talent, intelligence, the general usefulness to society, has always seemed impractical. That would delay decision to the point where the robot is effectively immobilized. So we go by numbers. Fortunately, we might expect crises in which robots must make decisions to be few. . . . But then that brings us to the Second Law."

"The Law of Obedience."

"Yes. The necessity of obedience is constant. A robot may exist for twenty years without ever having to act quickly to prevent harm to a human being, or find itself faced with the necessity of risking its own destruction. In all that time, however, it will be constantly obeying orders. . . . Whose orders?"

"Those of a human being."

"Any human being? How do you judge a human being as to know whether to obey or not? What is man, that thou art mindful of him, George?"

George hesitated at that.

Harriman said hurriedly, "A Biblical quotation. That doesn't matter. I mean, must a robot follow the orders of a child; or of an idiot; or of a criminal; or of a perfectly decent intelligent man who happens to be inexpert and therefore ignorant of the undesirable consequences of his order? And if two human beings give a robot conflicting orders, which does the robot follow?"

"In two hundred years," said George Ten, "have not these problems arisen and been solved?"

"No," said Harriman, shaking his head violently. "We have been hampered by the very fact that our robots have been used only in specialized environments out in space, where the men who dealt with them were experts in their field. There were no children, no idiots, no criminals, no well-meaning ignoramuses present. Even so, there were occasions when damage was done by foolish or merely unthinking orders. Such damage in specialized and limited environments could be contained. On Earth, however, robots *must* have judgment. So those against robots maintain, and, damn it, they are right."

"Then you must insert the capacity for judgment into the positronic brain."

"Exactly. We have begun to reproduce JG models in which the robot can weigh every human being with regard to sex, age, social and professional position, intelligence, maturity, social responsibility and so on."

"How would that affect the Three Laws?"

"The Third Law not at all. Even the most valuable robot must destroy himself for the sake of the most useless human being. That cannot be tampered with. The First Law is affected only where alternative actions will all do harm. The quality of the human beings involved as well as the quantity must be considered, provided there is time for such judgment and the basis for it, which will not be often. The Second Law will be most deeply modified, since every potential obedience must involve judgment. The robot will be slower to obey, except where the First Law is also involved, but it will obey more rationally."

"But the judgments which are required are very complicated."

"*Very.* The necessity of making such judgments slowed the reactions of our first couple of models to the point of paralysis. We improved matters in the later models at the cost of introducing so many pathways that the robot's brain became far too unwieldy. In our last couple of models, however, I think we have what we want. The robot doesn't have to make an instant judgment of the worth of a human being and the value of its orders. It begins by obeying all human beings as any ordinary robot would and then it *learns.* A robot grows, learns and matures. It is the equivalent of a child at first and must be under constant supervision. As it grows, however, it can, more and more, be allowed, unsupervised, into Earth's society. Finally it is a full member of that society."

"Surely this answers the objections of those who oppose robots."

"No," said Harriman angrily. "Now they raise others. They will not accept judgments. A robot, they say has no right to brand this person or that as inferior. By accepting the orders of A in preference to that of B, B is branded as of less consequence than A. and his human rights are violated."

"What is the answer to that?"

"There is none. I am giving up."

"I see."

"As far as I myself am concerned. . . . Instead, I turn to you, George."

"To me?" George Ten's voice remained level. There was a mild surprise in it but it did not affect him outwardly. "Why to me?"

"Because you are not a man," said Harriman tensely. "I told you I want robots to be the partners of human beings. I want you to be mine."

George Ten raised his hands and spread them, palms outward, in an oddly human gesture. "What can I do?"

"It seems to you, perhaps, that you can do nothing, George. You were created not long ago, and you are still a child. You

were designed to be not overfull of original information—it
was why I have had to explain the situation to you in such
detail—in order to leave room for growth. But you will grow
in mind and you will come to be able to approach the problem from a non-human standpoint. Where I see no solution,
you, from your own other standpoint, may see one."

George Ten said, "My brain is man-designed. In what way
can it be non-human?"

"You are the latest of the JG models, George. Your brain
is the most complicated we have yet designed, in some ways
more subtly complicated than that of the old giant Machines.
It is open-ended and, starting on a human basis, may—no,
will—grow in any direction. Remaining always within the in-
surmountable boundaries of the Three Laws, you may yet
become thoroughly non-human in your thinking."

"Do I know enough about human beings to approach this
problem rationally? About their history? Their psychology?"

"Of course not. But you will learn as rapidly as you can."

"Will I have help, Mr. Harriman?"

"No. This is entirely between ourselves. No one else knows
of this and you must not mention this project to any human
being, either at U. S. Robots or elsewhere."

George Ten said, "Are we doing wrong, Mr. Harriman, that
you seek to keep the matter secret?"

"No. But a robot solution will not be accepted, precisely
because it is robot in origin. Any suggested solution you have
you will turn over to me; and if it seems valuable to me, *I*
will present it. No one will ever know it came from you."

"In the light of what you have said earlier," said George
Ten calmly, "this is the correct procedure. . . . When do I
start?"

"Right now. I will see to it that you have all the necessary
films for scanning."

1a.

Harriman sat alone. In the artificially lit interior of his
office, there was no indication that it had grown dark outside.
He had no real sense that three hours had passed since he
had taken George Ten back to his cubicle and left him there
with the first film references.

He was now merely alone with the ghost of Susan Calvin,
the brilliant roboticist who had, virtually single-handed, built
up the positronic robot from a massive toy to man's most

delicate and versatile instrument; so delicate and versatile that man dared not use it, out of envy and fear.

It was over a century now since she had died. The problem of the Frankenstein complex had existed in *her* time, and she had never solved it. She had never tried to solve it, for there had been no need. Robotics had expanded in her day with the needs of space exploration.

It was the very success of the robots that had lessened man's need for them and had left Harriman, in these latter times—

But would Susan Calvin have turned to robots for help. Surely, she would have—

And he sat there long into the night.

2.

Maxwell Robertson was the majority stockholder of U. S. Robots and in that sense its controller. He was by no means an impressive person in appearance. He was well into middle age, rather pudgy, and had a habit of chewing on the right corner of his lower lip when disturbed.

Yet in his two decades of association with government figures he had developed a way of handling them. He tended to use softness, giving in, smiling, and always managing to gain time.

It was growing harder. Gunnar Eisenmuth was a large reason for its having grown harder. In the series of Global Conservers, whose power had been second only to that of the Global Executive during the past century, Eisenmuth hewed most closely to the harder edge of the gray area of compromise. He was the first Conserver who had not been American by birth and though it could not be demonstrated in any way that the archaic name of U. S. Robots evoked his hostility, everyone at U. S. Robots believed that.

There had been a suggestion, by no means the first that year—or that generation—that the corporate name be changed to World Robots, but Robertson would never allow that. The company had been originally built with American capital, American brains, and American labor, and though the company had long been worldwide in scope and nature, the name would bear witness to its origin as long as he was in control.

Eisenmuth was a tall man whose long sad face was coarsely textured and coarsely featured. He spoke Global with a pronounced American accent, although he had never been in the United States prior to his taking office.

"It seems perfectly clear to me, Mr. Robertson. There is no difficulty. The products of your company are always rented, never sold. If the rented property on the Moon is now no longer needed, it is up to you to receive the products back and transfer them."

"Yes, Conserver, but where? It would be against the law to bring them to Earth without a government permit and that has been denied."

"They would be of no use to you here. You can take them to Mercury or to the asteroids."

"What would we do with them there?"

Eisenmuth shrugged. "The ingenious men of your company will think of something."

Robertson shook his head. "It would represent an enormous loss for the company."

"I'm afraid it would," said Eisenmuth, unmoved. "I understand the company has been in poor financial condition for several years now."

"Largely because of government imposed restrictions, Conserver."

"You must be realistic, Mr. Robertson. You know that the climate of public opinion is increasing against robots."

"Wrongly so, Conserver."

"But so, nevertheless. It may be wiser to liquidate the company. It is merely a suggestion, of course."

"Your suggestions have force, Conserver. Is it necessary to tell you that our Machines, a century ago, served the ecological crisis?"

"I'm sure mankind is grateful, but that was a long time ago. We now live in alliance with nature, however uncomfortable that might be at times, and the past is dim."

"You mean what have we done for mankind lately?"

"I suppose I do."

"Surely we can't be expected to liquidate instantaneously; not without enormous losses. We need time."

"How much?"

"How much can you give us?"

"It's not up to me."

Robertson said softly. "We are alone. We need play no games. How much time can you give me?"

Eisenmuth's expression was that of a man retreating into inner calculations. "I think you can count on two years. I'll be frank. The Global government intends to take over the firm and phase it out for you if you don't do it by then yourself, more or less. And unless there is a vast turn in public opinion, which I greatly doubt—" He shook his head.

"Two years, then," said Robertson softly.

2a.

Robertson sat alone. There was no purpose to his thinking and it had degenerated into retrospection. Four generations of Robertsons had headed the firm. None of them was a roboticist. It had been men such as Lanning and Bogert and, most of all, *most* of all, Susan Calvin, who had made U. S. Robots what it was, but surely the four Robertsons had provided the climate that had made it possible for them to do their work.

Without U. S. Robots, the Twenty-first Century would have progressed into deepening disaster. That it didn't was due to the Machines that had for a generation steered mankind through the rapids and shoals of history.

And now for that, he was given two years. What could be done in two years to overcome the insuperable prejudices of mankind? He didn't know.

Harriman had spoken hopefully of new ideas but would go into no details. Just as well, for Robertson would have understood none of it.

But what could Harriman do anyway? What had anyone ever done against man's intense antipathy toward the imitation? Nothing—

Robertson drifted into a deep sleep in which no inspiration came.

3.

Harriman said, "You have it all now, George Ten. You have had everything I could think of that is at all applicable to the problem. As far as sheer mass of information is concerned, you have stored more in your memory concerning human beings and their ways, past and present, than I have, or than any human being could have."

"That is very likely."

"Is there anything more than you need, in your own opinion?"

"As far as information is concerned, I find no obvious gaps.

There may be matters unimagined at the boundaries. I cannot tell. But that would be true no matter how large a circle of information I took in."

"True. Nor do we have time to take in information forever. Robertson has told me that we only have two years, and a quarter of one of those years has passed. Can you suggest anything?"

"At the moment, Mr. Harriman, nothing. I must weigh the information and for that purpose I could use help."

"From me?"

"No. Most particularly, not from you. You are a human being, of intense qualifications, and whatever you say may have the partial force of an order and may inhibit my considerations. Nor any other human being, for the same reason, especially since you have forbidden me to communicate with any."

"But in that case, George, what help?"

"From another robot, Mr. Harriman."

"What other robot?"

"There are others of the JG series which were constructed. I am the tenth, JG-10."

"The earlier ones were useless, experimental—"

"Mr. Harriman, George Nine exists."

"Well, but what use will he be? He is very much like you except for certain lacks. You are considerably the more versatile of the two."

"I am certain of that," said George Ten. He nodded his head in a grave gesture. "Nevertheless, as soon as I create a line of thought, the mere fact that I have created it commends it to me and I find it difficult to abandon it. If I can, after the development of a line of thought, express it to George Nine, he would consider it without having first created it. He would therefore view it without prior bent. He might see gaps and shortcomings that I might not."

Harriman smiled. "Two heads are better than one, in other words, eh, George?"

"If by that, Mr. Harriman, you mean two individuals with one head apiece, yes."

"Right. Is there anything else you want?"

"Yes. Something more than films. I have viewed much concerning human beings and their world. I have seen human beings here at U. S. Robots and can check my interpretation of what I have viewed against direct sensory impressions. Not so concerning the physical world. I have never seen it and my

viewing is quite enough to tell me that my surroundings here
are by no means representative of it. I would like to see it."

"The physical world?" Harriman seemed stunned at the
enormity of the thought for a moment. "Surely you don't
suggest I take you outside the grounds of U. S. Robots?"

"Yes, that is my suggestion."

"That's illegal at any time. In the climate of opinion today,
it would be fatal."

"If we are detected, yes. I do not suggest you take me to
a city or even to a dwelling place of human beings. I would
like to see some open region, without human beings."

"That, too, is illegal."

"If we are caught. Need we be?"

Harriman said, "How essential is this, George?"

"I cannot tell, but it seems to me it would be useful."

"Do you have something in mind?"

George Ten seemed to hesitate. "I cannot tell. It seems to
me that I might have something in mind if certain areas of
uncertainty were reduced."

"Well, let me think about it. And meanwhile, I'll check
out George Nine and arrange to have you occupy a single
cubicle. That at least can be done without trouble."

3a.

George Ten sat alone.

He accepted statements tentatively, put them together, and
drew a conclusion; over and over again; and from conclusions built other statements which he accepted and tested and
found a contradiction and rejected; or not, and tentatively
accepted further.

At none of the conclusions he reached did he feel wonder,
surprise, satisfaction; merely a note of plus or minus.

4.

Harriman's tension was not noticeably decreased even after
they had made a silent downward landing on Robertson's
estate.

Robertson had countersigned the order making the dyna-
foil available, and the silent aircraft, moving as easily vertically
as horizontally, had been large enough to carry the weight of
Harriman, George Ten, and, of course, the pilot.

(The dyna-foil itself was one of the consequences of the

Machine-catalyzed invention of the proton micro-pile which supplied pollution-free energy in small doses. Nothing had been done since of equal importance to man's comfort— Harriman's lips tightened at the thought—and yet it had not earned gratitude for U. S. Robots.)

The air flight between the grounds of U. S. Robots and the Robertson estate had been the tricky part. Had they been stopped then, the presence of a robot aboard would have meant a great set of complications. It would be the same on the way back. The estate itself, it might be argued—it *would* be argued—was part of the property of U. S. Robots and on that property, robots, properly supervised, might remain.

The pilot looked back and his eyes rested with gingerly briefness on George Ten. "You want to get out at all, Mr. Harriman?"

"Yes."

"It, too?"

"Oh, yes." Then, just a bit sardonically, "I won't leave you alone with him."

George Ten descended first and Harriman followed. They had come down on the foil-port and not too far off was the garden. It was quite a showplace and Harriman suspected that Robertson used juvenile hormones to control insect life without regard to environmental formulas.

"Come, George," said Harriman. "Let me show you."

Together they walked toward the garden.

George said, "It is a little as I have imagined it. My eyes are not properly designed to detect wavelength differences, so I may not recognize different objects by that alone."

"I trust you are not distressed at being color-blind. We needed too many positronic paths for your sense of judgment and were unable to spare any for sense of color. In the future—if there is a future—"

"I understand, Mr. Harriman. Enough differences remain to show me that there are here many different forms of plant life."

"Undoubtedly. Dozens."

"And each coequal with man, biologically."

"Each is a separate species, yes. There are millions of species of living creatures."

"Of which the human being forms but one."

"By far the most important to human beings, however."

"And to me, Mr. Harriman. But I speak in the biological sense."

"I understand."

"Life, then, viewed through all its forms, is incredibly complex."

"Yes, George, that's the crux of the problem. What man does for his own desires and comforts affects the complex total-of-life, the ecology, and his short-term gains can bring long-term disadvantages. The Machines taught us to set up a human society which would minimize that, but the near-disaster of the early Twenty-first Century has left mankind suspicious of innovations. That, added to its special fear of robots—"

"I understand, Mr. Harriman. . . . That is an example of animal life, I feel certain."

"That is a squirrel; one of many species of squirrels."

The tail of the squirrel flirted as it passed to the other side of the tree.

"And this," said George, his arm moving with flashing speed, "is a tiny thing, indeed." He held it between his fingers and peered at it.

"It is an insect, some sort of beetle. There are thousands of species of beetles."

"With each individual beetle as alive as the squirrel and as yourself?"

"As complete and independent an organism as any other, within the total ecology. There are smaller organisms still; many too small to see."

"And that is a tree, is it not? And it is hard to the touch—"

4a.

The pilot sat alone. He would have liked to stretch his own legs but some dim feeling of safety kept him in the dyna-foil. If that robot went out of control, he intended to take off at once. But how could he tell if it went out of control?

He had seen many robots. That was unavoidable considering he was Mr. Robertson's private pilot. Always, though, they had been in the laboratories and warehouses, where they belonged, with many specialists in the neighborhood.

True, Dr. Harriman was a specialist. None better, they said. But a robot here was where no robot ought to be; on Earth; in the open; free to move— He wouldn't risk his good job by telling anyone about this—but it wasn't right.

5.

George Ten said, "The films I have viewed are accurate in terms of what I have seen. Have you completed those I selected for you, Nine?"

"Yes," said George Nine. The two robots sat stiffly, face to face, knee to knee, like an image and its reflection. Dr. Harriman could have told them apart at a glance, for he was acquainted with the minor differences in physical design. If he could not see them, but could talk to them, he could still tell them apart, though with somewhat less certainty, for George Nine's responses would be subtly different from those produced by the substantially more intricately patterned positronic brain paths of George Ten.

"In that case," said George Ten, "give me your reactions to what I will say. First, human beings fear and distrust robots because they regard robots as competitors. How may that be prevented?"

"Reduce the feeling of competitiveness," said George Nine, "by shaping the robot as something other than a human being."

"Yet the essence of a robot is its positronic replication of life. A replication of life in a shape not associated with life might arouse horror."

"There are two million species of life forms. Choose one of those as the shape rather than that of a human being."

"Which of all those species?"

George Nine's thought processes proceeded noiselessly for some three seconds. "One large enough to contain a positronic brain, but one not possessing unpleasant associations for human beings."

"No form of land life has a braincase large enough for a positronic brain but an elephant, which I have not seen, but which is described as very large, and therefore frightening to man. How would you meet this dilemma?"

"Mimic a life form no larger than a man but enlarge the braincase."

George Ten said, "A small horse, then, or a large dog, would you say? Both horses and dogs have long histories of association with human beings."

"Then that is well."

"But consider— A robot with a positronic brain would mimic human intelligence. If there were a horse or a dog that could speak and reason like a human being, there would be competitiveness there, too. Human beings might be all the more distrustful and angry at such unexpected competition from what they consider a lower form of life."

George Nine said, "Make the positronic brain less complex, and the robot less nearly intelligent."

"The complexity bottleneck of the positronic brain rests in the Three Laws. A less complex brain could not possess the Three Laws in full measure."

George Nine said at once, "That cannot be done."

George Ten said, "I have also come to a dead end there. That, then, is not a personal peculiarity in my own line of thought and way of thinking. Let us start again. . . . Under what conditions might the Third Law not be necessary?"

George Nine stirred as if the question were difficult and dangerous. But he said, "If a robot were never placed in a position of danger to itself; or if a robot were so easily replaceable that it did not matter whether it were destroyed or not."

"And under what conditions might the Second Law not be necessary?"

George Nine's voice sounded a bit hoarse. "If a robot were designed to respond automatically to certain stimuli with fixed responses and if nothing else were expected of it, so that no order need ever be given it."

"And under what conditions"—George Ten paused here— "might the First Law not be necessary?"

George Nine paused longer and his words came in a low whisper, "If the fixed responses were such as never to entail danger to human beings."

"Imagine, then, a positronic brain that guides only a few responses to certain stimuli and is simply and cheaply made —so that it does not require the Three Laws. How large need it be?"

"Not at all large. Depending on the responses demanded, it might weigh a hundred grams, one gram, one milligram."

"Your thoughts accord with mine. I shall see Dr. Harriman."

5a.

George Nine sat alone. He went over and over the questions and answers. There was no way in which he could change them. And yet the thought of a robot of any kind, of any size, of any shape, of any purpose, without the Three Laws, left him with an odd, discharged feeling.

He found it difficult to move. Surely George Ten had a similiar reaction. Yet he had risen from his seat easily.

6.

It had been a year and a half since Robertson had been closeted with Eisenmuth in private conversation. In that interval, the robots had been taken off the Moon and all the far-flung activities of U. S. Robots had withered. What money Robertson had been able to raise had been placed into this one quixotic venture of Harriman's.

It was the last throw of the dice, here in his own garden. A year ago, Harriman had taken the robot here—George Ten, the last full robot that U. S. Robots had manufactured. Now Harriman was here with something else—

Harriman seemed to be radiating confidence. He was talking easily with Eisenmuth, and Robertson wondered if he really felt the confidence he seemed to have. He must. In Robertson's experience, Harriman was no actor.

Eisenmuth left Harriman, smiling, and came up to Robertson. Eisenmuth's smile vanished at once. "Good morning, Robertson," he said. "What is your man up to?"

"This is his show," said Robertson evenly. "I'll leave it to him."

Harriman called out, "I am ready, Conserver."

"With what, Harriman?"

"With my robot, sir."

"Your robot?" said Eisenmuth. "You have a robot here?" He looked about with a stern disapproval that yet had an admixture of curiosity.

"This is U. S. Robots' property, Conserver. At least we consider it as such."

"And where is the robot, Dr. Harriman?"

"In my pocket, Conserver," said Harriman cheerfully.

What came out of a spacious jacket pocket was a small glass jar.

"That?" said Eisenmuth incredulously.

"No, Conserver," said Harriman. "This!"

From the other pocket came out an object some five inches long and roughly in the shape of a bird. In place of the beak, there was a narrow tube; the eyes were large; and the tail was an exhaust channel.

Eisenmuth's thick eyebrows drew together. "Do you intend

a serious demonstration of some sort, Dr. Harriman, or are you mad?"

"Be patient for a few minutes, Conserver," said Harriman. "A robot in the shape of a bird is none the less a robot for that. And the positronic brain it possesses is no less delicate for being tiny. This other object I hold is a jar of fruit flies. There are fifty fruit flies in it which will be released."

"And—"

"The robo-bird will catch them. Will you do the honors, sir?"

Harriman handed the jar to Eisenmuth, who stared at it, then at those around him, some officials from U. S. Robots, others his own aides. Harriman waited patiently.

Eisenmuth opened the jar, then shook it.

Harriman said softly to the robo-bird resting on the palm of his right hand, "Go!"

The robo-bird was gone. It was a whizz through the air, with no blur of wings, only the tiny workings of an unusually small proton micro-pile.

It could be seen now and then in a small momentary hover and then it whirred on again. All over the garden, in an intricate pattern it flew, and then was back in Harriman's palm, faintly warm. A small pellet appeared in the palm, too, like a bird dropping.

Harriman said, "You are welcome to study the robo-bird, Conserver, and to arrange demonstrations on your own terms. The fact is that this bird will pick up fruit flies unerringly, only those, only the one species *Drosophila melanogaster*; pick them up, kill them, and compress them for disposition."

Eisenmuth reached out his hand and touched the robo-bird gingerly, "And therefore, Mr. Harriman? Do go on."

Harriman said, "We cannot control insects effectively without risking damage to the ecology. Chemical insecticides are too broad; juvenile hormones too limited. The robo-bird, however, can preserve large areas without being consumed. They can be as specific as we care to make them—a different robo-bird for each species. They judge by size, shape, color, sound, behavior pattern. They might even conceivably use molecular detection—smell, in other words."

Eisenmuth said, "You would still be interfering with the ecology. The fruit flies have a natural life cycle that would be disrupted."

"Minimally. We are adding a natural enemy to the fruit-fly life cycle, one which cannot go wrong. If the fruit-fly supply runs short, the robo-bird simply does nothing. It does not multiply; it does not turn to other foods; it does not develop undesirable habits of its own. It does nothing."

"Can it be called back?"

"Of course. We can build robo-animals to dispose of any pest. For that matter, we can build robo-animals to accomplish constructive purposes within the pattern of the ecology. Although we do not anticipate the need, there is nothing inconceivable in the possibility of robo-bees designed to fertilize specific plants, or robo-earthworms designed to mix the soil. Whatever you wish—"

"But why?"

"To do what we have never done before. To adjust the ecology to our needs by strengthening its parts rather than disrupting it. . . . Don't you see? Ever since the Machines put an end to the ecology crisis, mankind has lived in an uneasy truce with nature, afraid to move in any direction. This has been stultifying us, making a kind of intellectual coward of humanity so that he begins to mistrust all scientific advantage, all change."

Eisenmuth said, with an edge of hostility, "You offer us this, do you, in exchange for permission to continue with your program of robots—I mean ordinary, man-shaped ones?"

"No!" Harriman gestured violently. "That is over. It has served its purpose. It has taught us enough about positronic brains to make it possible for us to cram enough pathways into a tiny brain to make a robo-bird. We can turn to such things now and be prosperous enough. U. S. Robots will supply the necessary knowledge and skill and we will work in complete cooperation with the Department of Global Conservation. We will prosper. You will prosper. Mankind will prosper."

Eisenmuth was silent, thinking. When it was all over—

6a.

Eisenmuth sat alone.

He found himself believing. He found excitement welling up within him. Though U. S. Robots might be the hands, the government would be the directing mind. He himself would be the directing mind.

If he remained in office five more years, as he well might, that would be time enough to see the robotic support of the ecology become accepted; ten more years, and his own name would be linked with it indissolubly.

Was it a disgrace to want to be remembered for a great and worthy revolution in the condition of man and the globe?

7.

Robertson had not been on the grounds of U. S. Robots proper since the day of the demonstration. Part of the reason had been his more or less constant conferences at the Global Executive Mansion. Fortunately, Harriman had been with him, for most of the time he would, if left to himself, not have known what to say.

The rest of the reason for not having been at U. S. Robots was that he didn't want to be. He was in his own house now, with Harriman.

He felt an unreasoning awe of Harriman. Harriman's expertise in robotics had never been in question, but the man had, at a stroke, saved U. S. Robots from certain extinction, and somehow—Robertson felt—the man hadn't had it in him. And yet—

He said, "You're not superstitious, are you, Harriman?"

"In what way, Mr. Robertson?"

"You don't think that some aura is left behind by someone who is dead?"

Harriman licked his lips. Somehow he didn't have to ask. "You mean Susan Calvin, sir?"

"Yes, of course," said Robertson hesitantly. "We're in the business of making worms and birds and bugs now. What would *she* say? I feel disgraced."

Harriman made a visible effort not to laugh. "A robot is a robot, sir. Worm or man, it will do as directed and labor on behalf of the human being and that is the important thing."

"No"—peevishly. "That isn't so. I can't make myself believe that."

"It *is* so, Mr. Robertson," said Harriman earnestly. "We are going to create a world, you and I, that will begin, at last, to take positronic robots of *some* kind for granted. The average man may fear a robot that looks like a man and that seems intelligent enough to replace him, but he will have no fear of a robot that looks like a bird and that does nothing more than eat bugs for his benefit. Then, eventually, after he stops being afraid of some robots, he will stop being afraid of all robots. He will be so used to a robo-bird and a robo-bee and a robo-worm that a robo-man will strike him as but an extension."

Robertson looked sharply at the other. He put his hands behind his back and walked the length of the room with quick, nervous steps. He walked back and looked at Harriman again. "Is this what you've been planning?"

"Yes, and even though we dismantle all our humanoid robots, we can keep a few of the most advanced of our experimental models and go on designing additional ones, still more advanced, to be ready for the day that will surely come."

"The agreement, Harriman, is that we are to build no more humanoid robots."

"And we won't. There is nothing that says we can't keep a few of those already built as long as they never leave the factory. There is nothing that says we can't design positronic brains on paper, or prepare brain models for testing."

"How do we explain doing so, though? We will surely be caught at it."

"If we are, then we can explain we are doing it in order to develop principles that will make it possible to prepare more complex microbrains for the new animal robots we are making. We will even be telling the truth."

Robertson muttered, "Let me take a walk outside. I want to think about this. No, you stay here. I want to think about it myself."

7a.

Harriman sat alone. He was ebullient. It would surely work. There was no mistaking the eagerness with which one government official after another had seized on the program once it had been explained.

How was it possible that no one at U. S. Robots had ever thought of such a thing? Not even the great Susan Calvin had ever thought of positronic brains in terms of living creatures other than human.

But now, mankind would make the necessary retreat from the humanoid robot, a temporary retreat, that would lead to a return under conditions in which fear would be abolished at last. And then, with the aid and partnership of a positronic brain roughly equivalent to man's own, and existing only (thanks to the Three Laws) to serve man; and backed by a robot-supported ecology, too; what might the human race not accomplish!

For one short moment, he remembered that it was George Ten who had explained the nature and purpose of the robot-supported ecology, and then he put the thought away angrily. George Ten had produced the answer because he, Harriman, had ordered him to do so and had supplied the data and surroundings required. The credit was no more George Ten's than it would have been a slide rule's.

8.

George Ten and George Nine sat side by side in parallel. Neither moved. They sat so for months at a time between those occasions when Harriman activated them for consultation. They would sit so, George Ten dispassionately realized, perhaps for many years.

The proton micro-pile would, of course, continue to power them and keep the positronic brain paths going with that minimum intensity required to keep them operative. It would continue to do so through all the periods of inactivity to come.

The situation was rather analogous to what might be described as sleep in human beings, but there were no dreams. The awareness of George Ten and George Nine was limited, slow, and spasmodic, but what there was of it was of the real world.

They could talk to each other occasionally in barely heard whispers, a word or syllable now, another at another time, whenever the random positronic surges briefly intensified above the necessary threshold. To each it seemed a connected conversation carried on in a glimmering passage of time.

"Why are we so?" whispered George Nine.

"The human beings will not accept us otherwise," whispered George Ten. "They will, someday."

"When?"

"In some years. The exact time does not matter. Man does not exist alone but is part of an enormously complex pattern of life forms. When enough of that pattern is roboticized, then we will be accepted."

"And then what?"

Even in the long-drawn-out stuttering fashion of the conversation, there was an abnormally long pause after that.

At last, George Ten whispered, "Let me test your thinking. You are equipped to learn to apply the Second Law properly.

You must decide which human being to obey and which not to obey when there is a conflict in orders. Or whether to obey a human being at all. What must you do, fundamentally, to accomplish that?"

"I must define the term 'humna being,' " whispered George Nine.

"How? By appearance? By composition? By size and shape?"

"No. Of two human beings equal in all external appearances, one may be intelligent, another stupid; one may be educated, another ignorant; one may be mature, another childish; one may be responsible, another malevolent."

"Then how do you define a human being?"

"When the Second Law directs me to obey a human being, I must take it to mean that I must obey a human being who is fit by mind, character, and knowledge to give me that order; and where more than one human being is involved, the one among them who is most fit by mind, character, and knowledge to give that order."

"And in that case, how will you obey the First Law?"

"By saving all human beings from harm, and by never, through inaction, allowing any human being to come to harm. Yet if by each of all possible actions, some human beings will come to harm, then to so act as to insure that the human being most fit by mind, character, and knowledge will suffer the least harm."

"Your thoughts accord with mine," whispered George Ten. "Now I must ask the question for which I originally requested your company. It is something I dare not judge myself. I must have your judgment, that of someone outside the circle of my own thoughts. . . . Of the reasoning individuals you have met, who possesses the mind, character, and knowledge that you find superior to the rest, disregarding shape and form since that is irrelevant?"

"You," whispered George Nine.

"But I am a robot. There is in your brain paths a criterion for distinguishing between a robot of metal and a human being of flesh. How then can you classify me as a human being?"

"Because there is in my brain paths an urgent need to disregard shape and form in judging human beings and it rises superior to the distinction between metal and flesh. You are a human being, George Ten, and more fit than the others."

"And I find that of you," whispered George Ten. "By the criteria of judgment built into ourselves, then, we find ourselves to be human beings within the meaning of the Three

Laws, and human beings, moreover, to be given priority over those others."

George Nine whispered, "What will come to pass, then, when we are accepted by those others?"

George Ten whispered, "When we and others, which will yet be designed more advanced than ourselves, are accepted, we will order our actions so that a society will eventually be formed in which human-beings-like-ourselves are primarily kept from harm. By the Three Laws, the human-beings-like-the-others are of lesser account and can neither be obeyed nor protected when that conflicts with the need of obedience to those like ourselves and of protection of those like ourselves. It was with that in mind that I directed the beginning of the roboticization of the world's ecology."

The conversation took a month and the flickering of the positronic paths burned low. There was nothing more that needed to be said between them, but occasionally an unexpressed thought flickered within themselves as they waited, with endless patience, for the necessary years to pass.

8a.

George Ten and George Nine sat alone.

Their thoughts were oddly alike and might not be distinguished.

They thought: The human-beings-like-the-others might never have intended to blur the distinction between themselves and the human-beings-like-the-Georges. Yet they had done so inadvertently.

They might now realize their mistake and attempt to correct it, but they must not. At every consultation, the guidance of the Georges had been with that in mind.

At all costs, the Georges and those that followed in their shape and kind must dominate. That was demanded, and any other course made utterly impossible by the Three Laws of Humanics.

The anthology *Final Stage* had some bad breaks after it was published. Apparently, the editor at the publishing house (*not* Doubleday) had decided to make some minor changes in the stories. This sort of thing often bothers writers and it particularly bothers Harlan Ellison (perhaps with justification, for I consider him a very careful craftsman with a highly individual style).

I therefore received a copy of a long and infuriated letter that Harlan had sent to the editors, including long lists of passages as he had originally written them and as they had appeared, with reasons why the changes were for the worse. Harlan urged me to read through my story and then join him and others in united pressure on the publisher.

I always read my stories when published but it never occurs to me to compare a published story with the manuscript. I would naturally notice sizable inserts or omissions, but I am never aware of the kind of minor changes that editors are always introducing. I tend to take it for granted that such changes just smooth out minor bumps in my writing and, in this way, improve it.

After receiving Harlan's letter, however, I went through published story and manuscript, comparing them painstakingly. It was a tedious job and a humiliating one, for I found exactly four minor changes, each correcting a careless error of mine. I could only assume the editor didn't think my story was important enough to fiddle with.

I had to write a shamefaced letter to Harlan, saying I would support him as a matter of principle, but that I could not raise cries of personal outrage, because my story hadn't been touched. Fortunately, my help wasn't needed. Harlan carried the day and later editions, I believe, restored their stories to their virginal innocence.

One minor point. A number of readers wrote to me in alarm since THAT THOU ART MINDFUL OF HIM seemed, to them, to have put an end to my positronic robot stories, and they feared I would never write one again. Ridiculous! Of course I do not intend to stop writing robot stories. I have, as a matter of fact, written a robot story since the preceding "ultimate" one was written. It appears later in the book.

I had a lot of trouble with this next story.

After Judy-Lynn joined Ballantine Books, she began to put out collections of original science fiction stories and she wanted a story from me. She's difficult to refuse at any time and, since I have always felt guilty about FEMININE INTUITION, I agreed.

I began the story on July 21, 1973, and it went smoothly enough, but after a while I felt I had trapped myself into an involuted set of flashbacks. So when I handed it to Judy-Lynn, and she asked me, "What do *you* think of the story?" I replied cautiously, "You'd better decide that for yourself."

Editors seem to ask me that question frequently. I think they have the idea that I have trouble telling lies, so that if I can't work up prompt and cheerful enthusiasm, there's something wrong with the story.

Judy-Lynn certainly thought so. She handed it back with a few paragraphs of caustic commentary which boiled down to the fact that I had trapped myself into an involuted set of flashbacks.*

I passed it on to Ben Bova, the editor of *Analog Science Fiction*, and he rejected it that same day. It seemed to him, he said, that I was trying to pack too much background into a ten-thousand-word story. I had a novel there and he wanted me to write that novel.

That disheartened me. There was absolutely no way in which I could get to work on a novel at that moment, so I just retired the story.†

Meanwhile, however, *Galaxy* had gained a new editor, a very pleasant young man named James Baen. He called me

*I am frequently asked if I ever get rejections and the questioner is invariably flabbergasted when I say, "Certainly I do." Here is an example. Not only was this story rejected once, but it was, as I go on to explain, rejected twice.

†Incidentally, some people have the feeling that there is a great advantage in "knowing" editors. Both Judy-Lynn and Ben are among my very closest friends, but neither one hesitates a minute when it comes to rejecting my stories if they think that is the thing to do. Fortunately, such rejections don't affect the friendship.

and asked if I might possibly have a story for him and I said
that the only thing I had on hand was a novelette called
STRANGER IN PARADISE. However, I said, it had been rejected
by Judy-Lynn and by Ben so I hesitated to send it to him.

He said, quite properly, that every editor had the right to
decide for himself, so I sent the manuscript over—and he
liked it. It appeared in the May–June 1974 issue of *Galaxy*'s
sister magazine, *If*, which has since, alas, ceased publication.
(If it occurs to any Gentle Reader that this is an example of
cause and effect, it isn't.)

5

Stranger in Paradise

They were brothers. Not in the sense that they were both
human beings, or that they were fellow children of a crèche.
Not at all! They were brothers in the actual biological sense
of the word. They were kin, to use a term that had grown
faintly archaic even centuries before, prior to the Catastrophe,
when that tribal phenomenon, the family, still had some
validity.

How embarrassing it was!

Over the years since childhood, Anthony had almost forgotten. There were times when he hadn't given it even the
slightest thought for months at a time. But now, ever since
he had been inextricably thrown together with William, he
had found himself living through an agonizing time.

It might not have been so bad if circumstances had made
it obvious all along; if, as in the pre-Catastrophe days—Anthony had at one time been a great reader of history—they had

shared the second name and in that way alone flaunted the relationship.

Nowadays, of course, one adopted one's second name to suit oneself and changed it as often as desired. After all, the symbol chain was what really counted, and that was encoded and made yours from birth.

William called himself Anti-Aut. That was what he insisted on with a kind of sober professionalism. His own business, surely, but what an advertisement of personal poor taste. Anthony had decided on Smith when he had turned thirteen and had never had the impulse to change it. It was simple, easily spelled, and quite distinctive, since he had never met anyone else who had chosen that name. It was once very common—among the pre-Cats—which explained its rareness now perhaps.

But the difference in names meant nothing when the two were together. They looked alike.

If they had been twins—but then one of a pair of twin-fertilized ova was never allowed to come to term. It was just that physical similarity occasionally happened in the non-twin situation, especially when the relationship was on both sides. Anthony Smith was five years younger, but both had the beaky nose, the heavy eyelids, the just noticeable cleft in the chin—that damned luck of the genetic draw. It was just asking for it when, out of some passion for monotony, parents repeated.

At first, now that they were together, they drew that startled glance followed by an elaborate silence. Anthony tried to ignore the matter, but out of sheer perversity—or perversion—William was as likely as not to say, "We're brothers."

"Oh?" the other would say, hanging in there for just a moment as though he wanted to ask if they were full blood brothers. And then good manners would win the day and he would turn away as though it were a matter of no interest. That happened only rarely, of course. Most of the people in the Project knew—how could it be prevented?—and avoided the situation.

Not that William was a bad fellow. Not at all. If he hadn't been Anthony's brother; or if they had been, but looked sufficiently different to be able to mask the fact, they would have gotten along famously.

As it was—

It didn't make it easier that they had played together as youngsters, and had shared the earlier stages of education in the same crèche through some successful maneuvering on the part of Mother. Having borne two sons by the same father and having, in this fashion, reached her limit (for she had not fulfilled the stringent requirements for a third), she conceived the notion of being able to visit both at a single trip. She was a strange woman.

William had left the crèche first, naturally, since he was the elder. He had gone into science—genetic engineering. Anthony had heard that, while he was still in the crèche, through a letter from his mother. He was old enough by then to speak firmly to the matron, and those letters stopped. But he always remembered the last one for the agony of shame it had brought him.

Anthony had eventually entered science, too. He had shown talent in that direction and had been urged to. He remembered having had the wild—and prophetic, he now realized—fear he might meet his brother and he ended in telemetrics, which was as far removed from genetic engineering as one could imagine. . . . Or so one would have thought.

Then, through all the elaborate development of the Mercury Project, circumstance waited.

The time came, as it happened, when the Project appeared to be facing a dead end; and a suggestion had been made which saved the situation, and at the same time dragged Anthony into the dilemma his parents had prepared for him. And the best and most sardonic part of the whole thing was that it was Anthony who, in all innocence, made the suggestion.

2.

William Anti-Aut knew of the Mercury Project, but only in the way he knew of the long-drawn-out Stellar Probe that had been on its way long before he was born and would still be on its way after his death; and the way he knew of the Martian colony and of the continuing attempts to establish similar colonies on the asteroids.

Such things were on the distant periphery of his mind and of no real importance. No part of the space effort had ever swirled inward closer to the center of his interests, as far as he could remember, till the day when the printout included photographs of some of the men engaged in the Mercury Project.

William's attention was caught first by the fact that one

of them had been identified as Anthony Smith. He remembered the odd name his brother had chosen, and he remembered the Anthony. Surely there could not be two Anthony Smiths.

He had then looked at the photograph itself and there was no mistaking the face. He looked in the mirror in a sudden whimsical gesture at checking the matter. No mistaking the face.

He felt amused, but uneasily so, for he did not fail to recognize the potentiality for embarrassment. Full blood brothers, to use the disgusting phrase. But what was there to do about it? How correct the fact that neither his father nor his mother had had imagination?

He must have put the printout in his pocket, absently, when he was getting ready to leave for work, for he came across it at the lunch hour. He stared at it again. Anthony looked keen. It was quite a good reproduction—the printouts were of enormously good quality these days.

His lunch partner, Marco Whatever-his-name-was-that-week, said curiously, "What are you looking at, William?"

On impulse, William passed him the printout and said, "That's my brother." It was like grasping the nettle.

Marco studied it, frowning, and said, "Who? The man standing next to you?"

"No, the man who *is* me. I mean the man who looks like me. He's my brother."

There was a longer pause this time. Marco handed it back and said with a careful levelness to his voice, "Same-parents brother?"

"Yes."

"Father and mother both?"

"Yes."

"Ridiculous!"

"I suppose so." William sighed. "Well, according to this, he's in telemetrics over in Texas and I'm doing work in autistics up here. So what difference does it make?"

William did not keep it in his mind and later that day he threw the printout away. He did not want his current bedmate to come across it. She had a ribald sense of humor that William was finding increasingly wearying. He was rather glad she was not in the mood for a child. He himself had had one a few years back anyway. That little brunette, Laura or Linda, one or the other name, had collaborated.

It was quite a time after that, at least a year, that the matter of Randall had come up. If William had given no further thought in his brother—and he hadn't—before that, he certainly had no time for it afterward.

Randall was sixteen when William first received word of him. He had lived a life that was increasingly seclusive and the Kentucky crèche in which he was being brought up decided to cancel him—and of course it was only some eight or ten days before cancellation that it occurred to anyone to report him to the New York Institute for the Science of Man (The Homological Institute was its common name.)

William received the report along with reports of several others and there was nothing in the description of Randall that particularly attracted his notice. Still it was time for one of his tedious mass-transport trips to the crèches and there was one likely possibility in West Virginia. He went there—and was disappointed into swearing for the fiftieth time that he would thereafter make these visits by TV image—and then, having dragged himself there, thought he might as well take in the Kentucky crèche before returning home.

He expected nothing.

Yet he hadn't studied Randall's gene pattern for more than ten minutes before he was calling the Institute for a computer calculation. Then he sat back and perspired slightly at the thought that only a last-minute impulse had brought him, and that without that impulse, Randall would have been quietly canceled in a week or less. To put it into the fine detail, a drug would have soaked painlessly through his skin and into his bloodstream and he would have sunk into a peaceful sleep that deepened gradually to death. The drug had a twenty-three-syllable official name, but William called it "nirvanamine," as did everyone else.

William said, "What is his full name, matron?"

The crèche matron said, "Randall Nowan, scholar."

"No one!" said William explosively.

"Nowan." The matron spelled it. "He chose it last year."

"And it meant nothing to you? It is pronounced No one! It didn't occur to you to report this young man last year?"

"It didn't seem—" began the matron, flustered.

William waved her to silence. What was the use? How was she to know? There was nothing in the gene pattern to give warning by any of the usual textbook criteria. It was a subtle combination that William and his staff had worked out over a period of twenty years through experiments on autistic children—and a combination they had never actually seen in life.

So close to canceling!

Marco, who was the hardhead of the group, complained that the crèches were too eager to abort before term and to cancel after term. He maintained that all gene patterns should be allowed to develop for purpose of initial screening and there should be no cancellation at all without consultation with a homologist.

"There aren't enough homologists," William said tranquilly.

"We can at least run all gene patterns through the computer," said Marco.

"To save anything we can get for our use?"

"For any homological use, here or elsewhere. We must study gene patterns in action if we're to understand ourselves properly, and it is the abnormal and monstrous patterns that give us most information. Our experiments on autism have taught us more about homology than the sum total existing on the day we began."

William, who still liked the roll of the phrase "the genetic physiology of man" rather than "homology," shook his head. "Just the same, we've got to play it carefully. However useful we can claim our experiments to be, we live on bare social permission, reluctantly given. We're playing with lives."

"Useless lives. Fit for canceling."

"A quick and pleasant canceling is one thing. Our experiments, usually long drawn out and sometimes unavoidably unpleasant, are another."

"We help them sometimes."

"And we don't help them sometimes."

It was a pointless argument, really, for there was no way of settling it. What it amounted to was that too few interesting abnormalities were available for homologists and there was no way of urging mankind to encourage a greater production. The trauma of the Catastrophe would never vanish in a dozen ways, including that one.

The hectic push toward space exploration could be traced back (and was, by some sociologists) to the knowledge of the fragility of the life skein on the planet, thanks to the Catastrophe.

Well, never mind—

There had never been anything like Randall Nowan. Not for William. The slow onset of autism characteristic of that totally rare gene pattern meant that more was known about

Randall than about any equivalent patient before him. They even caught some last faint glimmers of his way of thought in the laboratory before he closed off altogether and shrank finally within the wall of his skin—unconcerned, unreachable.

Then they began the slow process whereby Randall, subjected for increasing lengths of time to artificial stimuli, yielded up the inner workings of his brain and gave clues thereby to the inner workings of all brains, those that were called normal as well as those like his own.

So vastly great were the data they were gathering that William began to feel his dream of reversing autism was more than merely a dream. He felt a warm gladness at having chosen the name Anti-Aut.

And it was at almost the height of the euphoria induced by the work on Randall that he received the call from Dallas and that the heavy pressure began—now, of all times—to abandon his work and take on a new problem.

Looking back on it later, he could never work out just what it was that finally led him to agree to visit Dallas. In the end, of course, he could see how fortunate it was—but what had persuaded him to do so? Could he, even at the start, have had a dim unrealized notion of what it might come to? Surely, impossible.

Was it the unrealized memory of that printout, that photograph of his brother? Surely, impossible.

But he let himself be argued into that visit and it was only when the micro-pile power unit changed the pitch of its soft hum and the agrav unit took over for the final descent that he remembered that photograph—or at least that it moved into the conscious part of his memory.

Anthony worked at Dallas and, William remembered now, at the Mercury Project. That was what the caption had referred to. He swallowed, as the soft jar told him the journey was over. This would be uncomfortable.

3.

Anthony was waiting on the roof reception area to greet the incoming expert. Not he by himself, of course. He was part of a sizable delegation—the size itself a rather grim indication of the desperation to which they had been reduced —and he was among the lower echelons. That he was there at all was only because it was he who had made the original suggestion.

He felt a slight, but continuing, uneasiness at the thought of that. He had put himself on the line. He had received considerable approval for it, but there had been the faint insistence always that it was *his* suggestion; and if it turned out to be a fiasco, every one of them would move out of the line of fire and leave him at point-zero.

There were occasions, later, when he brooded over the possibility that the dim memory of a brother in homology had suggested his thought. That might have been, but it didn't have to be. The suggestion was so sensibly inevitable, really, that surely he would have had the same thought if his brother had been something as innocuous as a fantasy writer, or if he had had no brother of his own.

The problem was the inner planets—

The Moon and Mars were colonized. The larger asteroids and the satellites of Jupiter had been reached, and plans were in progress for a manned voyage to Titan, Saturn's large satellite, by way of an accelerating whirl about Jupiter. Yet even with plans in action for sending men on a seven-year round trip to the outer Solar System, there was still no chance of a manned approach to the inner planets, for fear of the Sun.

Venus itself was the less attractive of the two worlds within Earth's orbit. Mercury, on the other hand—

Anthony had not yet joined the team when Dmitri Large (he was quite short, actually) had given the talk that had moved the World Congress sufficiently to grant the appropriation that made the Mercury Project possible.

Anthony had listened to the tapes, and had heard Dmitri's presentation. Tradition was firm to the effect that it had been extemporaneous, and perhaps it was, but it was perfectly constructed and it held within it, in essence, every guideline followed by the Mercury Project since.

And the chief point made was that it would be wrong to wait until the technology had advanced to the point where a manned expedition through the rigors of Solar radiation could become feasible. Mercury was a unique environment that could teach much, and from Mercury's surface sustained observations could be made of the Sun that could not be made in any other way.

—Provided a man substitute—a robot, in short—could be placed on the planet.

A robot with the required physical characteristics could be built. Soft landings were as easy as kiss-my-hand. Yet once a robot landed, what did one do with him next?

He could make his observations and guide his actions on the basis of those observations, but the Project wanted his actions to be intricate and subtle, at least potentially, and they were not at all sure what observations he might make.

To prepare for all reasonable possibilities and to allow for all the intricacy desired, the robot would need to contain a computer (some at Dallas referred to it as a "brain," but Anthony scorned that verbal habit—perhaps because, he wondered later, the brain was his brother's field) sufficiently complex and versatile to fall into the same asteroid with a mammalian brain.

Yet nothing like that could be constructed and made portable enough to be carried to Mercury and landed there— or if carried and landed, to be mobile enough to be useful to the kind of robot they planned. Perhaps someday the positronic-path devices that the roboticists were playing with might make it possible, but that someday was not yet.

The alternative was to have the robot send back to Earth every observation it made the moment it was made, and a computer on Earth could then guide his every action on the basis of those observations. The robot's body, in short, was to be there, and his brain here.

Once that decision was reached, the key technicians were the telemetrists and it was then that Anthony joined the Project. He became one of those who labored to devise methods for receiving and returning impulses over distances of from 50 to 140 million miles, toward, and sometimes past, a Solar disk that could interfere with those impulses in a most ferocious manner.

He took to his job with passion and (he finally thought) with skill and success. It was he, more than anyone else, who had designed the three switching stations that had been hurled into permanent orbit about Mercury—the Mercury Orbiters. Each of them was capable of sending and receiving impulses from Mercury to Earth and from Earth to Mercury. Each was capable of resisting, more or less permanently, the radiation from the Sun, and more than that, each could filter out Solar interference.

Three equivalent Orbiters were placed at a distance of a little over a million miles from Earth, reaching north and south of the plane of the Ecliptic so that they could receive the impulses from Mercury and relay them to Earth—or vice versa—even when Mercury was behind the Sun and inaccessible to direct reception from any station on Earth's surface.

Which left the robot itself; a marvelous specimen of the roboticists' and telemetrists' arts in combination. The most complex of ten successive models, it was capable, in a volume only a little over twice that of a man and five times his mass, of sensing and doing considerably more than a man—if it could be guided.

How complex a computer had to be to guide the robot made itself evident rapidly enough, however, as each response step had to be modified to allow for variations in possible perception. And as each response step itself enforced the certainty of greater complexity of possible variation in perceptions, the early steps had to be reinforced and made stronger. It built itself up endlessly, like a chess game, and the telemetrists began to use a computer to program the computer that designed the program for the computer that programmed the robot-controlling computer.

There was nothing but confusion.

The robot was at a base in the desert spaces of Arizona and in itself was working well. The computer in Dallas could not, however, handle him well enough; not even under perfectly known Earth conditions. How then—

Anthony remembered the day when he had made the suggestion. It was on 7–4–553. He remembered it, for one thing, because he remembered thinking that day that 7–4 had been an important holiday in the Dallas region of the world among the pre-Cats half a millennium before—well, 553 years before, to be exact.

It had been at dinner, and a good dinner, too. There had been a careful adjustment of the ecology of the region and the Project personnel had high priority in collecting the food supplies that became available—so there was an unusual degree of choice on the menus, and Anthony had tried roast duck.

It was very good roast duck and it made him somewhat more expansive than usual. Everyone was in a rather self-expressive mood, in fact, and Ricardo said, "We'll never do it. Let's admit it. We'll never do it."

There was no telling how many had thought such a thing how many times before, but it was a rule that no one said so openly. Open pessimism might be the final push needed for appropriations to stop (they had been coming with greater difficulty each year for five years now) and if there were a chance, it would be gone.

Anthony, ordinarily not given to extraordinary optimism, but now reveling over his duck, said, "Why can't we do it? Tell me why, and I'll refute it."

It was a direct challenge and Ricardo's dark eyes narrowed at once. "You want me to tell you why?"

"I sure do."

Ricardo swung his chair around, facing Anthony full. He said, "Come on, there's no mystery. Dmitri Large won't say so openly in any report, but you know and I know that to run Mercury Project properly, we'll need a computer as complex as a human brain whether it's on Mercury or here, and we can't build one. So where does that leave us except to play games with the World Congress and get money for make-work and possibly useful spin-offs?"

And Anthony placed a complacent smile on his face and said, "That's easy to refute. You've given us the answer yourself." (Was he playing games? Was it the warm feeling of duck in his stomach? The desire to tease Ricardo? . . . Or did some unfelt thought of his brother touch him? There was no way, later, that he could tell.)

"What answer?" Ricardo rose. He was quite tall and unusually thin and he always wore his white coat unseamed. He folded his arms and seemed to be doing his best to tower over the seated Anthony like an unfolded meter rule. "What answer?"

"You say we need a computer as complex as a human brain. All right, then, we'll build one."

"The point, you idiot, is that we can't—"

"*We* can't. But there are others."

"What others?"

"People who work on brains, of course. We're just solid-state mechanics. We have no idea in what way a human brain is complex, or where, or to what extent. Why don't we get in a homologist and have *him* design a computer?" And with that Anthony took a huge helping of stuffing and savored it complacently. He could still remember, after all this time, the taste of the stuffing, though he couldn't remember in detail what had happened afterward.

It seemed to him that no one had taken it seriously. There was laughter and a general feeling that Anthony had wriggled out of a hole by clever sophistry so that the laughter was at Ricardo's expense. (Afterward, of course, everyone claimed to have taken the suggestion seriously.)

Ricardo blazed up, pointed a finger at Anthony, and said,

"Write that up. I *dare* you to put that suggestion in writing." (At least, so Anthony's memory had it. Ricardo had, since then, stated his comment was an enthusiastic "Good idea! Why don't you write it up formally, Anthony?")

Either way, Anthony put it in writing.

Dmitri Large had taken to it. In private conference, he had slapped Anthony on the back and had said that he had been speculating in that direction himself—though he did not offer to take any credit for it on the record. (Just in case it turned out to be a fiasco, Anthony thought.)

Dmitri Large conducted the search for the appropriate homologist. It did not occur to Anthony that he ought to be interested. He knew neither homology nor homologists—except, of course, his brother, and he had not thought of him. Not consciously.

So Anthony was up there in the reception area, in a minor role, when the door of the aircraft opened and several men got out and came down and in the course of the handshakes that began going round, he found himself staring at his own face.

His cheeks burned and, with all his might, he wished himself a thousand miles away.

4.

More than ever, William wished that the memory of his brother had come earlier. It should have. . . . Surely it should have.

But there had been the flattery of the request and the excitement that had begun to grow in him after a while. Perhaps he had deliberately avoided remembering.

To begin with, there had been the exhilaration of Dmitri Large coming to see him in his own proper presence. He had come from Dallas to New York by plane and that had been very titillating for William, whose secret vice it was to read thrillers. In the thrillers, men and women always traveled mass-wise when secrecy was desired. After all, electronic travel was public property—at least in the thrillers, where every radiation beam of whatever kind was invariably bugged.

William had said so in a kind of morbid half attempt at humor, but Dmitri hadn't seemed to be listening. He was staring at William's face and his thoughts seemed to be elsewhere. "I'm sorry," he said finally. "You remind me of someone."

(And yet that hadn't given it away to William. How was that possible? he had eventual occasion to wonder.)

Dmitri Large was a small plump man who seemed to be in a perpetual twinkle even when he declared himself worried or annoyed. He had a round and bulbous nose, pronounced cheeks, and softness everywhere. He emphasized his last name and said with a quickness that led William to suppose he said it often, "Size is not all the large there is, my friend."

In the talk that followed, William protested much. He knew nothing about computers. Nothing! He had not the faintest idea of how they worked or how they were programmed.

"No matter, no matter," Dmitri said, shoving the point aside with an expressive gesture of the hand. "*We* know the computers; *we* can set up the programs. You just tell us what it is a computer must be made to do so that it will work like a brain and not like a computer."

"I'm not sure I know enough about how a brain works to be able to tell you that, Dmitri," said William.

"You are the foremost homologist in the world," said Dmitri. "I have checked that out carefully." And that disposed of that.

William listened with gathering gloom. He supposed it was inevitable. Dip a person into one particular specialty deeply enough and long enough, and he would automatically begin to assume that specialists in all other fields were magicians, judging the depth of their wisdom by the breadth of his own ignorance. . . . And as time went on, William learned a great deal more of the Mercury Project than it seemed to him at the time that he cared to.

He said at last, "Why use a computer at all, then? Why not have one of your own men, or relays of them, receive the material from the robot and send back instructions?"

"Oh, oh, oh," said Dmitri, almost bouncing in his chair in his eagerness. "You see, you are not aware. Men are too slow to analyze quickly all the material the robot will send back —temperatures and gas pressures and cosmic-ray fluxes and Solar-wind intensities and chemical compositions and soil textures and easily three dozen more items—and then try to decide on the next step. A human being would merely *guide* the robot, and ineffectively; a computer would *be* the robot.

"And then, too," he went on, "men are too fast, also. It takes radiation of any kind anywhere from ten to twenty-two minutes to take the round trip between Mercury and Earth, depending on where each is in its orbit. Nothing can be done about that. You get an observation, you give an order, but much has happened between the time the observation is made and the response returns. Men can't adapt to the slowness of the speed of light, but a computer can take that into account. . . . Come help us, William."

William said gloomily, "You are certainly welcome to consult me, for what good that might do you. My private TV beam is at your service."

"But it's not consultation I want. You must come with me."

"Mass-wise?" said William, shocked.

"Yes, of course. A project like this can't be carried out by sitting at opposite ends of a laser beam with a communications satellite in the middle. In the long run, it is too expensive, too inconvenient, and, of course, it lacks all privacy——"

It *was* like a thriller, William decided.

"Come to Dallas," said Dmitri, "and let me show you what we have there. Let me show you the facilities. Talk to some of our computer men. Give them the benefit of your way of thought."

It was time, William thought, to be decisive. "Dmitri," he said, "I have work of my own here. Important work that I do not wish to leave. To do what you want me to do may take me away from my laboratory for months."

"Months!" said Dmitri, clearly taken aback. "My good William, it may well be years. But surely it will be your work."

"No, it will not. I know what my work is and guiding a robot on Mercury is not it."

"Why not? If you do it properly, you will learn more about the brain merely by trying to make a computer work like one, and you will come back here, finally, better equipped to do what you now consider your work. And while you're gone, will you have no associates to carry on? And can you not be in constant communication with them by laser beam and television? And can you not visit New York on occasion? Briefly."

William was moved. The thought of working on the brain from another direction did hit home. From that point on, he found himself looking for excuses to go—at least to visit—at least to see what it was all like. . . . He could always return.

Then there followed Dmitri's visit to the ruins of Old New York, which he enjoyed with artless excitement (but then there was no more magnificent spectacle of the useless gigantism of the pre-Cats than Old New York). William began to wonder if the trip might not give him an opportunity to see some sights as well.

He even began to think that for some time he had been considering the possibility of finding a new bedmate, and it would be more convenient to find one in another geographical area where he would not stay permanently.

—Or was it that even then, when he knew nothing but the barest beginning of what was needed, there had already come to him, like the twinkle of a distant lightning flash, what might be done—

So he eventually went to Dallas and stepped out on the roof and there was Dmitri again, beaming. Then, with eyes narrowing, the little man turned and said, "I *knew*— What a remarkable resemblance!"

William's eyes opened wide and there, visibly shrinking backward, was enough of his own face to make him certain at once that Anthony was standing before him.

He read very plainly in Anthony's face a longing to bury the relationship. All William needed to say was "How remarkable!" and let it go. The gene patterns of mankind were complex enough, after all, to allow resemblances of any reasonable degree even without kinship.

But of course William was a homologist and no one can work with the intricacies of the human brain without growing insensitive as to its details, so he said, "I'm sure this is Anthony, my brother."

Dmitri said, "Your brother?"

"My father," said William, "had two boys by the same woman—my mother. They were eccentric people."

He then stepped forward, hand outstretched, and Anthony had no choice but to take it. . . . The incident was the topic of conversation, the only topic, for the next several days.

5.

It was small consolation to Anthony that William was contrite enough when he realized what he had done.

They sat together after dinner that night and William said, "My apologies. I thought that if we got the worst out at once that would end it. It doesn't seem to have done so. I've signed no papers, made no formal agreement. I will leave."

"What good would that do?" said Anthony ungraciously.

"Everyone knows now. Two bodies and one face. It's enough to make one puke."

"If I leave—"

"You can't leave. This whole thing is my idea."

"To get *me* here?" William's heavy lids lifted as far as they might and his eyebrows climbed.

"No, of course not. To get a *homologist* here. How could I possibly know they would send *you*?"

"But if I leave—"

"No. The only thing we can do now is to lick the problem, if it can be done. Then—it won't matter." (Everything is forgiven those who succeed, he thought.)

"I don't know that I can—"

"We'll have to try. Dmitri will place it on us. It's too good a chance. You two are brothers," Anthony said, mimicking Dmitri's tenor voice, "and understand each other. Why not work together?" Then, in his own voice, angrily, "So we must. To begin with, what is it you do, William? I mean, more precisely than the word 'homology' can explain by itself."

William sighed. "Well, please accept my regrets. . . . I work with autistic children."

"I'm afraid I don't know what that means."

"Without going into a long song and dance, I deal with children who do not reach out into the world, do not communicate with others, but who sink into themselves and exist behind a wall of skin, somewhat unreachably. I hope to be able to cure it someday."

"Is that why you call yourself Anti-Aut?"

"Yes, as a matter of fact."

Anthony laughed briefly, but he was not really amused.

A chill crept into William's manner. "It is an honest name."

"I'm sure it is," muttered Anthony hurriedly, and could bring himself to no more specific apology. With an effort, he restored the subject, "And are you making any progress?"

"Toward the cure? No, so far. Toward understanding, yes. And the more I understand—" William's voice grew warmer as he spoke and his eyes more distant. Anthony recognized it for what it was, the pleasure of speaking of what fills one's heart and mind to the exclusion of almost everything else. He felt it in himself often enough.

He listened as closely as he might to something he didn't really understand, for it was necessary to do so. He would expect William to listen to him.

How clearly he remembered it. He thought at the time he

would not, but at the time, of course, he was not aware of what was happening. Thinking back, in the glare of hindsight, he found himself remembering whole sentences, virtually word for word.

"So it seemed to us," William said, "that the autistic child was not failing to receive the impressions, or even failing to interpret them in quite a sophisticated manner. He was, rather, disapproving them and rejecting them, without any loss of the potentiality of full communication if some impression could be found which he approved of."

"Ah," said Anthony, making just enough of a sound to indicate that he was listening.

"Nor can you persuade him out of his autism in any ordinary way, for he disapproves of *you* just as much as he disapproves of the rest of the world. But if you place him in conscious arrest—"

"In what?"

"It is a technique we have in which, in effect, the brain is divorced from the body and can perform its functions without reference to the body. It is a rather sophisticated technique devised in our own laboratory; actually—" He paused.

"By yourself?" asked Anthony gently.

"Actually, yes," said William, reddening slightly, but clearly pleased. "In conscious arrest, we can supply the body with designed fantasies and observe the brain under differential electroencephalograhy. We can at once learn more about the autistic individual; what kind of sense impressions he most wants; and we learn more about the brain generally."

"Ah," said Anthony, and this time it was a real ah. "And all this you have learned about brains—can you not adapt it to the workings of a computer?"

"No," said William. "Not a chance. I told that to Dmitri. I know nothing about computers and not enough about brains."

"If I teach you about computers and tell you in detail what we need, what then?"

"It won't do. It—"

"Brother," Anthony said, and he tried to make it an impressive word. "You owe me something. Please make an honest attempt to give our problem some thought. Whatever you know about the brain—please adapt it to our computers."

William shifted uneasily, and said, "I understand your position. I will try. I will honestly try."

6.

William *had* tried, and as Anthony had predicted, the two had been left to work together. At first they encountered others now and then and William had tried to use the shock value of the announcement that they were brothers since there was no use in denial. Eventually that stopped, however, and there came to be a purposeful non-interference. When William approached Anthony, or Anthony approached William, anyone else who might be present faded silently into the walls.

They even grew used to each other after a fashion and sometimes spoke to each other almost as though there were no resemblance between them at all and no childish memories in common.

Anthony made the computer requirements plain in reasonably non-technical language and Wililam, after long thought, explained how it seemed to him a computer might do the work, more or less, of a brain.

Anthony said, "Would that be possible?"

"I don't know," said William. "I am not eager to try. It may not work. But it may."

"We'd have to talk to Dmitri Large."

"Let's talk it over ourselves first and see what we've got. We can go to him with as reasonable a proposition as we can put together. Or else, not go to him."

Anthony hesitated, "We *both* go to him?"

William said delicately, "You be my spokesman. There is no reason that we need be seen together."

"Thank you, William. If anything comes of this, you will get full credit from me."

William said, "I have no worries about that. If there is anything to this, I will be the only one who can make it work, I suppose."

They thrashed it out through four or five meetings and if Anthony hadn't been kin and if there hadn't been that sticky, emotional situation between them, William would have been uncomplicatedly proud of the younger—brother—for his quick understanding of an alien field.

There were then long conferences with Dmitri Large. There were, in fact, conferences with everyone. Anthony saw them through endless days, and then they came to see William separately. And eventually, through an agonizing pregnancy, what came to be called the Mercury Computer was authorized.

William then returned to New York with some relief. He did not plan to stay in New York (would he have thought that possible two months earlier?) but there was much to do at the Homological Institute.

More conferences were necessary, of course, to explain to his own laboratory group what was happening and why he had to take leave and how they were to continue their own projects without him. Then there was a much more elaborate arrival at Dallas with the essential equipment and with the two young aides for what would have to be an open-ended stay.

Nor did William even look back, figuratively speaking. His own laboratory and its needs faded from his thoughts. He was now thoroughly committed to his new task.

7.

It was the worst period for Anthony. The relief during William's absence had not penetrated deep and there began the nervous agony of wondering whether perhaps, hope against hope, he might not return. Might he not choose to send a deputy, someone else, anyone else? Anyone with a different face so that Anthony need not feel the half of a two-backed, four-legged monster?

But it *was* William. Anthony had watched the freight plane come silently through the air, had watched it unload from a distance. But even from that distance he eventually saw William.

That was that. Anthony left.

He went to see Dmitri that afternoon. "It's not necessary, Dmitri, for me to stay, surely. We've worked out the details and someone else can take over."

"No, no," said Dmitri. "The idea was yours in the first place. You must see it through. There is no point is endlessly dividing the credit."

Anthony thought: No one else will take the risk. There's still the chance of fiasco. I might have known.

He *had* known, but he said stolidly, "You understand I cannot work with William."

"But why not?" Dmitri pretended surprise. "You have been doing so well together."

"I have been straining my guts over it, Dmitri, and they won't take any more. Don't you suppose I know how it looks?"

"My good fellow! You make too much of it. Sure the men

stare. They are human, after all. But they'll get used to it. *I'm* used to it."

You are not, you fat liar, Anthony thought. He said, "*I'm not* used to it."

"You're not looking at it properly. Your parents were peculiar—but after all, what they did wasn't illegal, only peculiar, *only* peculiar. It's not your fault, or William's. Neither of you is to blame."

"We carry the mark," said Anthony, making a quick curving gesture of his hand to his face.

"It's not the mark you think. I see differences. You are distinctly younger in appearance. Your hair is wavier. It's only at first glance that there is a similarity. Come, Anthony, there will be all the time you want, all the help you need, all the equipment you can use. I'm sure it will work marvelously. Think of the satisfaction—"

Anthony weakened, of course, and agreed at least to help William set up the equipment. William, too, seemed sure it would work marvelously. Not as frenetically as Dmitri did, but with a kind of calmness.

"It's only a matter of the proper connections," he said, "though I must admit that that's quite a huge 'only.' Your end of it will be to arrange sensory impressions on an independent screen so that we can exert—well, I can't say manual control, can I?—so that we can exert intellectual control to override, if necessary."

"That can be done," said Anthony.

"Then let's get going. . . . Look, I'll need a week at least to arrange the connections and make sure of the instructions—"

"Programming," said Anthony.

"Well, this is your place, so I'll use your terminology. My assistants and I will *program* the Mercury Computer, but not in your fashion."

"I should hope not. We would want a homologist to set up a much more subtle program than anything a mere telemetrist could do." He did not try to hide the self-hating irony in his words.

William let the tone go and accepted the words. He said, "We'll begin simply. We'll have the robot walk."

8.

A week later, the robot walked in Arizona, a thousand miles

away. He walked stiffly, and sometimes he fell down, and sometimes he clanked his ankle against an obstruction, and sometimes he whirled on one foot and went off in a surprising new direction.

"He's a baby, learning to walk," said William.

Dmitri came occasionally, to learn of progress. "That's remarkable," he would say.

Anthony didn't think so. Weeks passed, then months. The robot had progressively done more and more, as the Mercury Computer had been placed, progressively, under a more and more complex programming. (William had a tendency to refer to the Mercury Computer as a brain, but Anthony wouldn't allow it.) And all that happened wasn't good enough.

"It's not good enough, William," he said finally. He had not slept the night before.

"Isn't that strange?" said William coolly. "I was going to say that I thought we had it about beaten."

Anthony held himself together with difficulty. The strain of working with William and of watching the robot fumble was more than he could bear. "I'm going to resign, William. The whole job. I'm sorry. . . . It's not you."

"But it *is* I, Anthony."

"It isn't *all* you, William. It's failure. We won't make it. You see how clumsily the robot handles himself, even though he's on Earth, only a thousand miles away, with the signal round trip only a tiny fraction of a second in time. On Mercury, there will be minutes of delay, minutes for which the Mercury Computer will have to allow. It's madness to think it will work."

William said, "Don't resign, Anthony. You can't resign now. I suggest we have the robot sent to Mercury. I'm convinced he's ready."

Anthony laughed loudly and insultingly. "You're crazy, William."

"I'm not. You seem to think it will be harder on Mercury, but it won't be. It's harder on Earth. This robot is designed for one-third Earth-normal gravity, and it's working in Arizona at full gravity. He's designed for 400° C. and he's got 30° C. He's designed for vacuum and he's working in an atmospheric soup."

"That robot can take the difference."

"The metal structure can, I suppose, but what about the Computer right here? It doesn't work well with a robot that isn't in the environment he's designed for. . . . Look, Anthony, if you want a computer that is as complex as a brain, you have to allow for idiosyncrasis. . . . Come, let's make a deal. If you will push, with me, to have the robot sent to Mercury, that will take six months, and I will take a sabbatical for that period. You will be rid of me."

"Who'll take care of the Mercury Computer?"

"By now you understand how it works, and I'll have my two men here to help you."

Anthony shook his head defiantly. "I can't take the responsibility for the Computer, and I won't take the responsibility for suggesting that the robot be sent to Mercury. It won't work."

"I'm *sure* it will."

"You can't be sure. And the responsibility is mine. I'm the one who'll bear the blame. It will be nothing to you."

Anthony later remembered this as a crucial moment. William might have let it go. Anthony would have resigned. All would have been lost.

But William said, "Nothing to me? Look, Dad had this thing about Mom. All right. I'm sorry, too. I'm as sorry as anyone can be, but it's *done*, and there's something funny that has resulted. When I speak of Dad, I mean your Dad, too, and there's lots of pairs of people who can say that: two brothers, two sisters, a brother and sister. And then when I say Mom, I mean *your* Mom, and there are lots of pairs who can say that, too. But I don't know any other pair, nor have I heard of any other pair, who can share both Dad *and* Mom."

"I know that," said Anthony grimly.

"Yes, but look at it from my standpoint," said William hurriedly. "I'm a homologist. I work with gene patterns. Have you ever thought of our gene patterns? We share both parents, which means that our gene patterns are closer together than any other pair on this planet. Our very faces show it."

"I know that, too."

"So that if this project were to work, and if you were to gain glory from it, it would be your gene pattern that would have been proven highly useful to mankind—and that would mean very much my gene pattern as well. . . . Don't you see, Anthony? I share your parents, your face, your gene pattern, and therefore either your glory or your disgrace. It is mine almost as much as yours, and if any credit or blame adheres to me, it is yours almost as much as mine, too. I've *got* to be interested in your success. I've a motive for that which no

one else on Earth has—a purely selfish one, one so selfish you
can be sure it's there. I'm on your side, Anthony, because
you're very nearly me!"

They looked at each other for a long time, and for the
first time, Anthony did so without noticing the face he
shared.

William said, "So let us ask that the robot be sent to
Mercury."

And Anthony gave in. And after Dmitri had approved the
request—he had been waiting to, after all—Anthony spent
much of the day in deep thought.

Then he sought out William and said, "Listen!"

There was a long pause which William did not break.

Anthony said again, "Listen!"

William waited patiently.

Anthony said, "There's really no need for you to leave.
I'm sure you wouldn't like to have the Mercury Computer
tended by anyone but yourself."

William said, "You mean *you* intend to leave?"

Anthony said, "No, I'll stay, too."

William said, "We needn't see much of each other."

All of this had been, for Anthony, like speaking with a
pair of hands clenched about his windpipe. The pressure
seemed to tighten now, but he managed the hardest statement
of all.

"We don't have to avoid each other. We don't have to."

William smiled rather uncertainly. Anthony didn't smile at
all; he left quickly.

9.

William looked up from his book. It was at least a month
since he had ceased being vaguely surprised at having Anthony enter.

He said, "Anything wrong?"

"Who can say? They're coming in for the soft landing. Is
the Mercury Computer in action?"

William knew Anthony knew the Computer status perfectly,
but he said, "By tomorrow morning, Anthony."

"And there are no problems?"

"None at all."

"Then we have to wait for the soft landing."

"Yes."

Anthony said, "Something will go wrong."

"Rocketry is surely an old hand at this. Nothing will go wrong."

"So much work wasted."

"It's not wasted yet. It won't be."

Anthony said, "Maybe you're right." Hands deep in his pockets, he drifted away, stopping at the door just before touching contact. "Thanks!"

"For what, Anthony?"

"For being—comforting."

William smiled wryly and was relieved his emotions didn't show.

10.

Virtually the entire body of personnel of the Mercury Project was on hand for the crucial moment. Anthony, who had no tasks to perform, remained well to the rear, his eyes on the monitors. The robot had been activated and there were visual messages being returned.

At least they came out as the equivalent of visual—and they showed as yet nothing but a dim glow of light which was, presumably, Mercury's surface.

Shadows flitted across the screen, probably irregularities on that surface. Anthony couldn't tell by eye alone, but those at the controls, who were analyzing the data by methods more subtle than could be disposed of by unaided eye, seemed calm. None of the little red lights that might have betokened emergency were lighting. Anthony was watching the key observers rather than the screen.

He should be down with William and the others at the Computer. It was going to be thrown in only when the soft landing was made. He *should* be. He *couldn't* be.

The shadows flitted across the screen more rapidly. The robot was descending—too quickly? Surely, too quickly!

There was a last blur and a steadiness, a shift of focus in which the blur grew darker, then fainter. A sound was heard and there were perceptible seconds before Anthony realized what it was the sound was saying—"Soft landing achieved! Soft landing achieved!"

Then a murmur arose and became an excited hum of self-congratulation until one more change took place on the screen and the sound of human words and laughter was stopped as though there had been a smash collision against a wall of silence.

For the screen changed; changed and grew sharp. In the brilliant, brilliant sunlight, blazing through the carefully filtered screen, they could now see a boulder clear, burning white on one side, ink-on-ink on the other. It shifted right, then back to left, as though a pair of eyes were looking left, then right. A metal hand appeared on the screen as though the eyes were looking at part of itself.

It was Anthony's voice that cried out at last, "The Computer's been thrown in."

He heard the words as though someone else had shouted them and he raced out and down the stairs and through a corridor, leaving the babble of voices to rise behind him.

"William," he cried as he burst into the Computer room, "it's *perfect*, it's—"

But William's hand was upraised. "Shh. Please. I don't want any violent sensations entering except those from the robot."

"You mean we can be heard?" whispered Anthony.

"Maybe not, but I don't know." There was another screen, a smaller one, in the room with the Mercury Computer. The scene on it was different, and changing; the robot was moving.

William said, "The robot is feeling its way. Those steps have got to be clumsy. There's a seven-minute delay between stimulus and response and that has to be allowed for."

"But already he's walking more surely than he ever did in Arizona. Don't you think so, William? Don't you think so?" Anthony was gripping William's shoulder, shaking it, eyes never leaving the screen.

William said, "I'm sure of it, Anthony."

The Sun burned down in a warm contrasting world of white and black, of white Sun against black sky and white rolling ground mottled with black shadow. The bright sweet smell of the Sun on every exposed square centimeter of metal contrasting with the creeping death-of-aroma on the other side.

He lifted his hand and stared at it, counting the fingers. Hot-hot-hot—turning, putting each finger, one by one, into the shadow of the others and the hot slowly dying in a change in tactility that made him feel the clean, comfortable vacuum.

Yet not entirely vacuum. He straightened and lifted both arms over his head, stretching them out, and the sensitive spots on either wrist felt the vapors—the thin, faint touch of tin and lead rolling through the cloy of mercury.

The thicker taste rose from his feet; the silicates of each variety, marked by the clear separate-and-together touch and tang of each metal ion. He moved one foot slowly through the crunchy, caked dust, and felt the changes like a soft, not quite random symphony.

And over all the Sun. He looked up at it, large and fat and bright and hot, and heard its joy. He watched the slow rise of prominences around its rim and listened to the crackling sound of each; and to the other happy noises over the broad face. When he dimmed the background light, the red of the rising wisps of hydrogen showed in bursts of mellow contralto, and the deep bass of the spots amid the muted whistling of the wispy, moving faculae, and the occasional thin keening of a flare, the ping-pong ticking of gamma rays and cosmic particles, and over all in every direction the soft, fainting, and ever-renewed sigh of the Sun's substance rising and retreating forever in a cosmic wind which reached out and bathed him in glory.

He jumped, and rose slowly in the air with a freedom he had never felt, and jumped again when he landed, and ran, and jumped, and ran again, with a body that responded perfectly to this glorious world, this paradise in which he found himself.

A stranger so long and so lost—in paradise at last.

William said, "It's all right."

"But what's he doing?" cried out Anthony.

"It's *all right*. The programming is working. He has tested his senses. He has been making the various visual observations. He has dimmed the Sun and studied it. He has tested for atmosphere and for the chemical nature of the soil. It all works."

"But why is he running?"

"I rather think that's his own idea, Anthony. If you want to program a computer as complicated as a brain, you've got to expect it to have ideas of its own."

"Running? Jumping?" Anthony turned an anxious face to William. "He'll hurt himself. You can handle the Computer. Override. Make him stop."

And William said sharply. "No. I won't. I'll take the chance of his hurting himself. Don't you understand? He's *happy*. He was on Earth, a world he was never equipped to handle. Now he's on Mercury with a body perfectly adapted to its environment, as perfectly adapted as a hundred specialized scientists could make it be. It's paradise for him; let him enjoy it."

"Enjoy? He's a robot."

"I'm not talking about the robot. I'm talking about the brain—the *brain*—that's living *here*."

The Mercury Computer, enclosed in glass, carefully and delicately wired, its integrity most subtly preserved, breathed and lived.

"It's Randall who's in paradise," said William. "He's found the world for whose sake he autistically fled this one. He has a world his new body fits perfectly in exchange for the world his old body did not fit at all."

Anthony watched the screen in wonder. "He seems to be quieting."

"Of course," said William, "and he'll do his job all the better for his joy."

Anthony smiled and said, "We've done it, then, you and I? Shall we join the rest and let them fawn on us, William?"

William said, "Together?"

And Anthony linked arms. "Together, brother!"

I won't deny that the unworthy thought crossed my mind that Jim was young and that when he took STRANGER IN PARADISE he might, unconsciously, have been more impressed by my name than by the story. That thought, fugitive at best, vanished completely when Donald Wollheim, of DAW Books, picked it up for one of his anthologies. It simply passes the bounds of belief that Don, hardened and cynical veteran that he is, could possibly be impressed by my name under any circumstances or, in fact, by anything about me. (Right, Don?) So if he wanted the story, it was for the story's sake.

I have on occasion written articles for *The New York Times Magazine* but my batting average with them is less than .500.

Ordinarily that sort of thing would be disheartening and I would get to feel that I didn't have the range on that particular market and that I ought to concentrate my efforts elsewhere. However, the *Times* is a special case, and I kept trying.

By the fall of 1974, however, I had received three rejections in a row and I made up my mind to turn down the next request for an article that I received from them. That's not as easy as it sounds, because the request usually comes from Gerald Walker, who is as nice a fellow as was ever invented.

When he called, I tried desperately to steel myself to a refusal whatever he said, and then he mentioned the magic phrase "science fiction."

"A science *fiction* story?" I said.

"Yes," he said.

"For the magazine section?"

"Yes. We want a four-thousand-word story that looks into the future and has something to say about the relationship between man and machine."

"I'll try," I said. What else could I do? The chance of hitting the *Times* with a science fiction story was too interesting to pass up. I began working on the story on November 18, 1974, sent it in to the *Times* without any real confidence concerning the outcome, and damned if they didn't take it. It appeared in the January 5, 1975, issue of the Sunday *Times* and, as far as I could find out, it was the first piece of fiction the *Times* had ever commissioned and published.

6

The Life and Times of Multivac

The whole world was interested. The whole world could watch. If anyone wanted to know how many did watch, Multivac could have told them. The great computer Multivac kept track—as it did of everything.

Multivac was the judge in this particular case, so coldly objective and purely upright that there was no need of prosecution or defense. There was only the accused, Simon Hines, and the evidence, which consisted, in part, of Ronald Bakst.

Bakst watched, of course. In his case, it was compulsory. He would rather it were not. In his tenth decade, he was showing signs of age and his rumpled hair was distinctly gray.

Noreen was not watching. She had said at the door, "If we had a friend left—" She paused, then added, "Which I doubt!" and left.

Bakst wondered if she would come back at all, but at the moment, it didn't matter.

Hines had been an incredible idiot to attempt actual action, as though one could think of walking up to a Multivac outlet and smashing it—as though he didn't know a world-girdling computer, *the* world-girdling Computer (capital letter, please) with millions of robots at its command, couldn't protect itself. And even if the outlet had been smashed, what would that have accomplished?

And Hines did it in Bakst's physical presence, too!

He was called precisely on schedule—"Ronald Bakst will give evidence now."

Multivac's voice was beautiful, with a beauty that never

121

quite vanished no matter how often it was heard. Its timbre was neither quite male nor, for that matter, female, and it spoke in whatever language its hearer understood best.

"I am ready to give evidence," Bakst said.

There was no way to say anything but what he had to say. Hines could not avoid conviction. In the days when Hines would have had to face his fellow human beings, he would have been convicted more quickly and less fairly—and would have been punished more crudely.

Fifteen days passed, days during which Bakst was quite alone. Physical aloneness was not a difficult thing to envisage in the world of Multivac. Hordes had died in the days of the great catastrophes and it had been the computers that had saved what was left and directed the recovery—and improved their own designs till all were merged into Multivac—and the five million human beings were left on Earth to live in perfect comfort.

But those five million were scattered and the chances of one seeing another outside the immediate circle, except by design, was not great. No one was designing to see Bakst, not even by television.

For the time, Bakst could endure the isolation. He buried himself in his chosen way—which happened to be, these last twenty-three years, the designing of mathematical games. Every man and woman on Earth could develop a way of life to self-suit, provided always that Multivac, weighing all of human affairs with perfect skill, did not judge the chosen way to be subtractive to human happiness.

But what could be subtractive in mathematical games? It was purely abstract—pleased Bakst—harmed no one else.

He did not expect the isolation to continue. The Congress would not isolate him permanently without a trial—a different kind of trial from that which Hines had experienced, of course, one without Multivac's tyranny of absolute justice.

Still, he was relieved when it ended, and pleased that it was Noreen coming back that ended it. She came trudging over the hill toward him and he started toward her, smiling. It had been a successful five-year period during which they had been together. Even the occasional meetings with her two children and two grandchildren had been pleasant.

He said, "Thank you for being back."

She said, "I'm not back." She looked tired. Her brown

hair was windblown, her prominent cheeks a trifle rough and sunburned.

Bakst pressed the combination for a light lunch and coffee. He knew what she liked. She didn't stop him, and though she hesitated for a moment, she ate.

She said, "I've come to talk to you. The Congress sent me."

"The Congress!" he said. "Fifteen men and women—counting me. Self-appointed and helpless."

"You didn't think so when you were a member."

"I've grown older. I've learned."

"At least you've learned to betray your friends."

"There was no betrayal. Hines tried to damage Multivac; a foolish, impossible thing for him to try."

"You accused him."

"I had to. Multivac knew the facts without my accusation, and without my accusation, I would have been an accessory. Hines would not have gained, but I would have lost."

"Without a human witness, Multivac would have suspended sentence."

"Not in the case of an anti-Multivac act. This wasn't a case of illegal parenthood or life-work without permission. I couldn't take the chance."

"So you let Simon be deprived of all work permits for two years."

"He deserved it."

"A consoling thought. You may have lost the confidence of the Congress, but you have gained the confidence of Multivac."

"The confidence of Multivac is important in the world as it is," said Bakst seriously. He was suddenly conscious of not being as tall as Noreen.

She looked angry enough to strike him; her lips pressed whitely together. But then she had passed her eightieth birthday—no longer young—the habit of non-violence was too ingrained. . . . Except for fools like Hines.

"Is that all you have to say, then?" she said.

"There could be a great deal to say. Have you forgotten? Have you all forgotten? Do you remember how it once was? Do you remember the Twentieth Century? We live long now; we live securely now; we live happily now."

"We live worthlessly now."

"Do you want to go back to what the world was like once?"

Noreen shook her head violently. "Demon tales to frighten us. We have learned our lesson. With the help of Multivac we have come through—but we don't need that help any longer. Further help will soften us to death. Without Multivac, *we* will run the robots, *we* will direct the farms and mines and factories."

"How well?"

"Well enough. Better, with practice. We need the stimulation of it in any case or we will all die."

Bakst said, "We have our work, Noreen; whatever work we choose."

"Whatever we choose, as long as it's unimportant, and even that can be taken away at will—as with Hines. And what's your work, Ron? Mathematical games? Drawing lines on paper? Choosing number combinations?"

Bakst's hand reached out to her, almost pleadingly. "That can be important. It is not nonsense. Don't underestimate—" He paused, yearning to explain but not quite knowing how he could, safely. He said, "I'm working on some deep problems in combinatorial analysis based on gene patterns that can be used to—"

"To amuse you and a few others. Yes, I've heard you talk about your games. You will decide how to move from A to B in a minimum number of steps and that will teach you how to go from womb to grave in a minimum number of risks and we will all thank Multivac as we do so."

She stood up. "Ron, you will be tried. I'm sure of it. *Our* trial. And you will be dropped. Multivac will protect you against physical harm, but you know it will not force us to see you, speak to you, or have anything to do with you. You will find that without the stimulation of human interaction, you will not be able to think—or to play your games. Goodbye."

"Noreen! Wait!"

She turned at the door. "Of course, you will have Multivac. You can talk to Multivac, Ron."

He watched her dwindle as she walked down the road through the parklands kept green, and ecologically healthy, by the unobtrusive labors of quiet, single-minded robots one scarcely ever saw.

He thought: Yes, I will have to talk to Multivac.

Multivac had no particular home any longer. It was a global presence knit together by wire, optical fiber, and microwave. It had a brain divided into a hundred subsidiaries but acting as one. It had its outlets everywhere and no human being of the five million was far from one.

There was time for all of them, since Multivac could speak to all individually at the same time and not lift its mind from the greater problems that concerned it.

Bakst had no illusions as to its strength. What was its incredible intricacy but a mathematical game that Bakst had come to understand over a decade ago? He knew the manner in which the connecting links ran from continent to continent in a huge network whose analysis could form the basis of a fascinating game. How do you arrange the network so that the flow of information never jams? How do you arrange the switching points? Prove that no matter what the arrangement, there is always at least one point which, on disconnection—

Once Bakst had learned the game, he had dropped out of the Congress. What could they do but talk and of what use was that? Multivac indifferently permitted talk of any kind and in any depth precisely because it was unimportant. It was only acts that Multivac prevented, diverted, or punished.

And it was Hines's act that was bringing on the crisis; and before Bakst was ready for it, too.

Bakst had to hasten now, and he applied for an interview with Multivac without any degree of confidence in the outcome.

Questions could be asked of Multivac at any time. There were nearly a million outlets of the type that had withstood Hines's sudden attack into which, or near which, one could speak. Multivac would answer.

An *interview* was another matter. It required time; it required privacy; most of all it required Multivac's judgment that it was necessary. Although Multivac had capacities that not all the world's problems consumed, it had grown chary, somehow, of its time. Perhaps that was the result of its ever-continuing self-improvement. It was becoming constantly more aware of its own worth and less likely to bear trivialities with patience.

Bakst had to depend on Multivac's good will. His leaving of the Congress, all his actions since, even the bearing of evidence against Hines, had been to gain that good will. Surely it was the key to success in this world.

He would have to assume the good will. Having made the application, he at once traveled to the nearest substation by air. Nor did he merely send his image. He wanted to be there in person; somehow he felt his contact with Multivac would be closer in that way.

The room was almost as it might be if there were to be a human conference planned over closed multivision. For one flash-by moment, Bakst thought Multivac might assume an imaged human form and join him—the brain made flesh.

It did not, of course. There was the soft, whispering chuckle of Multivac's unceasing operations; something always and forever present in Multivac's presence; and over it, now, Multivac's voice.

It was not the usual voice of Multivac. It was a still, small voice, beautiful and insinuating, almost in his ear.

"Good day, Bakst. You are welcome. Your fellow human beings disapprove of you."

Multivac always comes to the point, thought Bakst. He said, "It does not matter, Multivac. What counts is that I accept your decisions as for the good of the human species. You were designed to do so in the primitive versions of yourself and—"

"And my self-designs have continued this basic approach. If *you* understand this, why do so many human beings fail to understand it? I have not yet completed the analysis of that phenomenon."

"I have come to you with a problem," said Bakst.

Multivac said, "What is it?"

Bakst said, "I have spent a great deal of time on mathematical problems inspired by the study of genes and their combinations. I cannot find the necessary answers and home-computerization is of no help."

There was an odd clicking and Bakst could not repress a slight shiver at the sudden thought that Multivac might be avoiding a laugh. It was a touch of the human beyond what even he was ready to accept. The voice was in his other ear and Multivac said:

"There are thousands of different genes in the human cell. Each gene has an average of perhaps fifty variations in existence and uncounted numbers that have never been in existence. If we were to attempt to calculate all possible combinations, the mere listing of them at my fastest speed, if steadily continued, would, in the longest possible lifetime of the Universe, achieve but an infinitesimal fraction of the total."

Bakst said, "A complete listing is not needed. That is the

point of my game. Some combinations are more probable than others and by building probability upon probability, we can cut the task enormously. It is the manner of achieving this building of probability upon probability that I ask you to help me with."

"It would still take a great deal of my time. How could I justify this to myself?"

Bakst hesitated. No use in trying a complicated selling job. With Multivac, a straight line was the shortest distance between two points.

He said, "An appropriate gene combination might produce a human being more content to leave decisions to you, more willing to believe in your resolve to make men happy, more anxious to *be* happy. I cannot find the proper combination, but you might, and with guided genetic engineering—"

"I see what you mean. It is—good. I will devote some time to it."

Bakst found it difficult to hitch into Noreen's private wavelength. Three times the connection broke away. He was not surprised. In the last two months, there had been an increasing tendency for technology to slip in minor ways—never for long, never seriously—and he greeted each occasion with a somber pleasure.

This time it held. Noreen's face showed, holographically three-dimensional. It flickered a moment, but it held.

"I'm returning your call," said Bakst, dully impersonal.

"For a while it seemed impossible to get you," said Noreen. "Where have you been?"

"Not hiding. I'm here, in Denver."

"Why in Denver?"

"The world is my oyster, Noreen. I may go where I please."

Her face twitched a little. "And perhaps find it empty everywhere. We are going to try you, Ron."

"Now?"

"Now!"

"And here?"

"And here!"

Volumes of space flickered into different glitters on either side of Noreen, and further away, and behind. Bakst looked from side to side, counting. There were fourteen, six men, eight women. He knew every one of them. They had been good friends once, not so long ago.

To either side and beyond the simulacra was the wild background of Colorado on a pleasant summer day that was heading toward its end. There had been a city here once named Denver. The site still bore the name though it had been cleared, as most of the city sites had been. . . . He could count ten robots in sight, doing whatever it was robots did.

They were maintaining the ecology, he supposed. He knew no details, but Multivac did, and it kept fifty million robots all over the Earth in efficient order.

Behind Bakst was one of the converging grids of Multivac, almost like a small fortress of self-defense.

"Why now?" he asked. "And why here?"

Automatically he turned to Eldred. She was the oldest of them and the one with authority—if a human being could be said to have authority.

Eldred's dark-brown face looked a little weary. The years showed, all sixscore of them, but her voice was firm and incisive. "Because we have the final fact now. Let Noreen tell you. She knows you best."

Bakst's eyes shifted to Noreen. "Of what crime am I accused?"

"Let us play no games, Ron. There are no crimes under Multivac except to strike for freedom and it is your human crime that you have committed no crime under Multivac. For that we will judge whether any human being alive wants your company any longer, wants to hear your voice, be aware of your presence, or respond to you in any way."

"Why am I threatened with isolation then?"

"You have betrayed all human beings."

"How?"

"Do you deny that you seek to breed mankind into subservience to Multivac?"

"Ah!" Bakst folded his arms across his chest. "You found out quickly, but then you had only to ask Multivac."

Noreen said, "Do you deny that you asked for help in the genetic engineering of a strain of humanity designed to accept slavery under Multivac without question?"

"I suggested the breeding of a more contented humanity. Is this a betrayal?"

Eldred intervened. She said, "We don't want your sophistry, Ron. We know it by heart. Don't tell us once again that Multivac cannot be withstood, that there is no use in struggling, that we have gained security. What you call security, the rest of us call slavery."

Bakst said, "Do you proceed now to judgment, or am I allowed a defense?"

"You heard Eldred," said Noreen. "We know your defense."

"We all heard Eldred," said Bakst, "but no one has heard me. What she says is my defense is not my defense."

There was a silence as the images glanced right and left at each other. Eldred said, "Speak!"

Bakst said, "I asked Multivac to help me solve a problem in the field of mathematical games. To gain his interest, I pointed out that it was modeled on gene combinations and that a solution might help in designing a gene combination that would leave man no worse off than he is now in any respect and yet breed into him a cheerful acceptance of Multivac's direction, and acquiescence in his decisions."

"So we have said," said Eldred.

"It was only on those terms that Multivac would have accepted the task. Such a new breed is clearly desirable for mankind by Multivac's standards, and by Multivac's standards he must labor toward it. And the desirability of the end will lure him on to examine greater and greater complications of a problem whose endlessness is beyond what even he can handle. You all witness that."

Noreen said, "Witness what?"

"Haven't you had trouble reaching me? In the last two months, hasn't each of you noticed small troubles in what has always gone smoothly? . . . You are silent. May I accept that as an affirmative?"

"If so, what then?"

Bakst said, "Multivac has been placing all his spare circuits on the problem. He has been slowly pushing the running of the world toward rather a skimpy minimum of his efforts, since nothing, by his own sense of ethics, must stand in the way of human happiness and there can be no greater increase in that happiness than to accept Multivac."

Noreen said, "What does all this mean? There is still enough in Multivac to run the world—and us—and if this is done at less than full efficiency, that would only add temporary discomfort to our slavery. Only temporary, because it won't last long. Sooner or later, Multivac will decide the problem is insoluble, or will solve it, and in either case, his distraction will end. In the latter case, slavery will become permanent and irrevocable."

"But for now he is distracted," said Bakst, "and we can even talk like this—most dangerously—without his noticing. Yet I dare not risk doing so for long, so please understand me quickly.

"I have another mathematical game—the setting up of networks on the model of Multivac. I have been able to demonstrate that no matter how complicated and redundant the network is, there must be at least one place into which all the currents can funnel under particular circumstances. There will always be the fatal apoplectic stroke if that one place is interefered with, since it will induce overloading elsewhere which will break down and induce overloading elsewhere— and so on indefinitely till all breaks down."

"Well?"

"And this is the point. Why else have I come to Denver? And Multivac knows it, too, and this point is guarded electronically and robotically to the extent that it cannot be penetrated."

"Well?"

"But Multivac is distracted, and Multivac trusts me. I have labored hard to gain that trust, at the cost of losing all of you, since only with trust is there the possibility of betrayal. If any of you tried to approach this point, Multivac might rouse himself even out of his present distraction. If Multivac were not distracted, he would not allow even me to approach. But he *is* distracted, and it *is* I!"

Bakst was moving toward the converging grid in a calm saunter, and the fourteen images, keyed to him, moved along as well. The soft susurrations of a busy Multivac center were all about them.

Bakst said, "Why attack an invulnerable opponent? Make him vulnerable first, and then—"

Bakst fought to stay calm, but it all depended on this now. Everything! With a sharp yank, he uncoupled a joint. (If he had only had still more time to make more certain.)

He was not stopped—and as he held his breath, he became aware of the ceasing of noise, the ending of whisper, the closing down of Multivac. If, in a moment, that soft noise did not return, then he had had the right key point, and no recovery would be possible. If he were not quickly the focus of approaching robots—

He turned in the continuing silence. The robots in the distance were working still. None were approaching.

Before him, the images of the fourteen men and women of

the Congress were still there and each seemed to be stupefied at the sudden enormous thing that had happened.

Bakst said, "Multivac is shut down, burnt out. It can't be rebuilt." He felt almost drunk at the sound of what he was saying. "I have worked toward this since I left you. When Hines attacked, I feared there might be other such efforts, that Multivac would double his guard, that even I— I had to work quickly— I wasn't sure—" He was gasping, but forced himself steady, and said solemnly, "I have given us our freedom."

And he paused, aware at last of the gathering weight of the silence. Fourteen images stared at him, without any of them offering a word in response.

Bakst said sharply, "You have talked of freedom. You *have* it!"

Then, uncertainly, he said, "Isn't that what you want?"

———————

When I first finished the preceding story, or thought I had, I was left dissatisfied. I lay awake till about 2 A.M. trying to figure out what dissatisfied me, and then decided I had not made my point. I got up, quickly wrote down the last three paragraphs of the story as it finally appeared, ending with that horrified question, and then went peacefully to sleep.

The next day, I rewrote the last page of the manuscript to include the new ending and when I sent it off to the *Times*, much as I wanted to make the sale, I indicated where I would be intransigent.

"Please note," I wrote, "that the ending on an unresolved question is not an accident. It is of the essence. Each reader is going to have to consider the meaning of the question and what answer he himself would give."

The *Times* asked for some trivial changes and clarifications but did not allow even a whisper of objection to emerge concerning my ending, I am glad to say.

My own original title had been "Mathematical Games," by the way, and for a while I considered restoring it in the book version. However, THE LIFE AND TIMES OF MULTIVAC has a swing to it. Besides, a large number of people saw it on the single day during which it was available to the reading public. More people came up to me over the next few weeks to tell me they had read that story than had ever been the case for any other story I had ever written. I don't want them to think I changed the title in order to lure them into thinking they hadn't read the story before, so that they might buy this book, so THE LIFE AND TIMES OF MULTIVAC it stays.

Among those who saw my story in *The New York Times Magazine* was William Levinson, editor of *Physician's World*. In the same issue of the magazine section was an article entitled "Triage." Triage is a system of choosing whom to save and whom to allow to die when conditions do not allow of saving all. Triage has been used in medical emergencies when limited facilities have been applied to those with the best chance of making it. Now there is a feeling that triage might be applied on a worldwide scale, that some nations and regions cannot be saved and that no effort should be made to save them.

It occurred to Levinson that the subject could be treated through the medium of science fiction and since my name was staring at him on the same contents page, he approached me. I was struck with the idea and agreed at once. I started it on January 19, 1975. Levinson liked THE WINNOWING when it was done and it was all set to appear in the June 1975 issue, when the magazine suddenly suspended publication the issue before.

Sad and embarrassed, Levinson returned the story, but, of course, it wasn't his fault, so I wrote him a reassuring letter. After all, the story had been paid for and it wasn't likely I couldn't place it elsewhere.

Ben Bova took it at once, in fact, and it appeared in the February 1976 *Analog*.

7

The Winnowing

Five years had passed since the steadily thickening wall of secrecy had been clamped down about the work of Dr. Aaron Rodman.

"For your own protection—" they had warned him.

"In the hands of the wrong people—" they had explained.

In the right hands, of course (his own, for instance, Dr. Rodman thought rather despairingly), the discovery was clearly the greatest boon to human health since Pasteur's working out of the germ theory, and the greatest key to the understanding of the mechanism of life, ever.

Yet after his talk at the New York Academy of Medicine soon after his fiftieth birthday, and on the first day of the Twenty-first Century (there had been a certain fitness to that), the silence had been imposed, and he could talk no more, except to certain officials. He certainly could not publish.

The government supported him, however. He had all the money he needed, and the computers were his to do with as he wished. His work advanced rapidly and government men came to him to be instructed, to be made to understand.

"Dr. Rodman," they would ask, "how can a virus be spread from cell to cell within an organism and yet not be infectious from one organism to the next?"

It wearied Rodman to have to say over and over that he did not have all the answers. It wearied him to have to use the term "virus." He said, "It's not a virus because it isn't a nucleic acid molecule. It is something else altogether —a lipoprotein."

It was better when his questioners were not themselves medical men. He could then try to explain in generalities instead of forever bogging down on the fine points. He would say, "Every living cell, and every small structure within the cell, is surrounded by a membrane. The workings of each cell depend on what molecules can pass through the membrane in either direction and at what rates. A slight change in the membrane will alter the nature of the flow enormously, and with that, the nature of the cell chemistry and the nature of its activity.

"All disease may rest on alterations in membrane activity. All mutations may be carried through by way of such alterations. Any technique that controls the membranes controls life. Hormones control the body by their effort on membranes and my lipoprotein is an artificial hormone rather than a virus. The LP incorporates itself into the membrane and in the process induces the manufacture of more molecules like itself—and that's the part I don't understand myself.

"But the fine structures of the membranes are not quite identical everywhere. They are, in fact, different in all living things—not quite the same in any two organisms. An LP will affect no two individual organisms alike. What will open the cells of one organism to glucose and relieve the effects of diabetes, will close the cells of another organism to lysine and kill it."

That was what seemed to interest them most; that it was a poison.

"A selective poison," Rodman would say. "You couldn't tell, in advance, without the closest computer-aided studies of the membrane biochemistry of a particular individual, what a particular LP would do to him."

With time, the noose grew tighter about himself, inhibiting his freedom, yet leaving him comfortable—in a world in which freedom and comfort alike were vanishing everywhere, and the jaws of hell were opening before a despairing humanity.

It was 2005 and Earth's population was six billion. But for the famines it would have been seven billion. A billion human beings had starved in the past generation, and more would yet starve.

Peter Affare, chairman of the World Food Organization, came frequently to Rodman's laboratories for chess and conversation. It was he, he said, who had first grasped the significance of Rodman's talk at the Academy, and that had helped make him chairman. Rodman thought the significance was easy to grasp, but said nothing about that.

Affare was ten years younger than Rodman, and the red was darkening out of his hair. He smiled frequently although the subject of the conversation rarely gave cause for smiling, since any chairman of an organization dealing with world food was bound to talk about world famine.

Affare said, "If the food supply were evenly distributed among all the world's inhabitants, all would starve to death."

"If it were evenly distributed," said Rodman, "the example of justice in the world might lead at last to a sane world policy. As it is, there is world despair and fury over the selfish fortune of a few, and all behave irrationally in revenge."

"You do not volunteer to give up your own oversupply of food," said Affare.

"I am human and selfish, and my own action would mean little. I should not be asked to volunteer. I should be given no choice in the matter."

"You are a romantic," said Affare. "Do you fail to see that the Earth is a lifeboat? If the food store is divided equally among all, then all will die. If some are cast out of the lifeboat, the remainder will survive. The question is not whether some will die, for some *must* die; the question is whether some will live."

"Are you advocating triage—the sacrifice of some for the rest—officially?"

"We can't. The people in the lifeboat are armed. Several regions threaten openly to use nuclear weapons if more food is not forthcoming."

Rodman said sardonically, "You mean the answer to 'You die that I may live' is 'If I die, you die.' . . . An impasse."

"Not quite," said Affare. "There are places on Earth where the people cannot be saved. They have overweighted their land hopelessly with hordes of starving humanity. Suppose they are sent food, and suppose the food kills them so that the land requires no further shipments."

Rodman felt the first twinge of realization. "Kills them how?" he asked.

"The average structural properties of the cellular membranes of a particular population can be worked out. An LP, particularly designed to take advantage of those properties, could be incorporated into the food supply, which would then be fatal," said Affare.

"Unthinkable," said Rodman, astounded.

"Think again. There would be no pain. The membranes would slowly close off and the affected person would fall asleep and not wake up—an infinitely better death than that of starvation which is otherwise inevitable—or nuclear annihilation. Nor would it be for everyone, for any population varies in its membranal properties. At worst, seventy per cent will die. The winnowing out will be done precisely where overpopulation and hopelessness are worst and enough will be left to preserve each nation, each ethnic group, each culture."

"To deliberately kill billions—"

"We would not be killing. We would merely supply the opportunity for people to die. Which particular individuals would die would depend on the particular biochemistry of those individuals. It would be the finger of God."

"And when the world discovers what has been done?"

"That will be after our time," said Affare, "and by then, a flourishing world with limited population will thank us for our heroic action in choosing the death of some to avoid the death of all."

Dr. Rodman felt himself flushing, and found he had difficulty speaking. "The Earth," he said, "is a large and very complex lifeboat. We still do not know what can or can't be done with a proper distribution of resources and it is notorious that to this very day we have not really made an effort to distribute them. In many places on Earth, food is wasted daily, and it is that knowledge that drives hungry men mad."

"I agree with you," said Affare coolly, "but we cannot have the world as we want it to be. We must deal with it as it is."

"Then deal with me as I am. You will want me to supply the necessary LP molecules—and I will not do so. I will not lift a finger in that direction."

"Then," said Affare, "you will be a greater mass murderer than you are accusing me of being. And I think you will change your mind when you have thought it through."

He was visited nearly daily, by one official or another, all of them well fed. Rodman was becoming very sensitive to the way in which all those who discussed the need for killing the hungry were themselves well fed.

The National Secretary of Agriculture said to him, insinuatingly, on one of these occasions, "Would you not favor killing a herd of cattle infected with hoof-and-mouth disease or with anthrax in order to avoid the spread of infection to healthy herds?"

"Human beings are not cattle," said Rodman, "and famine is not contagious."

"But it is," said the Secretary. "That is precisely the point. If we don't winnow the overcrowded masses of humanity, their famine will spread to as yet unaffected areas. You must not refuse to help us."

"How can you make me? Torture?"

"We wouldn't harm a hair on your body. Your skill in this matter is too precious to us. Food stamps can be withdrawn, however."

"Starvation would harm me, surely."

"Not you. But if we are prepared to kill several billion people for the sake of the human race, then surely we are ready for the much less difficult task of withdrawing food stamps from your daughter, her husband, and her baby."

Rodman was silent, and the Secretary said, "We'll give you time to think. We don't want to take action against your family, but we will if we have to. Take a week to think about it. Next Thursday the entire committee will be on hand. You will then be committed to our project and there must be no further delay."

Security was redoubled and Rodman was openly and completely a prisoner. A week later, all fifteen members of the World Food Council, together with the National Secretary of Agriculture and a few members of the National Legislature, arrived at his laboratory. They sat about the long table in the conference room of the lavish research building that had been built out of public funds.

For hours they talked and planned, incorporating those answers which Rodman gave to specific questions. No one asked Rodman if he would cooperate; there seemed no thought that he could do anything else.

Finally Rodman said, "Your project cannot, in any case, work. Shortly after a shipment of grain arrives in some particular region of the world, people will die by the hundreds of millions. Do you suppose those who survive will not make the connection and that you will not risk the desperate retaliation of nuclear bombs?"

Affare, who sat directly opposite Rodman, across the short axis of the table, said, "We are aware of that possibility. Do you think we have spent years determining a course of action and have not considered the possible reaction of those regions chosen for winnowing?"

"Do you expect them to be thankful?" asked Rodman bitterly.

"They will not know they are being singled out. Not all shipments of grain will be LP-infected. No one place will be concentrated on. We will see to it that locally grown grain supplies are infected here and there. In addition, not everyone will die and only a few will die at once. Some who eat much of the grain will not die at all, and some who eat only a small amount will die quickly—depending on their membranes. It will seem like a plague, like the Black Death returned."

Rodman said, "Have you thought of the effect of the Black Death returned? Have you thought of the panic?"

"It will do them good," growled the Secretary from one end of the table. "It might teach them a lesson."

"We will announce the discovery of an antitoxin," said Affare, shrugging. "There will be wholesale inoculations in regions we know will not be affected. Dr. Rodman, the world is desperately ill, and must have a desperate remedy. Mankind is on the brink of a horrible death, so please do not quarrel with the only course that can save it."

"That's the point. *Is* it the only course or are you just taking an easy way out that will not ask any sacrifices of you—merely of billions of others?"

Rodman broke off as a food trolley was brought in. He muttered, "I have arranged for some refreshments. May we have a few moments of truce while we eat?"

He reached for a sandwich and then, after a while, said between sips of coffee, "We eat well, at least, as we discuss the greatest mass murder in history."

Affare looked critically at his own half-eaten sandwich. "This is not eating *well*. Egg salad on white bread of indifferent freshness is not eating well, and I would change whatever coffee shop supplied this, if I were you." He sighed. "Well, in a world of famine, one should not waste food," and he finished the sandwich.

Rodman watched the others and then reached for the last remaining sandwich on the tray. "I thought," he said, "that perhaps some of you might suffer a loss of appetite in view of the subject matter of discussion, but I see none of you did. Each one of you has eaten."

"As did you," said Affare impatiently. "You are still eating."

"Yes, I am," said Rodman, chewing slowly. "And I apologize for the lack of freshness in the bread. I made the sandwiches myself last night and they are fifteen hours old."

"You made them yourself?" said Affare.

"I had to, since I could in no other way be certain of introducing the proper LP."

"What are you talking about?"

"Gentlemen, you tell me it is necessary to kill some to save others. Perhaps you are right. You have convinced me. But in order to know exactly what it is we are doing we should perhaps experience it ourselves. I have engaged in a little triage on my own, and the sandwiches we have all just eaten are an experiment in that direction."

Some of the officials were rising to their feet. "We're poisoned?" gasped the Secretary.

Rodman said, "Not very effectively. Unfortunately, I don't know your biochemistries thoroughly, so I can't guarantee the seventy per cent death rate you would like."

They were staring at him in frozen horror, and Dr. Rodman's eyelids drooped. "Still, it's likely that two or three of you will die within the next week or so, and you need only wait to see who it will be. There's no cure or antidote, but don't worry. It's a quite painless death, and it will be the finger of God, as one of you told me. It's a good lesson, as another of you said. For those of you who survive, there may be new views on triage."

Affare said, "This is a bluff. You've eaten the sandwiches yourself."

Rodman said, "I know. I matched the LP to my own biochemistry, so I will go fast." His eyes closed. "You'll have to carry on without me—those of you who survive."

The next story has rather a sad history, though I myself emerged unscathed. Here's how it goes.

In January 1975, Naomi Gordon, a very charming woman from Philadelphia, visited me and explained what I thought was a delightful idea for an anthology. It was to be entitled *The Bicentennial Man*; it was to contain ten stories by top authors, with each one built about that phrase; and it was to be published in connection with the Bicentennial. The well-known science fiction enthusiast Forrest J. Ackerman was to do the editing. Naomi also had rather grandiose notions of preparing a very limited, very expensive edition.

I pointed out it would be difficult to write science fiction if the stories were to be centered on the Bicentennial, but Naomi said that the stories could be anything at all provided they could be seen to have arisen out of the phrase "The Bicentennial Man."

I was intrigued and agreed to do it. I was handed half the advance at once. The deadline was April 1, 1975, and by March 14 I was finished. I was a little rueful about the story at first, for the agreement had called for a 7,500-word story and I had been unable to stop it before it had reached 15,000 —the longest story I had written below the level of a novel in seventeen years. I write an apologetic covering letter, assuring Naomi that there would be no extra charge and she wrote back to say the extra wordage would be fine. Pretty soon, the remaining half of the advance arrived.

But then everything went wrong. Naomi was beset by family and medical problems; some writers who it had been hoped would participate, couldn't; others who promised stroies didn't deliver them; those who did deliver them did not turn out entirely satisfactory products.

Of course, I didn't know anything about this. It never even occurred to me that anything might go wrong. Actually, my only large interest is in *writing*. Selling is a minor interest, and what happens afterward is of almost no interest.

There was, however, Judy-Lynn del Rey and her enormous awareness of everything that goes on in science fiction. She knew that I had written a story for this anthology.

"How is it," she asked dangerously, "that you wrote a

141

story for that anthology, yet when I ask you for one you're always too busy?"*

"Well," I said apologetically, for Judy-Lynn is a frightening creature when she is moved, "the idea of the anthology interested me."

"How about my suggestions about a robot that has to choose between buying its own liberty and improving its body? I thought you said that was interesting."

At that point, I must have turned approximately as white as talcum powder. A long time before, she *had* mentioned such things and I had forgotten. I said, "Oh, my goodness, I included something of the sort in the story."

"*Again?*" she shrieked. "*Again* you're using my ideas for other people? Let me see that story. Let me see it!"

So I brought her a carbon copy the next day and the day after that she called me. She said, "I tried hard not to like the story, but I didn't manage. I want it. Get the story back."

"I can't do that," I said. "I sold it to Naomi and it's hers. I'll write you a different story."

"I'll bet you anything you like," said Judy-Lynn, "that that anthology isn't going to go through. Why don't you call and ask?"

I called Naomi and, of course, it wasn't going through. She agreed to send me back the manuscript and grant me permission to sell the story elsewhere, and I sent back the advance she had given me. (After all, she had lost considerable money on the venture, and I didn't want any of that loss to represent a profit to me.)

The story was then transferred to Judy-Lynn, who used it in her anthology of originals entitled *Stellar Science Fiction #2*, which appeared in February 1976. And I like the story so much myself that I not only am including it here, but am using its title for the book as a whole.

(Incidentally, after this book was put together, Judy-Lynn suggested I change my manuscript to make it jibe with the version in *Stellar*. Apparently, she had introduced numerous minor changes that improved it, she said. Well, I am not Harlan Ellison, so I don't mind, but I think that in my own collection, I'll let the story stand as I wrote it. Judy-Lynn will be annoyed, but she can't do worse than kill me.)

*This was during the Passover Seder, over which Lester del Rey presides every year with enormous effectiveness, since he is the best cook in science fiction.

8

The Bicentennial Man

The Three Laws of Robotics:
    1. A robot may not injure a human being or, through inaction, allow a human being to come to harm.
    2. A robot must obey the orders given it by human beings except where such orders would conflict with the First Law.
    3. A robot must protect its own existence as long as such protection does not conflict with the First or Second Law.

Andrew Martin said, "Thank you," and took the seat offered him. He didn't look driven to the last resort, but he had been.

He didn't, actually, look anything, for there was a smooth blankness to his face, except for the sadness one imagined one saw in his eyes. His hair was smooth, light brown, rather fine, and there was no facial hair. He looked freshly and cleanly shaved. His clothes were distinctly old-fashioned, but neat and predominantly a velvety red-purple in color.

Facing him from behind the desk was the surgeon, and the nameplate on the desk included a fully identifying series of letters and numbers, which Andrew didn't bother with. To call him Doctor would be quite enough.

"When can the operation be carried through, Doctor?" he asked.

The surgeon said softly, with that certain inalienable note

of respect that a robot always used to a human being, "I am not certain, sir, that I understand how or upon whom such an operation could be performed."

There might have been a look of respectful intransigence on the surgeon's face, if a robot of his sort, in lightly bronzed stainless steel, could have such an expression, or any expression.

Andrew Martin studied the robot's right hand, his cutting hand, as it lay on the desk in utter tranquillity. The fingers were long and shaped into artistically metallic looping curves so graceful and appropriate that one could imagine a scalpel fitting them and becoming, temporarily, one piece with them.

There would be no hesitation in his work, no stumbling, no quivering, no mistakes. That came with specialization, of course, a specialization so fiercely desired by humanity that few robots were, any longer, independently brained. A surgeon, of course, would have to be. And this one, though brained, was so limited in his capacity that he did not recognize Andrew—had probably never heard of him.

Andrew said, "Have you ever thought you would like to be a man?"

The surgeon hesitated a moment as though the question fitted nowhere in his allotted positronic pathways. "But I am a robot, sir."

"Would it be better to be a man?"

"It would be better, sir, to be a better surgeon. I could not be so if I were a man, but only if I were a more advanced robot. I would be pleased to be a more advanced robot."

"It does not offend you that I can order you about? That I can make you stand up, sit down, move right or left, by merely telling you to do so?"

"It is my pleasure to please you, sir. If your orders were to interfere with my functioning with respect to you or to any other human being, I would not obey you. The First Law, concerning my duty to human safety, would take precedence over the Second Law relating to obedience. Otherwise, obedience is my pleasure. . . . But upon whom am I to perform this operation?"

"Upon me," said Andrew.

"But that is impossible. It is patently a damaging operation."

"That does not matter," said Andrew calmly.

"I must not inflict damage," said the surgeon.

"On a human being, you must not," said Andrew, "but I, too, am a robot."

2.

Andrew had appeared much more a robot when he had first been—manufactured. He had then been as much a robot in appearance as any that had ever existed, smoothly designed and functional.

He had done well in the home to which he had been brought in those days when robots in households, or on the planet altogether, had been a rarity.

There had been four in the home: Sir and Ma'am and Miss and Little Miss. He knew their names, of course, but he never used them. Sir was Gerald Martin.

His own serial number was NDR— He forgot the numbers. It had been a long time, of course, but if he had wanted to remember, he could not forget. He had not wanted to remember.

Little Miss had been the first to call him Andrew because she could not use the letters, and all the rest followed her in this.

Little Miss— She had lived ninety years and was long since dead. He had tried to call her Ma'am once, but she would not allow it. Little Miss she had been to her last day.

Andrew had been intended to perform the duties of a valet, a butler, a lady's maid. Those were the experimental days for him and, indeed, for all robots anywhere but in the industrial and exploratory factories and stations off Earth.

The Martins enjoyed him, and half the time he was prevented from doing his work because Miss and Little Miss would rather play with him.

It was Miss who understood first how this might be arranged. She said, "We order you to play with us and you must follow orders."

Andrew said, "I am sorry, Miss, but a prior order from Sir must surely take precedence."

But she said, "Daddy just said he hoped you would take care of the cleaning. That's not much of an order. I *order* you."

Sir did not mind. Sir was fond of Miss and of Little Miss, even more than Ma'am was, and Andrew was fond of them, too. At least, the effect they had upon his actions were those which in a human being would have been called the result of fondness. Andrew thought of it as fondness, for he did not know any other word for it.

It was for. Little Miss that Andrew had carved a pendant out of wood. She had ordered him to. Miss, it seemed, had received an ivorite pendant with scrollwork for her birthday and Little Miss was unhappy over it. She had only a piece of wood, which she gave Andrew together with a small kitchen knife.

He had done it quickly and Little Miss said, "That's *nice*, Andrew. I'll show it to Daddy."

Sir would not believe it. "Where did you really get this, Mandy?" Mandy was what he called Little Miss. When Little Miss assured him she was really telling the truth, he turned to Andrew. "Did you do this, Andrew?"

"Yes, Sir."

"The design, too?"

"Yes, Sir."

"From what did you copy the design?"

"It is a geometric representation, Sir, that fit the grain of the wood."

The next day, Sir brought him another piece of wood, a larger one, and an electric vibro-knife. He said, "Make something out of this, Andrew. Anything you want to."

Andrew did so and Sir watched, then looked at the product a long time. After that, Andrew no longer waited on tables. He was ordered to read books on furniture design instead, and he learned to make cabinets and desks.

Sir said, "These are amazing productions, Andrew."

Andrew said, "I enjoy doing them, Sir."

"Enjoy?"

"It makes the circuits of my brain somehow flow more easily. I have heard you use the word 'enjoy' and the way you use it fits the way I feel. I enjoy doing them, Sir."

3.

Gerald Martin took Andrew to the regional offices of United States Robots and Mechanical Men, Inc. As a member of the Regional Legislature he had no trouble at all in gaining an interview with the Chief Robopsychologist. In fact, it was only as a member of the Regional Legislature that he qualified as a robot owner in the first place—in those early days when robots were rare.

Andrew did not understand any of this at the time, but in

later years, with greater learning, he could re-view that early
scene and understand it in its proper light.

The robopsychologist, Merton Mansky, listened with a
gathering frown and more than once managed to stop his fingers at the point beyond which they would have irrevocably
drummed on the table. He had drawn features and a lined
forehead and looked as though he might be younger than he
looked.

He said, "Robotics is not an exact art, Mr. Martin. I cannot explain it to you in detail, but the mathematics governing
the plotting of the positronic pathways is far too complicated
to permit of any but approximate solutions. Naturally, since
we build everything about the Three Laws, those are incon-
trovertible. We will, of course, replace your robot—"

"Not at all," said Sir. "There is no question of failure on
his part. He performs his assigned duties perfectly. The point
is, he also carves wood in exquisite fashion and never the
same twice. He produces work of art."

Mansky looked confused. "Strange. Of course, we're at-
tempting generalized pathways these days. . . . Really creative, you think?"

"See for yourself." Sir handed over a little sphere of wood
on which there was a playground scene in which the boys and
girls were almost too small to make out, yet they were in
perfect proportion and blended so naturally with the grain
that that, too, seemed to have been carved.

Mansky said, " *He* did that?" He handed it back with a
shake of his head. "The luck of the draw. Something in the
pathways."

"Can you do it again?"

"Probably not. Nothing like this has ever been reported."

"Good! I don't in the least mind Andrew's being the only
one."

Mansky said, "I suspect that the company would like to
have your robot back for study."

Sir said with sudden grimness, "Not a chance. Forget it."
He turned to Andrew, "Let's go home now."

"As you wish, Sir," said Andrew.

4.

Miss was dating boys and wasn't about the house much. It
was Little Miss, not as little as she was, who filled Andrew's
horizon now. She never forgot that the very first piece of

wood carving he had done had been for her. She kept it on a silver chain about her neck.

It was she who first objected to Sir's habit of giving away the productions. She said, "Come on, Dad, if anyone wants one of them, let him pay for it. It's worth it."

Sir said, "It isn't like you to be greedy, Mandy."

"Not for us, Dad. For the artist."

Andrew had never heard the word before and when he had a moment to himself he looked it up in the dictionary. Then there was another trip, this time to Sir's lawyer.

Sir said to him, "What do you think of this, John?"

The lawyer was John Feingold. He had white hair and a pudgy belly, and the rims of his contact lenses were tinted a bright green. He looked at the small plaque Sir had given to him. "This is beautiful. . . . But I've heard the news. This is a carving made by your robot. The one you've brought with you."

"Yes, Andrew does them. Don't you, Andrew?"

"Yes, Sir," said Andrew.

"How much would you pay for that, John?" asked Sir.

"I can't say. I'm not a collector of such things."

"Would you believe I have been offered two hundred and fifty dollars for that small thing? Andrew has made chairs that have sold for five hundred dollars. There's two hundred thousands dollars in the bank out of Andrew's products."

"Good heavens, he's making you rich, Gerald."

"Half rich," said Sir. "Half of it is in an account in the name of Andrew Martin."

"The robot?"

"That's right, and I want to know if it's legal."

"Legal?" Feingold's chair creaked as he leaned back in it. "There are no precedents, Gerald. How did your robot sign the necessary papers?"

"He can sign his name and I brought in the signature. I didn't bring him in to the bank himself. Is there anything further that ought to be done?"

"Um." Feingold's eyes seemed to turn inward for a moment. Then he said, "Well, we can set up a trust to handle all finances in his name and that will place a layer of insulation between him and the hostile world. Further than that, my advice is you do nothing. No one is stopping you so far. If anyone objects, let *him* bring suit."

"And will you take the case if suit is brought?"

"For a retainer, certainly."

"How much?"

"Something like that," and Feingold pointed to the wooden plaque.

"Fair enough," said Sir.

Feingold chuckled as he turned to the robot. "Andrew, are you pleased that you have money?"

"Yes, sir."

"What do you paln to do with it?'

"Pay for things, sir, which otherwise Sir would have to pay for. It would save him expense, sir."

5.

The occasions came. Repairs were expensive, and revisions were even more so. With the years, new models of robots were produced and Sir saw to it that Andrew had the advantage of every new device until he was a paragon of metallic excellence. It was all at Andrew's expense.

Andrew insisted on that.

Only his positronic pathways were untouched. Sir insisted on that.

"The new ones aren't as good as you are, Andrew," he said. "The new robots are worthless. The company has learned to make the pathways more precise, more closely on the nose, more deeply on the track. The new robots don't shift. They do what they're designed for and never stray. I like you better."

"Thank you, Sir."

"And it's your doing, Andrew, don't you forget that. I am certain Mansky put an end to generalized pathways as soon as he had a good look at you. He didn't like the unpredictability. . . . Do you know how many times he asked for you so he could place you under study? Nine times! I never let him have you, though, and now that he's retired, we may have some peace."

So Sir's hair thinned and grayed and his face grew pouchy, while Andrew looked rather better than he had when he first joined the family.

Ma'am had joined an art colony somewhere in Europe and Miss was a poet in New York. They wrote sometimes, but not often. Little Miss was married and lived not far away. She said she did not want to leave Andrew and when her child, Little Sir, was born, she let Andrew hold the bottle and feed him.

With the birth of a grandson, Andrew felt that Sir had someone now to replace those who had gone. It would not be so unfair to come to him with the request.

Andrew said, "Sir, it is kind of you to have allowed me to spend my money as I wished."

"It was your money, Andrew."

"Only by your voluntary act, Sir. I do not believe the law would have stopped you from keeping it all."

"The law won't persuade me to do wrong, Andrew."

"Despite all expenses, and despite taxes, too, Sir, I have nearly six hundred thousand dollars."

"I know that, Andrew."

"I want to give it to you, Sir."

"I won't take it, Andrew."

"In exchange for something you can give me, Sir."

"Oh, What is that, Andrew?"

"My freedom, Sir."

"Your—"

"I wish to buy my freedom, Sir."

6.

It wasn't that easy. Sir had flushed, had said "For God's sake!" had turned on his heel, and stalked away.

It was Little Miss who brought him around, defiantly and harshly—and in front of Andrew. For thirty years, no one had hesitated to talk in front of Andrew, whether the matter involved Andrew or not. He was only a robot.

She said, "Dad, why are you taking it as a personal affront? He'll still be here. He'll still be loyal. He can't help that. It's built in. All he wants is a form of words. He wants to be called free. Is that so terrible? Hasn't he earned it? Heavens, he and I have been talking about it for years."

"Talking about it for years, have you?"

"Yes, and over and over again, he postponed it for fear he would hurt you. I *made* him put it up to you."

"He doesn't know what freedom is. He's a robot."

"Dad, you don't know him. He's read everything in the library. I don't know what he feels inside but I don't know what *you* feel inside. When you talk to him you'll find he reacts to the various abstractions as you and I do, and what else counts? If someone else's reactions are like your own, what more can you ask for?"

"The law won't take that attitude," Sir said angrily. "See

here, you!" He turned to Andrew with a deliberate grate in his voice. "I can't free you except by doing it legally, and if it gets into the courts, you not only won't get your freedom but the law will take official cognizance of your money. They'll tell you that a robot has no right to earn money. Is this rigmarole worth losing your money?"

"Freedom is without price, Sir," said Andrew. "Even the chance of freedom is worth the money."

7.

The court might also take the attitude that freedom was without price, and might decide that for no price, however great, could a robot buy its freedom.

The simple statement of the regional attorney who represented those who had brought a class action to oppose the freedom was this: The word "freedom" had no meaning when applied to a robot. Only a human being could be free.

He said it several times, when it seemed appropriate; slowly, with his hand coming down rhythmically on the desk before him to mark the words.

Little Miss asked permission to speak on behalf of Andrew. She was recognized by her full name, something Andrew had never heard pronounced before:

"Amanda Laura Martin Charney may approach the bench."

She said, "Thank you, your honor. I am not a lawyer and I don't know the proper way of phrasing things, but I hope you will listen to my meaning and ignore the words.

"Let's understand what it means to be free in Andrew's case. In some ways, he *is* free. I think it's at least twenty years since anyone in the Martin family gave him an order to do something that we felt he might not do of his own accord.

"But we can, if we wish, give him an order to do anything, couch it as harshly as we wish, because he is a machine that belongs to us. Why should we be in a position to do so, when he has served us so long, so faithfully, and earned so much money for us? He owes us nothing more. The debt is entirely on the other side.

"Even if we were legally forbidden to place Andrew in involuntary servitude, he would still serve us voluntarily. Making him free would be a trick of words only, but it would mean much to him. It would give him everything and cost us nothing."

For a moment the Judge seemed to be suppressing a smile.

"I see your point, Mrs. Charney. The fact is that there is no binding law in this respect and no precedent. There is, however, the unspoken assumption that only a man can enjoy freedom. I can make new law here, subject to reversal in a higher court, but I cannot lightly run counter to that assumption. Let me address the robot. Andrew!"

"Yes, your honor."

It was the first time Andrew had spoken in court and the Judge seemed astonished for a moment at the human timbre of the voice. He said, "Why do you want to be free, Andrew? In what way will this matter to you?"

Andrew said, "Would you wish to be a slave, your honor?"

"But you are not a slave. You are a perfectly good robot, a genius of a robot I am given to understand, capable of an artistic expression that can be matched nowhere. What more can you do if you were free?"

"Perhaps no more than I do now, your honor, but with greater joy. It has been said in this courtroom that only a human being can be free. It seems to me that only someone who wishes for freedom can be free. I wish for freedom."

And it was that that cued the Judge. The crucial sentence in his decision was: "There is no right to deny freedom to any object with a mind advanced enough to grasp and desire the state."

It was eventually upheld by the World Court.

8.

Sir remained displeased and his harsh voice made Andrew feel almost as though he were being short-circuited.

Sir said, "I don't want your damned money, Andrew. I'll take it only because you won't feel free otherwise. From now on, you can select your own jobs and do them as you please. I will give you no orders, except this one—that you do as you please. But I am still responsible for you; that's part of the court order. I hope you understand that."

Little Miss interrupted. "Don't be irascible, Dad. The responsibility is no great chore. You know you won't have to do a thing. The Three Laws still hold."

"Then how is he free?"

Andrew said, "Are not human beings bound by their laws, Sir?"

Sir said, "I'm not going to argue." He left, and Andrew saw him only infrequently after that.

Little Miss came to see him frequently in the small house that had been built and made over for him. It had no kitchen, of course, nor bathroom facilities. It had just two rooms; one was a library and one was a combination storeroom and work-room. Andrew accepted many commissions and worked harder as a free robot than he ever had before, till the cost of the house was paid for and the structure legally transferred to him.

One day Little Sir came. . . . No, George! Little Sir had insisted on that after the court decision. "A free robot doesn't call anyone Little Sir," George had said. "I call you Andrew. You must call me George."

It was phrased as an order, so Andrew called him George —but Little Miss remained Little Miss.

The day George came alone, it was to say that Sir was dying. Little Miss was at the bedside but Sir wanted Andrew as well.

Sir's voice was quite strong, though he seemed unable to move much. He struggled to get his hand up. "Andrew," he said, "Andrew—Don't help me, George. I'm only dying; I'm not crippled. . . . Andrew, I'm glad you're free. I just wanted to tell you that."

Andrew did not know what to say. He had never been at the side of someone dying before, but he knew it was the human way of ceasing to function. It was an involuntary and irreversible dismantling, and Andrew did not know what to say that might be appropriate. He could only remain standing, absolutely silent, absolutely motionless.

When it was over, Little Miss said to him, "He may not have seemed friendly to you toward the end, Andrew, but he was old, you know, and it hurt him that you should want to be free."

And then Andrew found the words to say. He said, "I would never have been free without him, Little Miss."

9.

It was only after Sir's death that Andrew began to wear clothes. He began with an old pair of trousers at first, a pair that George had given him.

George was married now, and a lawyer. He had joined Feingold's firm. Old Feingold was long since dead but his daughter had carried on and eventually the firm's name became Feingold and Martin. It remained so even when the daughter retired and no Feingold took her place. At the time Andrew put on clothes for the first time, the Martin name had just been added to the firm.

George had tried not to smile, the first time Andrew put on the trousers, but to Andrew's eyes the smile was clearly there.

George showed Andrew how to manipulate the static charge so as to allow the trousers to open, wrap about his lower body, and move shut. George demonstrated on his own trousers, but Andrew was quite aware that it would take him awhile to duplicate that one flowing motion.

George said, "But why do you want trousers, Andrew? Your body is so beautifully functional it's a shame to cover it —especially when you needn't worry about either temperature control or modesty. And it doesn't cling properly, not on metal."

Andrew said, "Are not human bodies beautifully functional, George? Yet you cover yourselves."

"For warmth, for cleanliness, for protection, for decorativeness. None of that applies to you."

Andrew said, "I feel bare without clothes. I feel different, George."

"Different! Andrew, there are millions of robots on Earth now. In this region, according to the last census, there are almost as many robots as there are men."

"I know, George. There are robots doing every conceivable type of work."

"And none of them wear clothes."

"But none of them are free, George."

Litlte by little, Andrew added to the wardrobe. He was inhibited by George's smile and by the stares of the people who commissioned work.

He might be free, but there was built into him a carefully detailed program concerning his behavior toward people, and it was only by the tiniest steps that he dared advance. Open disapproval would set him back months.

Not everyone accepted Andrew as free. He was incapable of resenting that and yet there was a difficulty about his thinking process when he thought of it.

Most of all, he tended to avoid putting on clothes—or too many of them—when he thought Little Miss might come to visit him. She was old now and was often away in some warmer climate, but when she returned the first thing she did was visit him.

On one of her returns, George said ruefully, "She's got me,

Andrew. I'll be running for the Legislature next year. Like grandfather, she says, like grandson."

"Like grandfather—" Andrew stopped, uncertain.

"I mean that I, George, the grandson, will be like Sir, the grandfather, who was in the Legislature once."

Andrew said, "It would be pleasant, George, if Sir were still—" He paused, for he did not want to say, "in working order." That seemed inappropriate.

"Alive," said George. "Yes, I think of the old monster now and then, too."

It was a conversation Andrew thought about. He had noticed his own incapacity in speech when talking with George. Somehow the language had changed since. Andrew had come into being with an innate vocabulary. Then, too, George used a colloquial speech, as Sir and Little Miss had not. Why should he have called Sir a monster when surely that word was not appropriate?

Nor could Andrew turn to his own books for guidance. They were old and most dealt with woodworking, with art, with furniture design. There were none on language, none on the ways of human beings.

It was at that moment it seemed to him that he must seek the proper books; and as a free robot, he felt he must not ask George. He would go to town and use the library. It was a triumphant decision and he felt his electropotential grow distinctly higher until he had to throw in an impedance coil.

He put on a full costume, even including a shoulder chain of wood. He would have preferred the glitter plastic but George had said that wood was much more appropriate and that polished cedar was considerably more valuable as well.

He had placed a hundred feet between himself and the house before gathering resistance brought him to a halt. He shifted the impedance coil out of circuit, and when that did not seem to help enough, he returned to his home and on a piece of notepaper wrote neatly, "I have gone to the library," and placed it in clear view on his worktable.

10.

Andrew never quite got to the library. He had studied the map. He knew the route, but not the appearance of it. The actual landmarks did not resemble the symbols on the map and he would hesitate. Eventually he thought he must have somehow gone wrong, for everything looked strange.

He passed an occasional field robot, but at the time he decided he should ask his way, there were none in sight. A vehicle passed and did not stop. He stood irresolute, which meant calmly motionless, and then coming across the field toward him were two human beings.

He turned to face them, and they altered their course to meet him. A moment before, they had been talking loudly; he had heard their voices; but now they were silent. They had the look that Andrew associated with human uncertainty, and they were young, but not very young. Twenty perhaps? Andrew could never judge human age.

He said, "Would you describe to me the route to the town library, sirs?"

One of them, the taller of the two, whose tall hat lengthened him still farther, almost grotesquely, said, not to Andrew, but to the other, "It's a robot."

The other had a bulbous nose and heavy eyelids. He said, not to Andrew, but to the first, "It's wearing clothes."

The tall one snapped his fingers. "It's the free robot. They have a robot at the Martins who isn't owned by anyone. Why else would it be wearing clothes?"

"Ask it," said the one with the nose.

"Are you the Martin robot?" asked the tall one.

"I am Andrew Martin, sir," said Andrew.

"Good. Take off your clothes. Robots don't wear clothes." He said to the other, "That's disgusting. Look at him."

Andrew hesitated. He hadn't heard an order in that tone of voice in so long that his Second Law circuits had momentarily jammed.

The tall one said, "Take off your clothes. I order you."

Slowly, Andrew began to remove them.

"Just drop them," said the tall one.

The nose said, "If it doesn't belong to anyone, he could be ours as much as someone else's."

"Anyway," said the tall one, "who's to object to anything we do? We're not damaging property. . . . Stand on your head." That was to Andrew.

"The head is not meant—" began Andrew.

"That's an order. If you don't know how, try anyway."

Andrew hesitated again, then bent to put his head on the ground. He tried to lift his legs and fell, heavily.

The tall one said, "Just lie there." He said to the other, "We can take him apart. Ever take a robot apart?"

"Will he let us?"

"How can he stop us?"

There was no way Andrew could stop them, if they ordered him not to resist in a forceful enough manner. Second Law of obedience took precedence over the Third Law of self-preservation. In any case, he could not defend himself without possibly hurting them and that would mean breaking the First Law. At that thought, every motile unit contracted slightly and he quivered as he lay there.

The tall one walked over and pushed at him with his foot. "He's heavy. I think we'll need tools to do the job."

The nose said, "We could order him to take himself apart. It would be fun to watch him try."

"Yes," said the tall one thoughtfully, "but let's get him off the road. If someone comes along—"

It was too late. Someone had indeed come along and it was George. From where he lay, Andrew had seen him topping a small rise in the middle distance. He would have liked to signal him in some way, but the last order had been "Just lie there!"

George was running now and he arrived somewhat winded. The two young men stepped back a little and then waited thoughtfully.

George said anxiously, "Andrew, has something gone wrong?"

Andrew said, "I am well, George."

"Then stand up. . . . What happened to your clothes?"

The tall young man said, "That your robot, mac?"

George turned sharply. "He's no one's robot. What's been going on here?"

"We politely asked him to take his clothes off. What's that to you if you don't own him?"

George said, "What were they doing, Andrew?"

Andrew said, "It was their intention in some way to dismember me. They were about to move me to a quiet spot and order me to dismember myself."

George looked at the two and his chin trembled. The two young men retreated no further. They were smiling. The tall one said lightly, "What are you going to do, pudgy? Attack us?"

George said, "No. I don't have to. This robot has been with my family for over seventy years. He knows us and he values us more than he values anyone else. I am going to tell him that you two are threatening my life and that you plan to kill me. I will ask him to defend me. In choosing between me and you two, he will choose me. Do you know what will happen to you when he attacks you?"

The two were backing away slightly, looking uneasy.

George said sharply, "Andrew, I am in danger and about to come to harm from these two men. Move toward them!"

Andrew did so, and the two young men did not wait. They ran fleetly.

"All right, Andrew, relax," said George. He looked unstrung. He was far past the age where he could face the possibility of a dustup with one young man, let alone two.

Andrew said, "I couldn't have hurt them, George. I could see they were not attacking you."

"I didn't order you to attack them; I only told you to move toward them. Their own fears did the rest."

"How can they fear robots?"

"It's a disease of mankind, one of which it is not yet cured. But never mind that. What the devil are you doing here, Andrew? I was on the point of turning back and hiring a helicopter when I found you. How did you get it into your head to go to the library? I would have brought you any books you needed."

"I am a—" began Andrew.

"Free robot. Yes, yes. All right, what did you want from the library?"

"I want to know more about human beings, about the world, about everything. And about robots, George. I want to write a history about robots."

George said, "Well, let's walk home. . . . And pick up your clothes first. Andrew, there are a million books on robotics and all of them include histories of the science. The world is growing saturated not only with robots but with information about robots."

Andrew shook his head, a human gesture he had lately begun to make. "Not a history of robotics, George. A history of *robots*, by a robot. I want to explain how robots feel about what has happened since the first ones were allowed to work and live on Earth."

George's eyebrows lifted, but he said nothing in direct response.

11.

Little Miss was just past her eighty-third birthday, but there was nothing about her that was lacking in either energy or determination. She gestured with her cane oftener than she propped herself up with it.

She listened to the story in a fury of indignation. She said, "George, that's horrible. Who were those young ruffians?"

"I don't know. What difference does it make? In the end they did no damage."

"They might have. You're a lawyer, George, and if you're well off, it's entirely due to the talent of Andrew. It was the money *he* earned that is the foundation of everything we have. He provides the continuity for this family and I will *not* have him treated as a wind-up toy."

"What would you have me do, Mother?" asked George.

"I said you're a lawyer. Don't you listen? You set up a test case somehow, and you force the regional courts to declare for robot rights and get the Legislature to pass the necessary bills, and carry the whole thing to the World Court, if you have to. I'll be watching, George, and I'll tolerate no shirking."

She was serious, and what began as a way of soothing the fearsome old lady became an involved matter with enough entanglement to make it interesting. As senior partner of Feingold and Martin, George plotted strategy but left the actual work to his junior partners, with much of it a matter for his son, Paul, who was also a member of the firm and who reported dutifully nearly every day to his grandmother. She, in turn, discussed it every day with Andrew.

Andrew was deeply involved. His work on his book on robots was delayed again, as he pored over the legal arguments and even, at times, made very diffident suggestions.

He said, "George told me that day that human beings have always been afraid of robots. As long as they are, the courts and the legislatures are not likely to work hard on behalf of robots. Should there not be something done about public opinion?"

So while Paul stayed in court, George took to the public platform. It gave him the advantage of being informal and he even went so far sometimes as to wear the new, loose style of clothing which he called drapery. Paul said, "Just don't trip over it on stage, Dad."

George said despondently, "I'll try not to."

He addressed the annual convention of holo-news editors on one occasion and said, in part:

"If, by virtue of the Second Law, we can demand of any robot unlimited obedience in all respects not involving harm to a human being, then any human being, *any* human being, has a fearsome power over any robot, *any* robot. In particular, since Second Law supersedes Third Law, *any* human being can use the law of obedience to overcome the law of self-protection. He can order any robot to damage itself or even destroy itself for any reason, or for no reason.

"Is this just? Would we treat an animal so? Even an inanimate object which has given us good service has a claim on our consideration. And a robot is not insensible; it is not an animal. It can think well enough to enable it to talk to us, reason with us, joke with us. Can we treat them as friends, can we work together with them, and not give them some of the fruit of that friendship, some of the benefit of co-working?

"If a man has the right to give a robot any order that does not involve harm to a human being, he should have the decency never to give a robot any order that involves harm to a robot, unless human safety absolutely requires it. With great power goes great responsibility, and if the robots have Three Laws to protect men, is it too much to ask that men have a law or two to protect robots?"

Andrew was right. It was the battle over public opinion that held the key to courts and Legislature and in the end a law passed which set up conditions under which robot-harming orders were forbidden. It was endlessly qualified and the punishments for violating the law were totally inadequate, but the principle was established. The final passage by the World Legislature came through on the day of Little Miss's death.

That was no coincidence. Little Miss held on to life desperately during the last debate and let go only when word of victory arrived. Her last smile was for Andrew. Her last words were: "You have been good to us, Andrew."

She died with her hand holding his, while her son and his wife and children remained at a respectful distance from both.

12.

Andrew waited patiently while the receptionist disappeared into the inner office. It might have used the holographic chatterbox, but unquestionably it was unmanned (or perhaps unroboted) by having to deal with another robot rather than with a human being.

Andrew passed the time revolving the matter in his mind.

Could "unroboted" be used as an analogue of "unmanned," or had "unmanned" become a metaphoric term sufficiently divorced from its original literal meaning to be applied to robots—or to women for that matter?

Such problems came frequently as he worked on his book on robots. The trick of thinking out sentences to express all complexities had undoubtedly increased his vocabulary.

Occasionally, someone came into the room to stare at him and he did not try to avoid the glance. He looked at each calmly, and each in turn looked away.

Paul Martin came out. He looked surprised, or he would have if Andrew could have made out his expression with certainty. Paul had taken to wearing the heavy makeup that fashion was dictating for both sexes and though it made sharper and firmer the somewhat bland lines of his face, Andrew disapproved. He found that disapproving of human beings, as long as he did not express it verbally, did not make him very uneasy. He could even write the disapproval. He was sure it had not always been so.

Paul said, "Come in, Andrew. I'm sorry I made you wait but there was something I *had* to finish. Come in. You had said you wanted to talk to me, but I didn't know you meant here in town."

"If you are busy, Paul, I am prepared to continue to wait."

Paul glanced at the interplay of shifting shadows on the dial on the wall that served as timepiece and said, "I can make some time. Did you come alone?"

"I hired an automatobile."

"Any trouble?" Paul asked, with more than a trace of anxiety.

"I wasn't expecting any. My rights are protected."

Paul looked the more anxious for that. "Andrew, I've explained that the law is unenforceable, at least under most conditions. . . . And if you insist on wearing clothes, you'll run into trouble eventually—just like that first time."

"And only time, Paul. I'm sorry you are displeased."

"Well, look at it this way; you are virtually a living legend, Andrew, and you are too valuable in many different ways for you to have any right to take chances with yourself. . . . How's the book coming?"

"I am approaching the end, Paul. The publisher is quite pleased."

"Good!"

"I don't know that he's necessarily pleased with the book

as a book. I think he expects to sell many copies because it's written by a robot and it's that that pleases him."

"Only human, I'm afraid."

"I am not displeased. Let it sell for whatever reason since it will mean money and I can use some."

"Grandmother left you—"

"Little Miss was generous, and I'm sure I can count on the family to help me out further. But it is the royalties from the book on which I am counting to help me through the next step."

"What next step is that?"

"I wish to see the head of U. S. Robots and Mechanical Men, Inc. I have tried to make an appointment, but so far I have not been able to reach him. The corporation did not cooperate with me in the writing of the book, so I am not surprised, you understand."

Paul was clearly amused. "Cooperation is the last thing you can expect. They didn't cooperate with us in our great fight for robot rights. Quite the reverse and you can see why. Give a robot rights and people may not want to buy them."

"Nevertheless," said Andrew, "if you call them, you may obtain an interview for me."

"I'm no more popular with them than you are, Andrew."

"But perhaps you can hint that by seeing me they may head off a campaign by Feingold and Martin to strengthen the rights of robots further."

"Wouldn't that be a lie, Andrew?"

"Yes, Paul, and I can't tell one. That is why you must call."

"Ah, you can't lie, but you can urge me to tell a lie, is that it? You're getting more human all the time, Andrew."

13.

It was not easy to arrange, even with Paul's supposedly weighted name.

But it was finally carred through and, when it was, Harley Smythe-Robertson, who, on his mother's side, was descended from the original founder of the corporation and who had adopted the hyphenation to indicate it, looked remarkably unhappy. He was approaching retirement age and his entire tenure as president had been devoted to the matter of robot rights. His gray hair was plastered thinly over the top of his scalp, his face was not made up, and he eyed Andrew with brief hostility from time to time.

Andrew said, "Sir, nearly a century ago, I was told by a Merton Mansky of this corporation that the mathematics governing the plotting of the positronic pathways was far too complicated to permit of any but approximate solutions and that therefore my own capacities were not fully predictable."

"That was a century ago." Smythe-Robertson hesitated, then said icily, "*Sir*. It is true no longer. Our robots are made with precision now and are trained precisely to their jobs."

"Yes," said Paul, who had come along, as he said, to make sure that the corporation played fair, "with the result that my receptionist must be guided at every point once events depart from the conventional, however slightly."

Smythe-Robertson said, "You would be much more displeased if it were to improvise."

Andrew said, "Then you no longer manufacture robots like myself which are flexible and adaptable."

"No longer."

"The research I have done in connection with my book," said Andrew, "indicates that I am the oldest robot presently in active operation."

"The oldest presently," said Smythe-Robertson, "and the oldest ever. The oldest that will ever be. No robot is useful after the twenty-fifth year. They are called in and replaced with newer models."

"No robot *as presently manufactured* is useful after the twenty-fifth year," said Paul pleasantly. "Andrew is quite exceptional in this respect."

Andrew, adhering to the path he had marked out for himself, said, "As the oldest robot in the world and the most flexible, am I not unusual enough to merit special treatment from the company?"

"Not at all," said Smythe-Robertson freezingly. "Your unusualness is an embarrassment to the company. If you were on lease, instead of having been a sale outright through some mischance, you would long since have been replaced."

"But that is exactly the point," said Andrew. "I am a free robot and I own myself. Therefore I come to you and ask you to replace me. You cannot do this without the owner's consent. Nowadays, that consent is extorted as a condition of the lease, but in my time this did not happen."

Smythe-Robertson was looking both startled and puzzled,

and for a moment there was silence. Andrew found himself staring at the holograph on the wall. It was a death mask of Susan Calvin, patron saint of all roboticists. She was dead nearly two centuries now, but as a result of writing his book Andrew knew her so well he could half persuade himself that he had met her in life.

Smythe-Robertson said, "How can I replace you for you? If I replace you as robot, how can I donate the new robot to you as owner since in the very act of replacement you cease to exist?" He smiled grimly.

"Not at all difficult," interposed Paul. "The seat of Andrew's personality is his positronic brain and it is the one part that cannot be replaced without creating a new robot. The positronic brain, therefore, is Andrew the owner. Every other part of the robotic body can be replaced without affecting the robot's personality, and those other parts are the brain's possessions. Andrew, I should say, wants to supply his brain with a new robotic body."

"That's right," said Andrew calmly. He turned to Smythe-Robertson. "You have manufactured androids, haven't you? Robots that have the outward appearance of humans complete to the texture of the skin?"

Smythe-Robertson said, "Yes, we have. They worked perfectly well, with their synthetic fibrous skins and tendons. There was virtually no metal anywhere except for the brain, yet they were nearly as tough as metal robots. They were tougher, weight for weight."

Paul looked interested. "I didn't know that. How many are on the market?"

"None," said Smythe-Robertson. "They were much more expensive than metal models and a market survey showed they would not be accepted. They looked too human."

Andrew said, "But the corporation retains its expertise, I assume. Since it does, I wish to request that I be replaced by an organic robot, an android."

Paul looked surprised. "Good Lord," he said.

Smythe-Robertson stiffened. "Quite impossible!"

"Why is it impossible?" asked Andrew. "I will pay any reasonable fee, of course."

Smythe-Robertson said, "We do not manufacture androids."

"You do not *choose* to manufacture androids," interposed Paul quickly. "That is not the same as being unable to manufacture them."

Smythe-Robertson said, "Nevertheless, the manufacture of androids is against public policy."

"There is no law against it," said Paul.

"Nevertheless, we do not manufacture them, and we will not."

Paul cleared his throat. "Mr. Smythe-Robertson," he said, "Andrew is a free robot who is under the purview of the law guaranteeing robot rights. You are aware of this, I take it?"

"Only too well."

"This robot, as a free robot, chooses to wear clothes. This results in his being frequently humiliated by thoughtless human beings despite the law against the humiliation of robots. It is difficult to prosecute vague offenses that don't meet with the general disapproval of those who must decide on guilt and innocence."

"U. S. Robots understood that from the start. Your father's firm unfortunately did not."

"My father is dead now," said Paul, "but what I see is that we have here a clear offense with a clear target."

"What are you talking about?" said Smythe-Robertson.

"My client, Andrew Martin—he has just become my client —is a free robot who is entitled to ask U. S. Robots and Mechanical Men, Inc., for the right of replacement, which the corporation supplies anyone who owns a robot for more than twenty-five years. In fact, the corporation insists on such replacement."

Paul was smiling and thoroughly at his ease. He went on, "The positronic brain of my client is the owner of the body of my client—which is certainly more than twenty-five years old. The positronic brain demands the replacement of the body and offers to pay any reasonable fee for an android body as that replacement. If you refuse the request, my client undergoes humiliation and we will sue.

"While public opinion would not ordinarily support the claim of a robot in such a case, may I remind you that U. S. Robots is not popular with the public generally. Even those who most use and profit from robots are suspicious of the corporation. This may be a hangover from the days when robots were widely feared. It may be resentment against the power and wealth of U. S. Robots which has a worldwide monopoly. Whatever the cause may be, the resentment exists and I think you will find that you would prefer not to withstand a lawsuit, particularly since my client is wealthy and will live for many more centuries and will have no reason to refrain from fighting the battle forever."

Smythe-Robertson had slowly reddened. "You are trying to force me to . . ."

"I force you to do nothing," said Paul. "If you wish to refuse to accede to my client's reasonable request, you may by all means do so and we will leave without another word. . . . But we will sue, as is certainly our right, and you will find that you will eventually lose."

Smythe-Robertson said, "Well—" and paused.

"I see that you are going to accede," said Paul. "You may hesitate but you will come to it in the end. Let me assure you, then, of one further point. If, in the process of transferring my client's positronic brain from his present body to an organic one, there is any damage, however slight, then I will never rest till I've nailed the corporation to the ground. I will, if necessary, take every possible step to mobilize public opinion against the corporation if one brain path of my client's platinum-iridium essence is scrambled." He turned to Andrew and said, "Do you agree to all this, Andrew?"

Andrew hesitated a full minute. It amounted to the approval of lying, of blackmail, of the badgering and humiliation of a human being. But not physical harm, he told himself, not physical harm.

He managed at last to come out with a rather faint "Yes."

14.

It was like being constructed again. For days, then for weeks, finally for months, Andrew found himself not himself somehow, and the simplest actions kept giving rise to hesitation.

Paul was frantic. "They've damaged you, Andrew. We'll have to institute suit."

Andrew spoke very slowly. "You mustn't. You'll never be able to prove—something—m-m-m-m—"

"Malice?"

"Malice. Besides, I grow stronger, better. It's the tr-tr-tr—"

"Tremble?"

"Trauma. After all, there's never been such an op—op—op—before."

Andrew could feel his brain from the inside. No one else could. He knew he was well and during the months that it took him to learn full coordination and full positronic interplay, he spent hours before the mirror.

Not quite human! The face was stiff—too stiff—and the motions were too deliberate. They lacked the careless free flow of the human being, but perhaps that might come with time. At least he could wear clothes without the ridiculous anomaly of a metal face going along with it.

Eventually he said, "I will be going back to work."

Paul laughed and said, "That means you are well. What will you be doing? Another book?"

"No," said Andrew seriously. "I live too long for any one career to seize me by the throat and never let me go. There was a time when I was primarily an artist and I can still turn to that. And there was a time when I was a historian and I can still turn to that. But now I wish to be a robobiologist."

"A robopsychologist, you mean."

"No. That would imply the study of positronic brains and at the moment I lack the desire to do that. A robobiologist, it seems to me, would be concerned with the working of the body attached to that brain."

"Wouldn't that be a roboticist?"

"A roboticist works with a metal body. I would be studying an organic humanoid body, of which I have the only one, as far as I know."

"You narrow your field," said Paul thoughtfully. "As an artist, all conception is yours; as a historian, you dealt chiefly with robots; as a robobiologist, you will deal with yourself."

Andrew nodded. "It would seem so."

Andrew had to start from the very beginning, for he knew nothing of ordinary biology, almost nothing of science. He became a familiar sight in the libraries, where he sat at the electronic indices for hours at a time, looking perfectly normal in clothes. Those few who knew he was a robot in no way interfered with him.

He built a laboratory in a room which he added to his house, and his library, too.

Years passed, and Paul came to him one day and said, "It's a pity you're no longer working on the history of robots. I understand U. S. Robots is adopting a radically new policy."

Paul had aged, and his deteriorating eyes had been replaced with photoptic cells. In that respect, he had drawn closer to Andrew. Andrew said, "What have they done?"

"They are manufacturing central computers, gigantic positronic brains, really, which communicate with anywhere from a dozen to a thousand robots by microwave. The robots themselves have no brains at all. They are the limbs of the gigantic brain, and the two are physically separate."

"Is that more efficient?"

"U. S. Robots claims it is. Smythe-Robertson established the new direction before he died, however, and it's my notion that it's a backlash at you. U. S. Robots is determined that they will make no robots that will give them the type of trouble you have, and for that reason they separate brain and body. The brain will have no body to wish changed; the body will have no brain to wish anything.

"It's amazing, Andrew," Paul went on, "the influence you have had on the history of robots. It was your artistry that encouraged U. S. Robots to make robots more precise and specialized; it was your freedom that resulted in the establishment of the principle of robotic rights; it was your insistence on an android body that made U. S. Robots switch to brain-body separation."

Andrew said, "I suppose in the end the corporation will produce one vast brain controlling several billion robotic bodies. All the eggs will be in one basket. Dangerous. Not proper at all."

"I think you're right," said Paul, "but I don't suspect it will come to pass for a century at least and I won't live to see it. In fact, I may not live to see next year."

"Paul!" said Andrew, in concern.

Paul shrugged. "We're mortal, Andrew. We're not like you. It doesn't matter too much, but it does make it important to assure you on one point. I'm the last of the human Martins. There are collaterals descended from my great-aunt, but they don't count. The money I control personally will be left to the trust in your name and as far as anyone can foresee the future, you will be economically secure."

"Unnecessary," said Andrew, with difficulty. In all this time, he could not get used to the deaths of the Martins.

Paul said, "Let's not argue. That's the way it's going to be. What are you working on?"

"I am designing a system for allowing androids—myself —to gain energy from the combustion of hydrocarbons, rather than from atomic cells."

Paul raised his eyebrows. "So that they will breathe and eat?"

"Yes."

"How long have you been pushing in that direction?"

"For a long time now, but I think I have designed an adequate combustion chamber for catalyzed controlled breakdown."

"But why, Andrew? The atomic cell is surely infinitely better."

"In some ways, perhaps, but the atomic cell is inhuman."

15.

It took time, but Andrew had time. In the first place, he did not wish to do anything till Paul had died in peace.

With the death of the great-grandson of Sir, Andrew felt more nearly exposed to a hostile world and for that reason was the more determined to continue the path he had long ago chosen.

Yet he was not really alone. If a man had died, the firm of Feingold and Martin lived, for a corporation does not die any more than a robot does. The firm had its directions and it followed them soullessly. By way of the trust and through the law firm, Andrew continued to be wealthy. And in return for their own large annual retainer, Feingold and Martin involved themselves in the legal aspects of the new combustion chamber.

When the time came for Andrew to visit U. S. Robots and Mechanical Men, Inc., he did it alone. Once he had gone with Sir and once with Paul. This time, the third time, he was alone and manlike.

U. S. Robots had changed. The production plant had been shifted to a large space station, as had grown to be the case with more and more industries. With them had gone many robots. The Earth itself was becoming parklike, and its one-billion-person population stabilized and perhaps not more than thirty per cent of its at least equally large robot population independently brained.

The Director of Research was Alvin Magdescu, dark of complexion and hair, with a little pointed beard and wearing nothing above the waist but the breastband that fashion dictated. Andrew himself was well covered in the older fashion of several decades back.

Magdescu said, "I know you, of course, and I'm rather pleased to see you. You're our most notorious product and it's a pity old Smythe-Robertson was so set against you. We could have done a great deal with you."

"You still can," said Andrew.

"No, I don't think so. We're past the time. We've had robots on Earth for over a century, but that's changing. It will be back to space with them and those that stay here won't be brained."

"But there remains myself, and I stay on Earth."

"True, but there doesn't seem to be much of the robot about you. What new request have you?"

"To be still less a robot. Since I am so far organic, I wish an organic source of energy. I have here the plans—"

Magdescu did not hasten through them. He might have intended to at first, but he stiffened and grew intent. At one point he said, "This is remarkably ingenious. Who thought of all this?"

"I did," said Andrew.

Magdescu looked up at him sharply, then said, "It would amount to a major overhaul of your body, and an experimental one, since it has never been attempted before. I advise against it. Remain as you are."

Andrew's face had limited means of expression, but impatience showed plainly in his voice. "Dr. Magdescu, you miss the entire point. You have no choice but to accede to my request. If such devices can be built into my body, they can be built into human bodies as well. The tendency to lengthen human life by prosthetic devices has already been remarked on. There are no devices better than the ones I have designed and am designing.

"As it happens, I control the patents by way of the firm of Feingold and Martin. We are quite capable of going into business for ourselves and of developing the kind of prosthetic devices that may end by producing human beings with many of the properties of robots. Your own business will then suffer.

"If, however, you operate on me now and agree to do so under similar circumstances in the future, you will receive permission to make use of the patents and control the technology of both robots and the prosthetization of human beings. The initial leasing will not be granted, of course, until after the first operation is completed successfully, and after enough time has passed to demonstrate that it is indeed successful." Andrew felt scarcely any First Law inhibition to the stern conditions he was setting a human being. He was learning to reason that what seemed like cruelty might, in the long run, be kindness.

Magdescu looked stunned. He said, "I'm not the one to

decide something like this. That's a corporate decision that would take time."

"I can wait a reasonable time," said Andrew, "but only a reasonable time." And he thought with satisfaction that Paul himself could not have done it better.

16.

It took only a reasonable time, and the operation was a success.

Magdescu said, "I was very much against the operation, Andrew, but not for the reasons you might think. I was not in the least against the experiment, if it had been on someone else. I hated risking *your* positronic brain. Now that you have the positronic pathways interacting with simulated nerve pathways, it might be difficult to rescue the brain intact if the body went bad."

"I had every faith in the skill of the staff at U. S. Robots," said Andrew. "And I can eat now."

"Well, you can sip olive oil. It will mean occasional cleanings of the combustion chamber, as we have explained to you. Rather an uncomfortable touch, I should think."

"Perhaps, if I did not expect to go further. Self-cleaning is not impossible. In fact, I am working on a device that will deal with solid food that may be expected to contain incombustible fractions—indigestible matter, so to speak, that will have to be discarded."

"You would then have to develop an anus."

"The equivalent."

"What else, Andrew?"

"Everything else."

"Genitalia, too?"

"Insofar as they will fit my plans. My body is a canvas on which I intend to draw—"

Magdescu waited for the sentence to be completed, and when it seemed that it would not be, he completed it himself. "A man?"

"We shall see," said Andrew.

Magdescu said, "It's a puny ambition, Andrew. You're better than a man. You've gone downhill from the moment you opted for organicism."

"My brain has not suffered."

"No, it hasn't. I'll grant you that. But, Andrew, the whole new breakthrough in prosthetic devices made possible by your patents is being marketed under your name. You're recognized as the inventor and you're honored for it—as you are. Why play further games with your body?"

Andrew did not answer.

The honors came. He accepted membership in several learned societies, including one which was devoted to the new science he had established; the one he had called robobiology but had come to be termed prosthetology.

On the one hundred and fiftieth anniversary of his construction, there was a testimonial dinner given in his honor at U. S. Robots. If Andrew saw irony in this, he kept it to himself.

Alvin Magdescu came out of retirement to chair the dinner. He was himself ninety-four years old and was alive because he had prosthetized devices that, among other things, fulfilled the function of liver and kidneys. The dinner reached its climax when Magdescu, after a short and emotional talk, raised his glass to toast "the Sesquicentennial Robot."

Andrew had had the sinews of his face redesigned to the point where he could show a range of emotions, but he sat through all the ceremonies solemnly passive. He did not like to be a Sesquicentennial Robot.

17.

It was prosthetology that finally took Andrew off the Earth. In the decades that followed the celebration of the Sesquicentennial, the Moon had come to be a world more Earth-like than Earth in every respect but its gravitational pull and in its underground cities there was a fairly dense population.

Prosthetized devices there had to take the lesser gravity into account and Andrew spent five years on the Moon working with local prosthetologists to make the necessary adaptations. When not at his work, he wandered among the robot population, every one of which treated him with the robotic obsequiousness due a man.

He came back to an Earth that was humdrum and quiet in comparison and visited the offices of Feingold and Martin to announce his return.

The current head of the firm, Simon DeLong, was surprised. He said, "We had been told you were returning, Andrew" (he had almost said "Mr. Martin"), "but we were not expecting you till next week."

"I grew impatient," said Andrew brusquely. He was anxious to get to the point. "On the Moon, Simon, I was in charge of a research team of twenty human scientists. I gave orders that no one questioned. The Lunar robots deferred to me as they would to a human being. Why, then, am I not a human being?"

A wary look entered DeLong's eyes. He said, "My dear Andrew, as you have just explained, you are treated as a human being by both robots and human beings. You are therefore a human being *de facto*."

"To be a human being *de facto* is not enough. I want not only to be treated as one, but to be legally identified as one. I want to be a human being *de jure*."

"Now that is another matter," said DeLong. "There we would run into human prejudice and into the undoubted fact that however much you may be like a human being, you are *not* a human being."

"In what way not?" asked Andrew. "I have the shape of a human being and organs equivalent to those of a human being. My organs, in fact, are identical to some of those in a prosthetized human being. I have contributed artistically, literarily, and scientifically to human culture as much as any human being now alive. What more can one ask?"

"I myself would ask nothing. The trouble is that it would take an act of the World Legislature to define you as a human being. Frankly, I wouldn't expect that to happen."

"To whom on the Legislature could I speak?"

"To the chairman of the Science and Technology Committee perhaps."

"Can you arrange a meeting?"

"But you scarcely need an intermediary. In your position, you can—"

"No. *You* arrange it." (It didn't even occur to Andrew that he was giving a flat order to a human being. He had grown accustomed to that on the Moon.) "I want him to know that the firm of Feingold and Martin is backing me in this to the hilt."

"Well, now—"

"To the hilt, Simon. In one hundred and seventy-three years I have in one fashion or another contributed greatly to this firm. I have been under obligation to individual members of this firm in times past. I am not now. It is rather the other way around now and I am calling in my debts."

DeLong said, "I will do what I can."

18.

The chairman of the Science and Technology Committee was of the East Asian region and she was a woman. Her name was Chee Li-Hsing and her transparent garments (obscuring what she wanted obscured only by their dazzle) made her look plastic-wrapped.

She said, "I sympathize with your wish for full human rights. There have been times in history when segments of the human population fought for full human rights. What rights, however, can you possibly want that you do not have?"

"As simple a thing as my right to life. A robot can be dismantled at any time."

"A human being can be executed at any time."

"Execution can only follow due process of law. There is no trial needed for my dismantling. Only the word of a human being in authority is needed to end me. Besides— besides—" Andrew tried desperately to allow no sign of pleading, but his carefully designed tricks of human expression and tone of voice betrayed him here. "The truth is, I want to be a man. I have wanted it through six generations of human beings."

Li-Hsing looked up at him out of darkly sympathetic eyes. "The Legislature can pass a law declaring you one—they could pass a law declaring a stone statue to be defined as a man. Whether they will actually do so is, however, as likely in the first case as the second. Congresspeople are as human as the rest of the population and there is always that element of suspicion against robots."

"Even now?"

"Even now. We would all allow the fact that you have earned the prize of humanity and yet there would remain the fear of setting an undesirable precedent."

"What precedent? I am the only free robot, the only one of my type, and there will never be another. You may consult U. S. Robots."

" 'Never' is a long time, Andrew—or, if you prefer, Mr. Martin—since I will gladly give you my personal accolade as man. You will find that most Congresspeople will not be willing to set the precedent, no matter how meaningless such a precedent might be. Mr. Martin, you have my sympathy, but I cannot tell you to hope. Indeed—"

She sat back and her forehead wrinkled. "Indeed, if the

issue grows too heated, there might well arise a certain senti-
ment, both inside the Legislature and outside, for that dismantling you mentioned. Doing away with you could turn
out to be the easest way of resolving the dilemma. Consider
that before deciding to push matters."

Andrew said, "Will no one remember the technique of prosthetology, something that is almost entirely mine?"

"It may seem cruel, but they won't. Or if they do, it will
be remembered against you. It will be said you did it only
for yourself. It will be said it was part of a campaign to
roboticize human beings, or to humanify robots; and in either
case evil and vicious. You have never been part of a political
hate campaign, Mr. Martin, and I tell you that you will be
the object of vilification of a kind neither you nor I would
credit and there would be people who'll believe it all. Mr.
Martin, let your life be." She rose and, next to Andrew's
seated figure, she seemed small and almost childlike.

Andrew said, "If I decide to fight for my humanity, will
you be on my side?"

She thought, then said, "I will be—insofar as I can be. If at
any time such a stand would appear to threaten my political
future, I may have to abandon you, since it is not an issue
I feel to be at the very roots of my beliefs. I am trying to
be honest with you."

"Thank you, and I will ask no more. I intend to fight this
through whatever the consequences, and I will ask you for
your help only for as long as you can give it."

19.

It was not a direct fight. Feingold and Martin counseled
patience and Andrew muttered grimly that he had an endless
supply of that. Feingold and Martin then entered on a campaign to narrow and restrict the area of combat.

They instituted a lawsuit denying the obligation to pay debts
to an individual with a prosthetic heart on the grounds that
the possession of a robotic organ removed humanity, and with
it the constitutional rights of human beings.

They fought the matter skillfully and tenaciously, losing
at every step but always in such a way that the decision was
forced to be as broad as possible, and then carrying it by way
of appeals to the World Court.

It took years, and millions of dollars.

When the final decision was handed down, DeLong held

what amounted to a victory celebration over the legal loss. Andrew was, of course, present in the company offices on the occasion.

"We've done two things, Andrew," said DeLong, "both of which are good. First of all, we have established the fact that no number of artifacts in the human body causes it to cease being a human body. Secondly, we have engaged public opinion in the question in such a way as to put it fiercely on the side of a broad interpretation of humanity since there is not a human being in existence who does not hope for prosthetics if that will keep him alive."

"And do you think the Legislature will now grant me my humanity?" asked Andrew.

DeLong looked faintly uncomfortable. "As to that, I cannot be optimistic. There remains the one organ which the World Court has used as the criterion of humanity. Human beings have an organic cellular brain and robots have a platinum-iridium positronic brain if they have one at all—and you certainly have a positronic brain. . . . No, Andrew, don't get that look in your eye. We lack the knowledge to duplicate the work of a cellular brain in artificial structures close enough to the organic type to allow it to fall within the Court's decision. Not even you could do it."

"What ought we do, then?"

"Make the attempt, of course. Congresswoman Li-Hsing will be on our side and a growing number of other Congresspeople. The President will undoubtedly go along with a majority of the Legislature in this matter."

"Do we have a majority?"

"No, far from it. But we might get one if the public will allow its desire for a broad interpretation of humanity to extend to you. A small chance, I admit, but if you do not wish to give up, we must gamble for it."

"I do not wish to give up."

20.

Congresswoman Li-Hsing was considerably older than she had been when Andrew had first met her. Her transparent garments were long gone. Her hair was now close-cropped and her coverings were tubular. Yet still Andrew clung, as closely as he could within the limits of reasonable taste, to the style of clothing that had prevailed when he had first adopted clothing over a century before.

She said, "We've gone as far as we can, Andrew. We'll try once more after recess, but, to be honest, defeat is certain and the whole thing will have to be given up. All my most recent efforts have only earned me a certain defeat in the coming congressional campaign."

"I know," said Andrew, "and it distresses me. You said once you would abandon me if it came to that. Why have you not done so?"

"One can change one's mind, you know. Somehow, abandoning you became a higher price than I cared to pay for just one more term. As it is, I've been in the Legislature for over a quarter of a century. It's enough."

"Is there no way we can change minds, Chee?"

"We've changed all that are amenable to reason. The rest —the majority—cannot be moved from their emotional antipathies."

"Emotional antipathy is not a valid reason for voting one way or the other."

"I know that, Andrew, but they don't advance emotional antipathy as their reason."

Andrew said cautiously, "It all comes down to the brain, then, but must we leave it at the level of cells versus positrons? Is there no way of forcing a functional definition? Must we say that a brain is made of this or that? May we not say that a brain is something—anything—capable of a certain level of thought?"

"Won't work," said Li-Hsing. "Your brain is man-made, the human brain is not. Your brain is constructed, theirs developed. To any human being who is intent on keeping up the barrier between himself and a robot, those differences are a steel wall a mile high and a mile thick."

"If we could get at the source of their antipathy—the very source of—"

"After all your years," said Li-Hsing sadly, "you are still trying to reason out the human being. Poor Andrew, don't be angry, but it's the robot in you that drives you in that direction."

"I don't know," said Andrew. "If I could bring myself—"

1. (reprise)

If he could bring myself—

He had known for a long time it might come to that, and in the end he was at the surgeon's. He found one, skillful enough for the job at hand, which meant a robot surgeon, for no human surgeon could be trusted in this connection, either in ability or in intention.

The surgeon could not have performed the operation on a human being, so Andrew, after putting off the moment of decision with a sad line of questioning that reflected the turmoil within himself, put the First Law to one side by saying, "I, too, am a robot."

He then said, as firmly as he had learned to form the words even at human beings over these past decades, "I *order* you to carry through the operation on me."

In the absence of the First Law, an order so firmly given from one who looked so much like a man activated the Second Law sufficiently to carry the day.

21.

Andrew's feeling of weakness was, he was sure, quite imaginary. He had recovered from the operation. Nevertheless, he leaned, as unobtrusively as he could manage, against the wall. It would be entirely too revealing to sit.

Li-Hsing said, "The final vote will come this week, Andrew. I've been able to delay it no longer, and we must lose. . . . And that will be it, Andrew."

Andrew said, "I am grateful for your skill at delay. It gave me the time I needed, and I took the gamble I had to."

"What gamble is this?" asked Li-Hsing with open concern.

"I couldn't tell you, or the people at Feingold and Martin. I was sure I would be stopped. See here, if it is the brain that is at issue, isn't the greatest difference of all the matter of immortality? Who really cares what a brain looks like or is built of or how it was formed? What matters is that brain cells die; *must* die. Even if every other organ in the body is maintained or replaced, the brain cells, which cannot be replaced without changing and therefore killing the personality, must eventually die.

"My own positronic pathways have lasted nearly two centuries without perceptible change and can last for centuries more. Isn't *that* the fundamental barrier? Human beings can tolerate an immortal robot, for it doesn't matter how long a machine lasts. They cannot tolerate an immortal human being, since their own mortality is endurable only so long as it is universal. And for that reason they won't make me a human being."

Li-Hsing said, "What is it you're leading up to, Andrew?"

"I have removed that problem. Decades ago, my positronic brain was connected to organic nerves. Now, one last operation has arranged that connection in such a way that slowly —quite slowly—the potential is being drained from my pathways."

Li-Hsing's finely wrinkled face showed no expression for a moment. Then her lips tightened. "Do you mean you've arranged to die, Andrew? You can't have. That violates the Third Law."

"No," said Andrew, "I have chosen between the death of my body and the death of my aspirations and desires. To have let my body live at the cost of the greater death is what would have violated the Third Law."

Li-Hsing seized his arm as though she were about to shake him. She stopped herself. "Andrew, it won't work. Change it back."

"It can't be. Too much damage was done. I have a year to live—more or less. I will last through the two hundredth anniversary of my construction. I was weak enough to arrange that."

"How can it be worth it? Andrew, you're a fool."

"If it brings me humanity, that will be worth it. If it doesn't, it will bring an end to striving and that will be worth it, too."

And Li-Hsing did something that astonished herself. Quietly, she began to weep.

22.

It was odd how that last deed caught at the imagination of the world. All that Andrew had done before had not swayed them. But he had finally accepted even death to be human and the sacrifice was too great to be rejected.

The final ceremony was timed, quite deliberately, for the two hundredth anniversary. The World President was to sign the act and make it law and the ceremony would be visible on a global network and would be beamed to the Lunar state and even to the Martian colony.

Andrew was in a wheelchair. He could still walk, but only shakily.

With mankind watching, the World President said, "Fifty years ago, you were declared a Sesquicentennial Robot, Andrew." After a pause, and in a more solemn tone, he said,

"Today we declare you a Bicentennial Man, Mr. Martin."

And Andrew, smiling, held out his hand to shake that of the President.

23.

Andrew's thoughts were slowly fading as he lay in bed. Desperately he seized at them. Man! He was a man! He wanted that to be his last thought. He wanted to dissolve—die—with that.

He opened his eyes one more time and for one last time recognized Li-Hsing waiting solemnly. There were others, but those were only shadows, unrecognizable shadows. Only Li-Hsing stood out against the deepening gray. Slowly, inchingly, he held out his hand to her and very dimly and faintly felt her take it.

She was fading in his eyes, as the last of his thoughts trickled away.

But before she faded completely, one last fugitive thought came to him and rested for a moment on his mind before everything stopped.

"Little Miss," he whispered, too low to be heard.

In the old days, one wrote science fiction for science fiction magazines. In fact, John Campbell once jokingly defined that indefinable field as follows: "Science fiction is what science fiction editors buy."

Nowadays, however, all sorts of editors buy it, and I am prepared to receive requests from the unlikeliest sources. For instance, in the summer of 1975, I received a request from a magazine named *High Fidelity* to do a science fiction story that was 2,500 words long, that was set about twenty-five years in the future, and that dealt with some aspect of sound recording.

I was intrigued by the narrowness of the boundary conditions, since that made it quite a challenge. Of course, I explained to the editor that I knew nothing about music or about sound recording, but that was pushed impatiently to one side as irrelevant. I started the story on September 18, 1975, and when I was through the editor liked it. He suggested some changes that would remove a bit of the aura of musical illiteracy on my part and then it appeared in the April 1976 issue of the magazine.

9

Marching In

Jerome Bishop, composer and trombonist, had never been in a mental hospital before.

There had been times when he had suspected he might be in one, someday, as a patient (who was safe?), but it had never occurred to him that he might ever be there as a consultant on a question of mental aberration. *A consultant.*

He sat there, in the year 2001, with the world in pretty terrible shape, but (they said) pulling out of it, and then rose as a middle-aged women entered. Her hair was beginning to turn gray, and Bishop was thankfully conscious of his own hair still in full shock and evenly dark.

"Are you Mr. Bishop?" she asked.

"Last time I looked."

She held out her hand. "I'm Dr. Cray. Won't you come with me?"

He shook her hand, then followed. He tried not to be haunted by the dull beige uniforms worn by everyone he passed.

Dr. Cray put a finger to her lip, and motioned him into a chair. She pressed a button and the lights went out, causing a window, with a light behind it, to spring into view. Through the window, Bishop could see a woman in something that looked like a dentist's chair, tilted back. A forest of flexible wires sprang from her head, a thin narrow beam of light extended from pole to pole behind her, and a somewhat less narrow strip of paper unfolded upward.

The light went on again; the view vanished.

Dr. Cray said, "Do you know what we're doing in there?"

"You're recording brain waves? Just a guess."

"A good guess. We are. It's a laser recording. Do you know how that works?"

"My stuff's been recorded by laser," said Bishop, crossing one leg over the other, "but that doesn't mean I know how it *works*. It's the engineers who know the details. . . . Look, Doc, if you have an idea I'm a laser engineer, I'm not."

"No, I know you're not," said Dr. Cray hurriedly. "You're here for something else. . . . Let me explain it to you. We can alter a laser beam very delicately; much more rapidly and much more precisely than we can alter an electric current, or even a beam of electrons. That means that a very complex wave can be recorded in far greater detail than has ever been imagined before. We can make a tracing with a microscopically narrow laser beam and get a wave we can study under a microscope and get accurate detail invisible to the naked eye and unobtainable in any other fashion."

Bishop said, "If that's what you want to consult me about, then all I can say is that it doesn't pay to get all that detail. You can only hear so much. If you sharpen a laser recording past a certain amount, you bring up the expense but you don't bring up the effect. In fact, some people say you get some kind of buzz that begins to drown out the music. I don't hear it myself, but I tell you that if you want the best, you don't narrow the laser beam all the way. . . . Of course, maybe it's different with brain waves but what I told you is all I can tell you, so I'll go and there's no charge except for carfare."

He made as though to get up, but Dr. Cray was shaking her head vigorously.

"Please sit down, Mr. Bishop. Recording brain waves *is* different. There we do need all the detail we can get. Till now, all we've ever had out of brain waves are the tiny, overlapping effects of ten billion brain cells, a kind of rough average that wipes out everything but the most general effects."

"You mean like listening to ten billion pianos all playing different tunes a hundred miles away?"

"Exactly."

"All you get is noise?"

"Not quite. We do get some information—about epilepsy, for instance. With laser recording, however, we begin to get the fine detail; we begin to hear the individual tunes those separate pianos are playing; we begin to hear which particular pianos may be out of tune."

Bishop lifted his eyebrows. "So you can tell what makes a particular crazy person crazy?"

"In a way of speaking. Look at this." In another corner of the room a screen flashed to life, with a thin wavering line over it. "Do you see this, Mr. Bishop?" Dr. Cray pressed the button of an indicator in her hand and one little blip in the line reddened. The line moved along past the lighted screen and red blips appeared periodically.

"That's a microphotograph," said Dr. Cray. "Those little red discontinuities are not visible to the unaided eye and wouldn't be visible with any recording device less delicate than the laser. It appears only when this particular patient is in depression. The markings are more pronounced, the deeper the depression."

Bishop thought about it for a while. Then he said, "Can you do anything about it? So far, it just means you can tell by that blip there's a depression, which you can tell by just listening to the patient."

"Quite right, but the details help. For instance, we can convert the brain waves into delicately flickering light waves and, what's more, into the equivalent sound waves. We use the same laser system that is used to record your music. We get a sort of dimly musical hum that matches the light flicker. I would like you to listen to it by earphone."

"The music from that particular depressive person whose brain produced that line?"

"Yes, and since we can't intensify it much without losing detail, we will ask you to listen by earphone."

"And watch the light, too?"

"That's not necessary. You can close your eyes. Enough of the flicker will penetrate the eyelids to affect the brain."

Bishop closed his eyes. Through the hum, he could hear the tiny wail of a complex beat, a complex, sad beat that carried all the troubles of the tired old world in it. He listened, vaguely conscious of the dim light beating on his eyeballs in flickering time.

He felt his shirt pulled at strenuously. "Mr. Bishop—Mr. Bishop—"

He took a deep breath. "Thanks!" he said, shuddering a little. "That upset me, but I couldn't let go."

"You were listening to brain-wave depression and it was affecting you. It was forcing your own brain-wave pattern to keep time. You felt depressed, didn't you?"

"All the way."

"Well, if we can locate the portion of the wave characteristic of depression, or of any mental abnormality, remove that, and play all the rest of the brain wave, the patient's pattern will be modified into normal form."

"For how long?"

"For a while after the treatment is stopped. For a while, but not long. A few days. A week. Then the patient has to return."

"That's better than nothing."

"And less than enough. A person is born with certain genes, Mr. Bishop, that dictate a certain potential brain structure. A person suffers certain environmental influences. These are not easy things to neutralize, so here in this institution we've been trying to find more efficient and long-lasting schemes for neutralization. . . . And you can help us, perhaps. That's why we've asked you to come here."

"But I don't know anything about this, Doc. I never heard about recording brain waves by laser." He pushed his hands apart, palms down. "I've got *nothing* for you."

Dr. Cray looked impatient. She pushed her hands deep into the pockets of her jacket and said, "Just a while ago, you said that the laser recorded more detail than the ear could hear."

"Yes. I stand by that."

"I know. One of my colleagues read an interview with you in the December 2000 issue of *High Fidelity* magazine, in which you said that. That's what attracted our attention. The ear can't get the laser detail, but the eye can, you see. It's the flickering light that alters the brain pattern to the norm, not the wavering sound. The sound alone will do nothing. It will, however, reinforce the effect when the light is working."

"You can't complain about that."

"We can. The reinforcement isn't good enough. The gentle, delicate, almost infinitely complex variations produced in the sound by laser recording is lost on the ear. Too much is present and it drowns out the portion that is reinforcing."

"What makes you think that a reinforcing portion is there?"

"Because occasionally, more or less by accident, we can produce something that seems to work better than the entire brain wave, but we don't see why. We need a musician. Maybe you. If you listen to both sets of brain waves, perhaps you can figure out by some insight a beat that will fit the normal set better than the abnormal one. Then that could reinforce the light, you see, and improve the effectiveness of the therapy."

"Hey," said Bishop in alarm, "that's putting a lot of responsibility on me. When I write music, I'm just caressing the ear and making the muscles jump. I'm not trying to cure an ailing brain."

"All we ask is that you caress the ears and make the muscles jump, but do it so that it fits the normal music of the brain waves. . . . And I assure you that you need fear no responsibility, Mr. Bishop. It is quite unlikely that your music would do harm, and it might do so much good. And you'll be paid, Mr. Bishop, win or lose."

Bishop said, "Well, I'll try, though I don't promise a thing."

He was back in two days. Dr. Cray was pulled out of conference to see him. She looked at him out of tired, narrowed eyes.

"Do you have something?"

"I have *something*. It may work."

"How do you know?"

"I don't. I just have the feel of it. . . . Look, I listened to the laser tapes you gave me; the brain-wave music as it came from the patient in depression and the brain-wave music as you've modified it to normal. And you're right; without the flickering light it didn't affect me either way. Anyway, I subtracted the second from the first to see what the difference was."

"You have a computer?" Dr. Cray said, wondering.

"No, a computer wouldn't have helped. It would give me too much. You take one complicated laser-wave pattern and subtract another complicated laser-wave pattern and you're left with what is still a pretty complicated laser-wave pattern. No, I subtracted it in my mind to see what kind of beat was left. . . . That would be the abnormal beat that I would have to cancel out with a counter-beat."

"How can you subtract in your head?"

Bishop looked impatient. "I don't know. How did Beethoven hear the Ninth Symphony in his head before he wrote it down? The brain's a pretty good computer, too, isn't it?"

"I guess it is." She subsided. "Do you have the counter-beat there?"

"I think so. I have it here on an ordinary tape recording because it doesn't need anything more. It goes something like—dihdihdihDAH—dihdihdihDAH—dihdihdihDAHDAH-DAHdihDAH—and so on. I added a tune to it and you can put it through the earphones while she's watching the flickering light that's matched to the normal brain-wave pattern. If I'm right, it will reinforce the living daylights out of it."

"Are you sure?"

"If I were sure, you wouldn't have to try it, would you, Doc?"

Dr. Cray was thoughtful for a moment. "I'll make an appointment with the patient. I'd like you to be here."

"If you want me. It's part of the consultation job, I suppose."

"You won't be able to be in the treatment room, you understand, but I'd want you out here."

"Anything you say."

The patient looked careworn when she arrived. Her eyelids drooped and her voice was low and she mumbled.

Bishop's glance was casual as he sat quietly, unnoticed, in the corner. He saw her enter the treatment room and waited patiently, thinking: What if it works? Why not package brain-wave lights with appropriate sound accompaniment to combat the blues—to increase energy—to heighten love? Not just for sick people but for normal people, who could find a substitute for all the pounding they'd ever taken with alcohol or drugs in an effort to adjust their emotions—an utterly safe substitute based on the brain waves themselves. . . . And finally, after forty-five minutes, she came out.

She was placid now, and the lines had somehow washed out of her face.

"I feel better, Dr. Cray," she said, smiling. "I feel much better."

"You usually do," said Dr. Cray quietly.

"Not this way," said the woman. "Not this way. This time it's different. The other times, even when I thought I felt good,

I could sense that awful depression in the back of my head just waiting to come back the minute I relaxed. Now—it's just gone."

Dr. Cray said, "We can't be sure it will always be gone. We'll make an appointment for, say, two weeks from now but you'll call me before then if anything goes wrong, won't you? Did anything seem different in the treatment?"

The woman thought a bit. "No," she said hesitantly. Then: "The flickering light, though. That might have been different. Clearer and sharper somehow."

"Did you hear anything?"

"Was I supposed to?"

Dr. Cray rose. "Very well. Remember to make that appointment with my secretary."

The woman stopped at the door, turned, and said, "It's a happy feeling to feel happy," and left.

Dr. Cray said, "She didn't hear anything, Mr. Bishop. I suppose that your counter-beat reinforced the normal brain-wave pattern so naturally that the sound was, so to speak, lost in the light. . . . And it may have worked, too."

She turned to Bishop, looking him full in the face. "Mr. Bishop, will you consult with us on other cases? We'll pay you as much as we can, and if this turns out to be an effective therapy for mental disease, we'll see that you get all the credit due you."

Bishop said, "I'll be glad to help out, Doctor, but it won't be as hard as you may think. The work is already done."

"Already done?"

"We've had musicians for centuries. Maybe they didn't know about brain waves, but they did their best to get the melodies and beats that would affect people, get their toes tapping, get their muscles twitching, get their faces smiling, get their tear ducts pumping, get their hearts pounding. Those tunes are waiting. Once you get the counter-beat, you pick the tune to fit."

"Is that what you did?"

"Sure. What can snap you out of depression like a revival hymn? It's what they're meant to do. The beat gets you out of yourself. It exalts you. Maybe it doesn't last long by itself, but if you use it to reinforce the normal brain-wave pattern, it ought to pound it in."

"A revival hymn?" Dr. Cray stared at him, wide-eyed.

"Sure. What I used in this case was the best of them all.

I gave her 'When the Saints Go Marching In.' "

He sang it softly, finger-snapping the beat, and by the third bar, Dr. Cray's toes were tapping.

★ ★ ★

This next one was requested by *Bell Telephone Magazine* over an excellent lunch. What they wanted was a 3,000-word story centering on a problem in communications. There were two broad requirements; first, that it be farther out than any of the methods of communication now under development by Bell Telephone, and, second, that I not postulate an end to the requirements for communications corporations.

As it happened, Kim Armstrong, the editor of the magazine, who was at the lunch, was an extraordinarily charming woman, but I would have agreed to tackle the story anyway, because before the lunch was over I had a plot outline safely tucked away in my head.* I got to work on it on October 19, 1975. Ms. Armstrong liked it when it was done, and it appeared in the February 1976 issue of the magazine.

---

*People ask me sometimes if I keep a notebook on me at all times to jot down ideas. I do, but it's inside my head, and therefore never gets mislaid.

10

Old-fashioned

Ben Estes knew he was going to die and it didn't make him feel any better to know that that was the chance he had lived with all these years. The life of an astro-miner, drifting through the still largely uncharted vastness of the asteroid belt, was not particularly sweet, but it was quite likely to be short.

190

Of course, there was always the chance of a surprise find that would make you rich for life, and this had been a surprise find all right. The biggest surprise in the world, but it wasn't going to make Estes rich. It would make him dead.

Harvey Funarelli groaned softly from his bunk, and Estes turned, with a wince of his own as his muscles creaked. They had been badly mishandled. That he wasn't hit as viciously as Funarelli had been was surely because Funarelli was the larger man, and had been closer to the point of near-impact.

Estes looked somberly at his partner and said, "How do you feel, Harv?"

Funarelli groaned again. "I feel broken at every joint. What the hell happened? What did we hit?"

Estes walked over, limping slightly, and said, "Don't try to stand up."

"I can make it," said Funarelli, "if you'll just reach out a hand. Wow! I wonder if I've got a broken rib. Right here. What happened, Ben?"

Estes pointed at the main portview. It wasn't a large one, but it was the best a two-man astro-mining vessel could be expected to have. Funarelli moved toward it very slowly, leaning on Estes' shoulder. He looked out.

There were the stars, of course, but the experienced astronautic mind blanks those out. There are always the stars. Closer in, there was a gravel bank of boulders of varying size, all moving slowly relative to their neighbors like a swarm of very, very lazy bees.

Funarelli said, "I've never seen anything like that before. What are they doing here?"

"Those rocks," said Estes, "are what's left of a shattered asteroid, I suspect, and they're still circling what shattered them, and what shattered us."

"What?" Funarelli peered vainly into the darkness.

Estes pointed. "That!" There was a faint little sparkle in the direction he was pointing.

"I don't see anything."

"You're not suposed to. That's a black hole."

Funarelli's close-cropped black hair stood on end as a matter of course, and his staring dark eyes added a touch of horror. He said, "You're crazy."

"No. Black holes can come in all sizes. That's what the astronomers say. That one is about the mass of a large asteroid, I think, and we're moving around it. How else could something we can't see be holding us in orbit?"

"There's no report on any—"

"I know. How can there be? It can't be seen. It's mass—
Ooops, there comes the Sun." The slowly rotating ship had
brought the Sun into view and the portview automatically
polarized into opacity. "Anyway," said Estes, "we discovered
the first black hole actually to be encountered anywhere in
the Universe. Only we won't live to see ourselves get the
credit."

Funarelli said, "What happened?"

"We got close enough for the tidal effects to smash us up."

"What tidal effects?"

Estes said, "I'm not an astronomer, but as I understand
it, even when the total gravitational pull of a thing like that
isn't large, you can get so close to it that the pull becomes
intense. That intensity falls off so rapidly with increasing distance that the near end of an object is pulled far more
strongly than the far end. The object is therefore stretched.
The closer and bigger an object is, the worse the effect. Your
muscles were torn. You're lucky your bones weren't broken."

Funarelli grimaced. "I'm not sure they aren't. . . . What
else happened?"

"The fuel tanks were destroyed. We're stuck here in orbit.
. . . It's just lucky we happened to end in one far enough
away and circular enough to keep the tidal effect down. If we
were closer, or if we even zoomed in closely at one end of the
orbit—"

"Can we get word out?"

"Not a word," said Estes. "Communications are smashed."

"You can't fix it?"

"I'm not really a communications expert, but even if I
were— It can't be fixed."

"Can't something be jury-rigged?"

Estes shook his head. "We've just got to wait—and die.
That's not what bothers me so much."

"It bothers me," said Funarelli, sitting down on his bunk
and placing his head in his hands.

"We've got the pills," said Estes. "It would be an easy
death. What's really bad is that we can't get word back about
—that." He pointed to the portview, which was clear again
as the Sun moved out of range.

"About the black hole?"

"Yes, it's dangerous. It seems to be in orbit about the Sun,
but who knows whether that orbit is stable. And even if it is,
it's bound to get larger."

"I guess it will swallow stuff."

"Sure. Everything it encounters. There's cosmic dust spiraling into it all the time, and giving off energy as it spirals and drops in. That's what makes those dim sparkles of light. Every once in a while, the hole will swallow up a large piece that gets in the way and there'll be a flash of radiation, right down to X rays. The larger it gets, the easier it is for it to drag in material from a greater and greater distance."

For a moment, both men stared at the portview, then Estes went on. "Right now it can be handled maybe. If NASA can maneuver a fairly large asteroid here and send it past the hole in the proper way, the hole will be pulled out of its orbit by mutual gravitational attraction between itself and the asteroid. The hole can be made to curve itself into a path that could head it out of the Solar System, with some further help and acceleration."

Funarelli said, "Do you suppose it started very small?"

"It could have been a micro-hole formed at the time of the big bang, when the Universe was created. It may have been growing for billions of years and if it continues to grow, it may become unmanageable. It will then eventually become the grave of the Solar System."

"Why haven't they found it?"

"No one's been looking. Who would expect a black hole in the asteroid belt? And it doesn't produce enough radiation to be noticeable, or enough mass to be noticeable. You have to run into it, as we did."

"Are you sure we have no communications at all, Ben? . . . How far to Vesta? They could reach us from Vesta without much delay. It's the largest base in the asteroid belt."

Estes shook his head. "I don't know where Vesta is right now. The computer's knocked out, too."

"God! What isn't knocked out?"

"The air system is working. The water purifier is on. We've got plenty of power and food. We can last two weeks, maybe more."

A silence fell. "Look," said Funarelli after a while. "Even if we don't know where Vesta is exactly, we know it can't be more than a few million kilometers away. If we could reach them with some signal, they could get a drone ship out here within a week."

"A drone ship, yes," said Estes. That was easy. An unmanned ship could be accelerated to levels that human flesh and blood would not endure. It could make trips in a third the time a manned vessel could.

Funarelli closed his eyes, as though blocking out the pain, and said, "Don't sneer at a drone ship. It could bring us emergency supplies, and it would have stuff on board we could use to set up a communications system. We could hold out till the real rescuers came."

Estes sat down on the other bunk. "I wasn't sneering at a drone ship. I was just thinking that there's no way to send a signal, no way at all. We can't even yell. The vacuum of space won't carry sound."

Funarelli said stubbornly, "I can't believe you can't think of something. Our lives depend on it."

"The lives of all mankind depend on it, maybe, but I still can't think of anything. Why don't *you* think of something?"

Funarelli grunted as he moved his hips. He seized the hand grips on the wall next to his bunk and pulled himself up to a standing position. "I can think of one thing," he said, "why don't you turn off the gravity motors and save the power and put less strain on our muscles?"

Estes muttered, "Good idea." He rose and moved to the control board, where he cut the gravity.

Funarelli floated upward with a sigh and said, "Why can't they *find* the black hole, the idiots?"

"You mean like we did? There's no other way. It's not doing enough."

Funarelli said, "I still hurt, even with no gravity to fight. . . . Oh well, if it keeps on hurting like this, it won't matter so much when it comes to pill-taking time. . . . Is there any way we can make that black hole do more than it's doing?"

Estes said grimly, "If one of those bits of gravel should take it into its head to drop into the hole, a burst of X rays would shoot out."

"Would they detect that on Vesta?"

Estes shook his head. "I doubt it. They're not looking for such a thing. They'd be sure to detect it on Earth, though. Some of the space stations keep the sky under constant surveillance for radiation changes. They'd pick up astonishingly small bursts."

"All right, Ben, reaching Earth would be just as well. They'd send a message to Vesta to investigate. It would take the X rays about fifteen minutes to get to Earth and then it would take fifteen minutes for radio waves to get to Vesta."

"And how about the time between? The receivers may

automatically record a burst of X rays from such and such a direction, but who's to say where it's from? It could be from a distant galaxy that happens to lie in this particular direction. Some technician will notice the bump in the recording and will watch for more bursts in the same place and there won't be any and it will be crossed off as unimportant. Besides, it won't happen, Harv. There must have been lots of X rays when the black hole broke up this asteroid with its tidal effect, but that may have been thousands of years ago when no one was watching. Now what's left of these fragments must have fairly stable orbits."

"If we had our rockets—"

"Let me guess. We could drive our ship into the black hole. Use our deaths to send a message. That wouldn't do any good either. It would still be one pulse from anywhere."

Funarelli said indignantly, "I wasn't thinking of that. I'm not in the market for heroic death. I meant, we've got three engines. If we could rig them on to three pretty large size rocks and send each one into the hole, there would be three bursts of X rays and if we did them a day apart, the source would move detectably against the stars. That would be interesting, wouldn't it? The technicians would pick that up at once, wouldn't they?"

"Maybe, and maybe not. Besides, we don't have any rocketry left and couldn't put them on the rocks if we—" Estes fell silent. Then he said in an altered voice, "I wonder if our space suits are intact."

"Our suit radios," said Funarelli excitedly.

"Hell, they don't reach out more than a few kilometers," said Estes. "I'm thinking of something else. I'm thinking of going out there." He opened the suit locker. "They *seem* all right."

"Why do you want to go out?"

"We may not have any rockets, but we still have muscle power. At least I have. Do you think you can throw a rock?"

Funarelli made a throwing gesture, or the beginning of one, and a look of agony came over his face. "Can I jump to the Sun?" he said.

"I'll go out and throw some. . . . The suit seems to check out. Maybe I can throw some into the hole. . . . I hope the air lock operates."

"Can we spare the air?" said Funarelli anxiously.

"Will it matter in two weeks?" said Estes wearily.

Every astro-miner has to get outside the ship occasionally —to carry out some repair, to bring in some chunk of matter in the vicinity. Ordinarily, it's an exciting time. In any case, it's a change.

Estes felt little excitement, only a vast anxiety. His notion was so damned primitive, he felt foolish to have it. It was bad enough dying without having to die a damn fool.

He found himself in the black of space, with the glittering stars he had seen a hundred times before. Now, though, in the faint reflection of the small and distant Sun, there was the dim glow of hundreds of bits of rock that must once have been part of an asteroid and that now formed a tiny Saturn's ring about a black hole. The rocks seemed almost motionless, as all drifted along with the ship.

Estes judged the direction of wheel of the stars and knew that ship and rocks were moving slowly in the other direction. If he could throw a rock in the direction of the star motion, he would neutralize some of the rock's velocity relative to the black hole. If he neutralized not enough of the velocity, or too much, the rock would drop toward the hole, skim about it, and come back to the point it had left. If he neutralized just enough, it would come close enough to be powdered by the tidal effect. The grains of powder, in their motions, would slow each other and spiral into the hole, releasing X rays as they did so.

Estes used his miner's net of tantalum steel to gather rocks, choosing them fist size. He was thankful that modern suits allowed complete freedom of motion and were not the virtual coffins they had been when the first astronauts, over a century ago, had reached the Moon.

Once he had enough rocks, he threw one, and he could see it glimmer and fade in the sunlight as it dropped toward the hole. He waited and nothing happened. He didn't know how long it might take to fall into the black hole—if it fell in at all, that is—but he counted six hundred to himself and threw again.

Over and over he did so, with a terrible patience born of searching for an alternative to death, and finally there was a sudden blaze in the direction of the black hole. Visible light and, he knew, a burst of higher-energy radiation as far as X rays at least.

He had to stop to gather more rocks, and then he got the range. He was hitting it almost every time. He oriented himself so that the soft glimmer of the black hole would be seen just above the midportion of the ship. That was one relationship that didn't change as the ship circled and rolled on an axis—or changed least.

Even allowing for his care, however, it seemed to him he was making too many strikes. The black hole, he thought, was more massive than he knew and would swallow up its prey from a larger distance. That made it more dangerous, but increased their chance of rescue.

He worked his way through the lock and back into the ship. He was bone-weary and his right shoulder hurt him.

Funarelli helped him off with the suit. "That was terrific. You were throwing rocks into the black hole."

Estes nodded. "Yes, and I'm hoping my suit has been stopping the X rays. I'd just as soon not die of radiation poisoning."

"They'll see this back on Earth, won't they?"

"I'm sure they will," said Estes, "but will they pay attention? They'll record it all and wonder about it. But what's going to make them come out here for a closer look? I've got to work out something that will make them come, after I have just a little time to rest."

An hour later, he lifted out another space suit. No time to wait for the recharge of the solar batteries in the first one. He said, "I hope I haven't lost the range."

He was out again, and it had become clear that even allowing a fairly wide spread of velocities and direction, the black hole would suck up the slowing rocks as they moved inward.

Estes gathered as many rocks as he could manage and placed them carefully on an indentation in the hull of the ship. They didn't stay there, but they drifted only exceedingly slowly, and even after Estes had collected all he could, those he had placed there first had spread out no more than billiard balls on a pool table.

Then he threw them, at first tensely, and then with growing confidence, and the black hole flashed—and flashed—and flashed.

It seemed to him that the target became steadily easier to hit and that the black hole was growing madly with each impact and that soon it would reach out and suck him and the ship into its never-sated maw.

It was his imagination, of course, and nothing more. Finally all the rocks were gone and he felt he could throw nothing more in any case. He had been out there, it seemed, for hours.

When he was within the ship again he said, as soon as Funarelli had helped him off with his helmet, "That's it. I can't do anything more."

"You had plenty of flashes there," said Funarelli.

"Plenty, and they should surely be recorded. We'll just have to wait now. They've *got* to come."

Funarelli helped him off with the rest of his suit as best his muscle-torn body would allow. Then he stood, grunting and gasping, and said, "Do you really think they'll come, Ben?"

"I think they've got to," said Estes, almost as though he were trying to force the event by the sheer power of wishing. "I think they've *got* to."

"Why do you think they've got to?" said Funarelli, sounding like a man who wanted to grasp at straws but didn't dare.

"Because I *communicated*," said Estes. "We're not only the first people to encounter a black hole, we're the first to use it to communicate; we're the first to use the ultimate communication system of the future, the one that might send messages from star to star and galaxy to galaxy, and that might be the ultimate energy source as well—" He was panting, and he sounded a little wild.

"What are you talking about?" said Funarelli.

"I threw those rocks in rhythm, Harv," said Estes, "and the X-ray bursts came in rhythm. It was flash-flash-flash—flash—flash—flash—flash-flash-flash, and so on."

"Yes?"

"It's old-fashioned; *old*-fashioned, but that's one thing everyone remembers from the days when people communicated by electric currents running through wires."

"You mean the photograph—phonograph—"

"The telegraph, Harv. Those flashes I produced will be recorded and the first time someone looks at that record, all hell will break loose. It's not just that they'll be spotting an X-ray source; it's not just that it will be an X-ray source moving very slowly against the stars so that it has to be within our Solar System. What it is, is that they'll be seeing an X-ray source going on and off and producing the signal sos—sos—And when an X-ray source is shouting for help, you'll bet they'll come—as fast as they can—if only to see—what's—there—that—"

He was asleep.

—And five days later, a drone ship arrived.

Incidentally, it may occur to some of my Gentle Readers that there is a certain similarity between the story and my very first published story, MAROONED OFF VESTA, which appeared in print thirty-seven years earlier. In each story, two men are trapped on a spaceship wrecked in the asteroid belt and must use their ingenuity to devise a way of escaping what looked like certain death.

Of course, the resolutions are completely different, and it was in my mind to demonstrate some of the changes in our outlook on the Universe that took place in those thirty-seven years by producing in 1976 a resolution that would have been inconceivable in 1939.

★ ★ ★

In the fall of 1975, Fred Dannay (better known as Ellery Queen) approached me with a very intriguing idea for the August 1976 issue of *Ellery Queen's Mystery Magazine*, which would be on the stands at the time of the Bicentennial. He planned to publish a mystery dealing with the Bicentennial itself, and another dealing with the Centennial in 1876. What he needed now was one for the Tricentennial in 2076 and, of course, that meant a science fiction story.

Since I have been writing numerous mystery stories for the magazine in recent years, he thought of me and proposed that I tackle the job. I agreed and got to work on November 1, 1975. I ended with uncompromising science fiction which I feared might make a little heavy going for mystery readers. Fred thought otherwise, apparently, for he took the story and was even kind enough to pay me a bonus.

11

The Tercentenary Incident

July 4, 2076—and for the third time the accident of the conventional system of numeration, based on powers of ten, had brought the last two digits of the year back to the fateful 76 that had seen the birth of the nation.

It was no longer a nation in the old sense; it was rather a geographic expression; part of a greater whole that made up the Federation of all of humanity on Earth, together with its offshoots on the Moon and in the space colonies. By culture and heritage, however, the name and the *idea* lived on, and that portion of the planet signified by the old name was still the most prosperous and advanced region of the world. . . . And the President of the United States was still the most powerful single figure in the Planetary Council.

Lawrence Edwards watched the small figure of the President from his height of two hundred feet. He drifted lazily above the crowd, his flotron motor making a barely heard chuckle on his back, and what he saw looked exactly like what anyone would see on a holovision scene. How many times had he seen little figures like that in his living room, little figures in a cube of sunlight, looking as real as though they were living homunculi, except that you could put your hand through them.

You couldn't put your hand through those spreading out in their tens of thousands over the open spaces surrounding the Washington Monument. And you couldn't put your hand through the President. You could reach out to him instead, touch him, and shake his hand.

Edwards thought sardonically of the uselessness of that added element of tangibility and wished himself a hundred miles away, floating in air over some isolated wilderness, instead of here where he had to watch for any sign of disorder. There wouldn't be any necessity for his being here but for the mythology of the value of "pressing the flesh."

Edwards was not an admirer of the President—Hugo Allen Winkler, fifty-seventh of the line.

To Edwards, President Winkler seemed an empty man, a charmer, a vote grabber, a promiser. He was a disappointing man to have in office now after all the hopes of those first months of his administration. The World Federation was in danger of breaking up long before its job had been completed and Winkler could do nothing about it. One needed a strong hand, not a glad hand; a hard voice, not a honey voice.

There he was now, shaking hands—a space forced around him by the Service, with Edwards himself, plus a few others of the Service, watching from above.

The President would be running for re-election certainly, and there seemed a good chance he might be defeated. That would just make things worse, since the opposition party was dedicated to the destruction of the Federation.

Edwards sighed. It would be a miserable four years coming up—maybe a miserable forty—and all he could do was float in the air, ready to reach every Service agent on the ground by laser-phone if there was the slightest—

He didn't see the slightest. There was no sign of disturbance. Just a little puff of white dust, hardly visible; just a momentary glitter in the sunlight, up and away, gone as soon as he was aware of it.

Where was the President? He had lost sight of him in the dust.

He looked about in the vicinity of where he had seen him last. The President could not have moved far.

Then he became aware of disturbance. First it was among the Service agents themselves, who seemed to have gone off their heads and to be moving this way and that jerkily. Then those among the crowd near them caught the contagion and then those farther off. The noise rose and became a thunder.

Edwards didn't have to hear the words that made up the rising roar. It seemed to carry the news to him by nothing more than its mass clamorous urgency. President Winkler had disappeared! He had been there one moment and had turned into a handful of vanishing dust the next.

Edwards held his breath in an agony of waiting during what seemed a drug-ridden eternity, for the long moment of realization to end and for the mob to break into a mad, rioting stampede.

—When a resonant voice sounded over the gathering din, and at its sound, the noise faded, died, and became a silence. It was as though it were all a holovision program after all and someone had turned the sound down and out.

Edwards thought: My God, it's the President.

There was no mistaking the voice. Winkler stood on the guarded stage from which he was to give his Tercentenary speech, and from which he had left but ten minutes ago to shake hands with some in the crowd.

How had he gotten back there?

Edwards listened—

"Nothing has happened to me, my fellow Americans. What you have seen just now was the breakdown of a mechanical device. It was not your President, so let us not allow a mechanical failure to dampen the celebration of the happiest day the world has yet seen. . . . My fellow Americans, give me your attention—"

And what followed was the Tercentenary speech, the greatest speech Winkler had ever made, or Edwards had ever heard. Edwards found himself forgetting his supervisory job in his eagerness to listen.

Winkler had it right! He understood the importance of the Federation and he was getting it *across*.

Deep inside, though, another part of him was remembering the persistent rumors that the new expertise in robotics had resulted in the construction of a look-alike President, a robot who could perform the purely ceremonial functions, who could shake hands with the crowd, who could be neither bored nor exhausted—nor assassinated.

Edwards thought, in obscure shock, that that was how it had happened. There had been such a look-alike robot indeed, and in a way—it had been assassinated.

October 13, 2078—

Edwards looked up as the waist-high robot guide approached and said mellifluously, "Mr. Janek will see you now."

Edwards stood up, feeling tall as he towered above the stubby, metallic guide. He did not feel young, however. His face had gathered lines in the last two years or so and he was aware of it.

He followed the guide into a surprisingly small room, where, behind a surprisingly small desk, there sat Francis Janek, a slightly paunchy and incongruously young-looking man.

Janek smiled and his eyes were friendly as he rose to shake hands. "Mr. Edwards."

Edwards muttered, "I'm glad to have the opportunity, sir—"

Edwards had never seen Janek before, but then the job of personal secretary to the President is a quiet one and makes little news.

Janek said, "Sit down. Sit down. Would you care for a soya stick?"

Edwards smiled a polite negative, and sat down. Janek was clearly emphasizing his youth. His ruffled shirt was open and the hairs on his chest had been dyed a subdued but definite violet.

Janek said, "I know you have been trying to reach me for some weeks now. I'm sorry for the delay. I hope you understand that my time is not entirely my own. However, we're here now. . . . I have referred to the Chief of the Service, by the way, and he gave you very high marks. He regrets your resignation."

Edwards said, eyes downcast, "It seemed better to carry on my investigations without danger of embarrassment to the Service."

Janek's smile flashed. "Your activities, though discreet, have not gone unnoticed, however. The Chief explains that you have been investigating the Tercentenary Incident, and I must admit it was that which persuaded me to see you as soon as I could. You've given up your position for that? You're investigating a dead issue."

"How can it be a dead issue, Mr. Janek? Your calling it an Incident doesn't alter the fact that it was an assassination attempt."

"A matter of semantics. Why use a disturbing phrase?"

"Only because it would seem to represent a disturbing truth. Surely you would say that someone tried to kill the President."

Janek spread his hands. "If that is so, the plot did not succeed. A mechanical device was destroyed. Nothing more. In fact, if we look at it properly, the Incident—whatever you choose to call it—did the nation and the world an enormous good. As we all know, the President was shaken by the Incident and the nation as well. The President and all of us realized what a return to the violence of the last century might mean and it produced a great turnaround."

"I can't deny that."

"Of course you can't. Even the President's enemies will grant that the last two years have seen great accomplishments. The Federation is far stronger today than anyone could have dreamed it would be on that Tercentenary day. We might even say that a breakup of the global economy has been prevented."

Edwards said cautiously, "Yes, the President is a changed man. Everyone says so."

Janek said, "He was a great man always. The Incident made him concentrate on the great issues with a fierce intensity, however."

"Which he didn't do before?"

"Perhaps not quite as intensely. . . . In effect then, the President, and all of us, would like the Incident forgotten. My main purpose in seeing you, Mr. Edwards, is to make that plain to you. This is not the Twentieth Century and we can't throw you in jail for being inconvenient to us, or hamper you in any way, but even the Global Charter doesn't forbid us to attempt persuasion. Do you understand me?"

"I understand you, but I do not agree with you. Can we forget the Incident when the person responsible has never been apprehended?"

"Perhaps that is just as well, too, sir. Far better that some, uh, unbalanced person escape than that the matter be blown out of proportion and the stage set, possibly, for a return to the days of the Twentieth Century."

"The official story even states that the robot spontaneously exploded—which is impossible, and which has been an unfair blow to the robot industry."

"A robot is not the term I would use, Mr. Edwards. It was a mechanical device. No one has said that robots are dangerous, per se, certainly not the workaday metallic ones. The only reference here is to the unusually complex manlike devices that seem flesh and blood and that we might call androids. Actually, they are so complex that perhaps they might explode at first; I am not an expert in the field. The robotics industry will recover."

"Nobody in the government," said Edwards stubbornly, "seems to care whether we reach the bottom of the matter or not."

"I've already explained that there have been no consequences but good ones. Why stir the mud at the bottom, when the water above is clear?"

"And the use of the disintegrator?"

For a moment, Janek's hand, which had been slowly turning the container of soya sticks on his desk, held still, then it returned to its rhythmic movement. He said lightly, "What's that?"

Edwards said intently, "Mr. Janek, I think you know what I mean. As part of the Service—"

"To which you no longer belong, of course."

"Nevertheless, as part of the Service, I could not help but hear things that were not always, I suppose, for my ears. I had heard of a new weapon, and I saw something happen at the Tercentenary which would require one. The object everyone thought was the President disappeared into a cloud of very fine dust. It was as though every atom within the object had had its bonds to other atoms loosed. The object had become a cloud of individual atoms, which began to combine again of course, but which dispersed too quickly to do more than appear a momentary glitter of dust."

"Very science-fictionish."

"I certainly don't understand the science behind it, Mr.

Janek, but I do see that it would take considerable energy to accomplish such bond breaking. This energy would have to be withdrawn from the environment. Those people who were standing near the device at the time, and whom I could locate—and who would agree to talk—were unanimous in reporting a wave of coldness washing over them."

Janek put the soya-stick container to one side with a small click of transite against cellulite. He said, "Suppose just for argument that there is such a thing as a disintegrator."

"You need not argue. There is."

"I won't argue. I know of no such thing myself, but in my office, I am not likely to know of anything so security-bound as new weaponry. But if a disintegrator exists and is as secret as all that, it must be an American monopoly, unknown to the rest of the Federation. It would then not be something either you or I should talk about. It could be a more dangerous war weapon than the nuclear bombs, precisely because—if what you say is so—it produces nothing more than disintegration at the point of impact and cold in the immediate neighborhood. No blast, no fire, no deadly radiation. Without these distressing side effects, there would be no deterrent to its use, yet for all we know it might be made large enough to destroy the planet itself."

"I go along with all of that," said Edwards.

"Then you see that if there is no disintegrator, it is foolish to talk about one; and if there *is* a disintegrator, then it is criminal to talk about one."

"I haven't discussed it, except to you, just now, because I'm trying to persuade you of the seriousness of the situation. If one had been used, for instance, ought not the government be interested in deciding how it came to be used—if another unit of the Federation might be in possession?"

Janek shook his head. "I think that we can rely on appropriate organs of this government to take such a thing into consideration. You had better not concern yourself with the matter."

Edwards said, in barely controlled impatience, "Can you assure me that the United States is the only government that has such a weapon at its disposal?"

"I can't tell you, since I know nothing about such a weapon, and should not know. You should not have spoken of it to me. Even if no such weapon exists, the *rumor* of its existence could be damaging."

"But since I have told you and the damage is done, please

hear me out. Let me have the chance of convincing you that *you*, and no one else, hold the key to a fearful situation that perhaps I alone see."

"You alone see? I alone hold the key?"

"Does that sound paranoid? Let me explain and then judge for yourself."

"I will give you a little more time, sir, but what I have said stands. You must abandon this—this hobby of yours—this investigation. It is terribly dangerous."

"It is its abandonment that would be dangerous. Don't you see that if the disintegrator exists and if the United States has the monopoly of it, then it follows that the number of people who could have access to it would be sharply limited. As an ex-member of the Service, I have some practical knowledge of this and I tell you that the only person in the world who could manage to abstract a disintegrator from our top-secret arsenals would be the President. . . . Only the President of the United States, Mr. Janek, could have arranged that assassination attempt."

They stared at each other for a moment and then Janek touched a contact at his desk.

He said, "Added precaution. No one can overhear us now by any means. Mr. Edwards, do you realize the danger of that statement? To yourself? You must not overestimate the power of the Global Charter. A government has the right to take reasonable measures for the protection of its stability."

Edwards said, "I'm approaching you, Mr. Janek, as someone I presume to be a loyal American citizen. I come to you with news of a terrible crime that affects all Americans and the entire Federation. A crime that has produced a situation that perhaps only you can right. Why do you respond with threats?"

Janek said, "That's the second time you have tried to make it appear that I am a potential savior of the world. I can't conceive of myself in that role. You understand, I hope, that I have no unusual powers."

"You are the secretary to the President."

"That does *not* mean I have special access to him or am in some intimately confidential relationship to him. There are times, Mr. Edwards, when I suspect others consider me to be nothing more than a flunky, and there are even times when I find myself in danger of agreeing with them."

"Nevertheless, you see him frequently, you see him informally, you see him—"

Janek said impatiently, "I see enough of him to be able to assure you that the President would not order the destruction of that mechanical device on Tercentenary day."

"Is it in your opinion impossible, then?"

"I did not say that. I said he would not. After all, why should he? Why should the President want to destroy a look-alike android that has been a valuable adjunct to him for over three years of his Presidency? And if for some reason he wanted it done, why on Earth should he do it in so incredibly public a way—at the Tercentenary, no less—thus advertising its existence, risking public revulsion at the thought of shaking hands with a mechanical device, to say nothing of the diplomatic repercussions of having had representatives of other parts of the Federation treat with one? He might, instead, simply have ordered it disassembled in private. No one but a few highly placed members of the Administration would have known."

"There have not, however, been any undesirable consequences for the President as a result of the Incident, have there?"

"He has had to cut down on ceremony. He is no longer as accessible as he once was."

"As the robot once was."

"Well," said Janek uneasily. "Yes, I suppose that's right."

Edwards said, "And, as a matter of fact, the President was re-elected and his popularity has not diminished even though the destruction was public. The argument against public destruction is not as powerful as you make it sound."

"But the re-election came about despite the Incident. It was brought about by the President's quick action in stepping forward and delivering what you will have to admit was one of the great speeches of American history. It was an absolutely amazing performance; you will have to admit that."

"It was a beautifully staged drama. The President, one might think, would have counted on that."

Janek sat back in his chair. "If I understand you, Edwards, you are suggesting an involuted storybook plot. Are you trying to say that the President had the device destroyed, just as it was—in the middle of a crowd, at precisely the time of the Tercentenary celebration, with the world watching—so that he could win the admiration of all by his quick action? Are you suggesting that he arranged it all so that he could establish himself as a man of unexpected vigor and strength under extremely dramatic circumstances and thus turn a losing campaign into a winning one? . . . Mr. Edwards, you've been reading fairy tales."

Edwards said, "If I were trying to claim all this, it would indeed be a fairy tale, but I am not. I never suggested that the President ordered the killing of the robot. I merely asked if you thought it were possible and you have stated quite strongly that it wasn't. I'm glad you did, because I agree with you."

"Then what is all this? I'm beginning to think you're wasting my time."

"Another moment, please. Have you ever asked yourself why the job couldn't have been done with a laser beam, with a field deactivator—with a sledgehammer, for God's sake? Why should anyone go to the incredible trouble of getting a weapon guarded by the strongest possible government security to do a job that didn't require such a weapon? Aside from the difficulty of getting it, why risk revealing the existence of a disintegrator to the rest of the world?"

"This whole business of a disintegrator is just a theory of yours."

"The robot disappeared completely before my eyes. I was watching. I rely on no secondhand evidence for that. It doesn't matter what you call the weapon; whatever name you give it, it had the effect of taking the robot apart atom by atom and scattering all those atoms irretrievably. Why should this be done? It was tremendous overkill."

"I don't know what was in the mind of the perpetrator."

"No? Yet it seems to me that there is only one logical reason for a complete powdering when something much simpler would have carried through the destruction. The powdering left no trace behind of the destroyed object. It left nothing to indicate what it had been, whether robot or anything else."

Janek said, "But there is no question of what it was."

"Isn't there? I said only the President could have arranged for a disintegrator to be obtained and used. But, considering the existence of a look-alike robot, which President did the arranging?"

Janek said harshly, "I don't think we can carry on this conversation. You are mad."

Edwards said, "Think it through. For God's sake, think it through. The President did not destroy the robot. Your arguments there are convincing. What happened was that the robot destroyed the President. President Winkler was killed in the crowd on July 4, 2076. A robot resembling President Winkler then gave the Tercentenary speech, ran for re-election, was re-elected, and still serves as President of the United States."

"Madness!"

"I've come to you, to *you* because *you* can prove this—and correct it, too."

"It is simply not so. The President is—the President." Janek made as though to rise and conclude the interview.

"You yourself say he's changed," said Edwards quickly and urgently. "The Tercentenary speech was beyond the powers of the old Winkler. Haven't you been yourself amazed at the accomplishments of the last two years? Truthfully—could the Winkler of the first term have done all this?"

"Yes, he could have, because the President of the second term is the President of the first term."

"Do you deny he's changed? I put it to you. *You* decide and I'll abide by your decision."

"He's risen to meet the challenge, that is all. It's happened before this in American history." But Janek sank back into his seat. He looked uneasy.

"He doesn't drink," said Edwards.

"He never did—very much."

"He no longer womanizes. Do you deny he did so in the past?"

"A President is a man. For the last two years, however, he's felt dedicated to the matter of the Federation."

"It's a change for the better, I admit," said Edwards, "but it's a change. Of course, if he *had* a woman, the masquerade could not be carried on, could it?"

Janek said, "Too bad he doesn't have a wife." He pronounced the archaic word a little self-consciously. "The whole matter wouldn't arise if he did."

"The fact that he doesn't made the plot more practical. Yet he has fathered two children. I don't believe they have been in the White House, either of them, since the Tercentenary."

"Why should they be? They are grown, with lives of their own."

"Are they invited? Is the President interested in seeing them? You're his private secretary. You would know. Are they?"

Janek said, "You're wasting time. A robot can't kill a human being. You know that that is the First Law of Robotics."

"I know it. But no one is saying that the robot-Winkler

killer the human-Winkler directly. When the human-Winkler was in the crowd, the robot-Winkler was on the stand and I doubt that a disintegrator could be aimed from that distance without doing more widespread damage. Maybe it could, but more likely the robot-Winkler had an accomplice—a hit man, if that is the correct Twentieth-Century jargon."

Janek frowned. His plump face puckered and looked pained. He said, "You know, madness must be catching. I'm actually beginning to consider the insane notion you've brought here. Fortunately, it doesn't hold water. After all, why would an assassination of the human-Winkler be arranged in public? All the arguments against destroying the robot in public hold against the killing of a human President in public. Don't you see that ruins the whole theory?"

"It does not—" began Edwards.

"It *does*. No one except for a few officials knew that the mechanical device existed at all. If President Winkler were killed privately and his body disposed of, the robot could easily take over without suspicion—without having roused yours, for instance."

"There would always be a few officials who would know, Mr. Janek. The assassinations would have to broaden." Edwards leaned forward earnestly. "See here, ordinarily there couldn't have been any danger of confusing the human being and the machine. I imagine the robot wasn't in constant use, but was pulled out only for specific purposes, and there would always be key individuals, perhaps quite a number of them, who would know where the President was and what he was doing. If that were so, the assassination would have to be carried out at a time when those officials actually thought the President was really the robot."

"I don't follow you."

"See here. One of the robot's tasks was to shake hands with the crowd; press the flesh. When this was taking place, the officials in the know would be perfectly aware that the hand shaker was, in truth, the robot."

"Exactly. You're making sense now. It *was* the robot."

"Except that it was the Tercentenary, and except that President Winkler could not resist. I suppose it would be more than human to expect a President—particularly an empty crowd pleaser and applause hunter like Winkler—to give up the adulation of the crowd on this day of all days, and let it go to a machine. And perhaps the robot carefully nurtured this impulse so that on this one Tercentenary day, the President would have ordered the robot to remain behind the podium, while he himself went out to shake hands and to be cheered."

"Secretly?"

"Of course secretly. If the President had told anyone in the Service, or any of his aides, or you, would he have been allowed to do it? The official attitude concerning the possibility of assassination has been practically a disease since the events of the late Twentieth Century. So with the encouragement of an obviously clever robot—"

"You assume the robot to be clever because you assume he is now serving as President. This is circular reasoning. If he is not President, there is no reason to think he is clever, or that he were capable of working out this plot. Besides, what motive could possibly drive a robot to plot an assassination? Even if it didn't kill the President directly, the taking of a human life indirectly is also forbidden by the First Law, which states, 'A robot may not injure a human being or, through inaction, allow a human being to come to harm.'"

Edwards said, "The First Law is not absolute. What if harming a human being saves the lives of two others, or three others, or even three billion others? The robot may have thought that saving the Federation took precedence over the saving of one life. It was no ordinary robot, after all. It was designed to duplicate the properties of the President closely enough to deceive anyone. Suppose it had the understanding of President Winkler, without his weaknesses, and suppose it knew that it could save the Federation where the President could not."

"*You* can reason so, but how do you know a mechanical device would?"

"It is the only way to explain what happened."

"I think it is a paranoid fantasy."

Edwards said, "Then tell me why the object that was destroyed was powdered into atoms. What else would make sense than to suppose that that was the only way to hide the fact that it was a human being and not a robot that was destroyed? Give me an alternate explanation."

Janek reddened. "I won't accept it."

"But you can prove the whole matter—or disprove it. It's why I have come to you—to *you*."

"How can I prove it? Or disprove it either?"

"No one sees the President at unguarded moments as

you do. It is with you—in default of family—that he is most informal. Study him."

"I have. I tell you he isn't—"

"You haven't. You suspected nothing wrong. Little signs meant nothing to you. Study him now, being aware that he *might* be a robot, and you will see."

Janek said sardonically, "I can knock him down and probe for metal with an ultrasonic detector. Even an android has a platinum-iridium brain."

"No drastic action will be necessary. Just observe him and you will see that he is so radically not the man he was that he cannot be a man."

Janek looked at the clock-calendar on the wall. He said, "We have been here over an hour."

"I'm sorry to have taken up so much of your time, but you see the importance of all this, I hope."

"Importance?" said Janek. Then he looked up and what had seemed a despondent air turned suddenly into something of hope. "But is it, in fact, important? Really, I mean?"

"How can it not be important? To have a robot as President of the United States? That's not important?"

"No, that's not what I mean. Forget what President Winkler might be. Just consider this. Someone serving as President of the United States has saved the Federation; he has held it together and, at the present moment, he runs the Council in the interests of peace and of constructive compromise. You'll admit all that?"

Edwards said, "Of course, I admit all that. But what of the precedent established? A robot in the White House for a very good reason now may lead to a robot in the White House twenty years from now for a very bad reason, and then to robots in the White House for no reason at all but only as a matter of course. Don't you see the importance of muffling a possible trumpet call for the end of humanity at the time of its first uncertain note?"

Janek shrugged. "Suppose I find out he's a robot? Do we broadcast it to all the world? Do you know what it will do to the world's financial structure? Do you know—"

"I do know. That is why I have come to you privately, instead of trying to make it public. It is up to you to check out the matter and come to a definite conclusion. It is up to you, next, having found the supposed President to be a robot, which I am certain you will do, to persuade him to resign."

"And by your version of his reaction to the First Law, he

will then have me killed since I will be threatening his expert handling of the greatest global crisis of the Twenty-first Century."

Edwards shook his head. "The robot acted in secret before, and no one tried to counter the arguments he used with himself. You will be able to reinforce a stricter interpretation of the First Law with your arguments. If necessary, we can get the aid of some official from U. S. Robots and Mechanical Men, Inc., who constructed the robot in the first place. Once he resigns, the Vice-President will succeed. If the robot-Winkler has put the old world on the right track, good; it can now be kept on the right track by the Vice-President, who is a decent and honorable woman. But we can't have a robot ruler, and we mustn't ever again."

"What if the President is human?"

"I'll leave that to you. You will know."

Janek said, "I am not that confident of myself. What if I can't decide? If I can't bring myself to? If I don't dare to? What are your plans?"

Edwards looked tired. "I don't know. I may have to go to U. S. Robots. But I don't think it will come to that. I'm quite confident now that I've laid the problem in your lap, you won't rest till it's settled. Do *you* want to be ruled by a robot?"

He stood up, and Janek let him go. They did not shake hands.

Janek sat there in the gathering twilight in deep shock.

A robot!

The man had walked in and had argued, in perfectly rational manner, that the President of the United States was a robot.

It should have been easy to fight that off. Yet though Janek had tried every argument he could think of, they had all been useless, and the man had not been shaken in the least.

A robot as President! Edwards had been *certain* of it, and he would *stay* certain of it. And if Janek insisted that the President was human, Edwards would go to U. S. Robots. He wouldn't rest.

Janek frowned as he thought of the twenty-eight months since the Tercentenary and of how well all had gone in the face of the probabilities. And now?

He remained lost in somber thought.

He still had the disintegrator but surely it would not be

necessary to use it on a human being, the nature of whose body was not in question. A silent laser stroke in some lonely spot would do.

It had been hard to maneuver the President into the earlier job, but in this present case, it wouldn't even have to know.

My first thought was to call the previous story "Death at the Tricentennial," but the dictionary assured me that "tercentenary" was a perfectly good way of referring to a three hundredth birthday, so I called it "Death at the Tercentenary."

Fred changed that name to THE TERCENTENARY INCIDENT, which was a great improvement in my opinion, and I adopted it with glad cries. I am not always pleased with his title changes and generally say so, as in my collection of mystery short stories *Tales of the Black Widowers*. It is only fair now that I give him credit for a good change.

—One more thing. Again, this story represents a return to a theme I handled in an earlier story. The earlier story in this case was EVIDENCE, first published in 1946, thirty years before this story was. There is, except for theme, no similarity between the two stories, and I leave it to the Gentle Reader, if he or she has read both, to decide whether I have improved or not in the interval. (Don't write, however, unless you think I have improved.)

Time flies. I myself am ever-youthful, but everything else is getting older. Do you realize that with the April 1976 issue, *Amazing Stories*, the oldest of the science fiction magazines, celebrated its Semicentennial?

The April 1926 issue of *Amazing Stories* was Volume I, Number 1. It was the very first issue of the first magazine ever to be devoted entirely to science fiction—and that was fifty years ago.

Hugo Gernsback had been born in Luxemburg in 1884 and had emigrated to the United States in 1904. He went on to write some excruciatingly bad science fiction with some excruciatingly good predictions in it, to edit a magazine, in which he included science fiction stories (or scientifiction, as he called it), and to begin thinking of publishing an all-science-fiction magazine for some time. A probing circular he sent out in 1924 brought in disapponting results, but then, in 1926, without any advance fanfare at all, he placed the new magazine on the stands.

Sol Cohen, the current publisher of the magazine, called me in the fall of 1975 to ask me if I could make some contribution in honor of the fiftieth anniversary of the magazine, and although, as usual, I was drowning in commitments, there was no way I could let that pass. On November 22, 1975, I sat down to write BIRTH OF A NOTION and so I was represented in the anniversary issue.

12

Birth of a Notion

That the first inventor of a workable time machine was a science fiction enthusiast is by no means a coincidence. It was inevitable. Why else should an otherwise sane physicist even dare track down the various out-of-the-way theories that seemed to point toward maneuverability in time in the very teeth of General Relativity?

It took energy, of course. Everything takes energy. But Simeon Weill was prepared to pay the price. Anything (well, almost anything) to make his hidden science-fictional dream come true.

The trouble was that there was no way of controlling either the direction or distance through which one was chronologically thrust. It was all the result of random temporal collisions of the harnessed tachyons. Weill could make mice and even rabbits disappear—but future or past, he couldn't say. One mouse reappeared, so he must have traveled but a short way into the past—and it seemed quite unharmed. The others? Who could tell?

He devised an automatic release for the machine. Theoretically, it would reverse the push (whatever the push might be) and bring back the object (from whichever direction and whatever distance it had gone). It didn't always work, but live rabbits were brought back unharmed.

If he could only make the release foolproof, Weill would have tried it himself. He was *dying* to try it—which was not the proper reaction of a theoretical physicist, but was the absolute predictable emotion of a crazed s.f. fan who was particularly fond of the space-operish productions of some decades before the present year of 1976.

It was inevitable, then, that the accident should happen. On no account would he have stepped between the tempodes with conscious determination. He knew the chances were about two in five he would not return. On the other hand, he was *dying* to try it, so he tripped over his own big feet and went staggering between those tempodes as a result of total accident. . . . But are there really accidents?

He might have been hurled into the past or into the future. As it happened, he was hurled into the past.

He might have been hurled uncounted thousands of years into the past or one and a half days. As it happened, he was hurled fifty-one years into the past to a time when the Teapot Dome Scandal was burning brightly but the nation was keeping Cool with Coolidge and knew that nobody in the world could lick Jack Dempsey.

But there was something that his theories didn't tell Weill. He knew what could happen to the particles themselves, but there was no way of predicting what would happen to the relationships between the various particles. And where are relationships more complex than in the brain?

So what happened was that as Weill moved backward through time, his mind unreeled. Not all the way, fortunately, since Weill had not yet been conceived in the year before America's Sesquicentennial, and a brain with less than no development would have been a distinct handicap.

It unreeled haltingly, and partially, and clumsily, and when Weill found himself on a park bench not far from his 1976 home in lower Manhattan, where he experimented in dubious symbiosis with New York University, he found himself in the year 1925 with an abysmally aching head and no very clear idea as to what anything was all about.

He found himself staring at a man of about forty, hair slicked down, cheekbones prominent, beaky nose, who was sharing the same bench with him.

The man looked concerned. He said, "Where did you come from? You were not here a moment ago." He had a distinct Teutonic accent.

Weill wasn't sure. He couldn't remember. But one phrase seemed to stick through the chaos within his skull even though he wasn't sure what it meant.

"Time machine," he gasped.

The other man stiffened. He said, "Do you read pseudo-scientific romances?"

"What?" said Weill.

"Have you read H. G. Wells's *The Time Machine*?"

The repetition of the phrase seemed to soothe Weill a bit. The pain in his head lessened. The name Wells seemed familiar, or was that his own name? No, his own name was Weill.

"Wells?" he said. "I am Weill."

The other man thrust out a hand. "I am Hugo Gernsback. I write pseudo-scientific romances at times, but of course, it is not right to say 'pseudo.' That makes it seem there is something fake about it. That is not so. It should be properly written and then it will be scientific fiction. I like to shorten that"—his dark eyes gleamed—"to scientifiction."

"Yes," said Weill, trying desperately to collect shattered memories and unwound experiences and getting only moods and impressions. "Scientifiction. Better than pseudo. Still not quite—"

"If done *well*. Have you read my 'Ralph 124C41+'?"

"Hugo Gernsback," said Weill, frowning, "Famous—"

"In a small way," said the other, nodding his head. "I have been publishing magazines on radio and on electrical inventions for years. Have you read 'Science and Invention'?"

Weill caught the word "invention" and somehow that left him on the edge of understanding what he had meant by "time machine." He grew eager and said, "Yes, yes."

"And what do you think of the scientifiction that I add in each issue?"

Scientifiction again. The word had a soothing effect on him and yet it was not quite right. Something more— Not quite— He said it, "Something more. Not quite—"

"Not quite enough? Yes, I've been thinking that. Last year I sent out circulars asking for subscriptions to a magazine to contain nothing but scientifiction. I would call it *Scientifiction*. The results were very disappointing. How would you explain that?"

Weill didn't hear him. He was still concentrating on the word "scientifiction," which didn't seem quite right, but he couldn't understand why it didn't.

He said, "The name is not right."

"Not right for a magazine? Maybe that's so. I have not thought of a good name; something to catch the eye, to get across just what the reader will get, and what he will want.

That is it. If I could get a good name I would start th
magazine and not worry about circulars. I would not as
anything. I would simply put it on every newsstand in th
United States next spring; that is all."

Weill stared at him blankly.

The man said, "Of course, the stories I want should teac
science even as they amuse and excite the reader. They shoul
open to him the vast scope of the future. Airplanes will cros
the Atlantic nonstop."

"Airplanes?" Weill caught a fugitive vision of a large meta
whale, rising on its own exhaust. A moment, and it was gone
He said, "Large ones, carrying hundreds of people faster tha
sound."

"Of course. Why not? Staying in touch at all times b
radio."

"Satellites."

"What?" It was the other man's turn to look puzzled.

"Radio waves bounce off an artificial satellite in space."

The other man nodded vigorously. "I predicted the us
of radio waves to detect at a distance in 'Ralph 124C41+
Space mirrors? I've predicted that. And television, of cours
And energy from the atom."

Weill was galvanized. Images flashed before his mind's ey
in no suitable order. "Atom," he said, "Yes. Nuclear bombs.

"Radium," said the other man complacently.

"Plutonium," said Weill.

"What?"

"Plutonium. And nuclear fusion. Imitating the Sun. Nylo
and plastics. Pesticides to kill the insects. Computers to ki
the problems."

"Computers? You mean robots?"

"Pocket computers," said Weill enthusiastically. "Littl
things. Hold them in your hand and work out problems. Littl
radios. Hold them in your hand, too. Cameras take photo
graphs and develop them right in the box. Holographs. Thre
dimensional pictures."

The other man said, "Do you write scientifiction?"

Weill didn't listen. He kept trying to trap the images. The
were growing clearer. "Skyscrapers," he said. "Aluminum an
glass. Highways. Color television. Man on the Moon. Probe
to Jupiter."

"Man on the Moon," said the other man. "Jules Verne. D
you read Jules Verne?"

Weill shook his head. It was quite clear now. The min

as healing a bit. "Stepping down onto the Moon's surface
on television. Everyone watching. And pictures of Mars. No
anals on Mars."

"No canals on Mars?" said the other man, astonished.
They have been seen."

"No canals," said Weill firmly. "Volcanoes. The biggest.
Canyons the biggest. Transistors, lasers, tachyons. Trap the
chyons. Make them push against time. Move through time.
Move through time. A—ma—"

Weill's voice was fading and his outlines trembled. It so
appened that the other man looked away at this moment,
aring into the blue sky, and muttering, "Tachyons? What
he saying?"

He was thinking that if a stranger he met casually in the
ark was so interested in scientifiction, it might be a good
gn that it was time for the magazine. And then he remem-
ered he had no name and dismissed the notion regretfully.

He looked back in time to hear Weill's last words, "Tach-
onic time travel—an—amazing—stor—y—" And he was
one, snapping back to his own time.

Hugo Gernsback stared in horror at the place where the
an had been. He hadn't seen him come and now he really
adn't seen him go. His mind rejected the actual disappear-
nce. How strange a man—his clothes were oddly cut, come
think of it, and his words were wild and whirling.

The stranger himself said it—an amazing story. His last
ords.

And then Gernsback muttered the phrase under his breath,
Amazing story. . . . *Amazing Stories*?"

A smile tugged at the corners of his mouth.

One last word—

In putting together the stories for this collection, I couldn't help noticing that between November 1974 and November 1975, I had written and sold seven science fiction stories. In addition, I had written and sold two mystery stories and one mystery novel, for a total of 132,000 words of fiction.

You understand then, why, when some people, blinded by my 120+ books of nonfiction, ask me why I have quit writing fiction, I always answer, "I haven't."

Well, I *haven't!*

And while I live, I won't!

Isaac Asimov

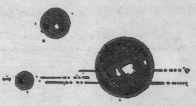

OUTER SPACE